PRAISE FOR BARRY MAITLAND

JOINT WINNER OF THE 1995 NED KELLY AWARD

SHORTLISTED FOR THE CWA JOHN CREASEY AWARD
FOR BEST FIRST CRIME NOVEL OF 1994

THE BELLTREE TRILOGY I: *Crucifixion Creek*
SHORTLISTED FOR THE 2015 NED KELLY AWARD

'A hard-boiled plummet into damaged lives.'
Australian

'Takes off at a frantic gallop towards a
heart-thumping finale that promises only a
brief respite. Be prepared to stay up late.'
Age

'An unqualified triumph.'
West Australian

'An adrenaline-filled ride through
Sydney's seedy underbelly.'
AustCrimeFiction.org

THE BELLTREE TRILOGY II: *Ash Island*
SHORTLISTED FOR THE 2016 NED KELLY AWARD

'Maitland does not flinch from a brutal denouement...
Prepare for a long and gripping haul.'
Sydney Morning Herald

'This is crime fiction at its very best with a local twist.'
Newcastle Herald

Barry Maitland was born in Scotland and in 1984 moved to Australia to head the architecture school at the University of Newcastle in New South Wales. *The Marx Sisters*, the first in his Brock and Kolla crime series, was published in 1994. Barry now writes full time and his books are read throughout the English-speaking world and in translation in a number of other countries. He lives in the Hunter Valley.

Barry Maitland

SLAUGHTER PARK

THE BELLTREE TRILOGY

TEXT PUBLISHING MELBOURNE AUSTRALIA

The Text Publishing Company
Swann House
22 William Street
Melbourne Victoria 3000
Australia
textpublishing.com.au

First published in 2016 by The Text Publishing Company

Cover design by W. H. Chong
Page design by Imogen Stubbs
Typeset by J & M Typesetting

Printed and bound in the US by Lightning Source

National Library of Australia Cataloguing-in-Publication entry
Creator: Maitland, Barry, author.
Title: Slaughter Park/by Barry Maitland.
ISBN: 9781925355697 (paperback)
             9781925410129 (ebook)
Series: Maitland, Barry. Belltree trilogy; bk. 3.
Subjects: Detective and mystery stories, Australian.
             Murder—Investigation—New South Wales—Sydney—Fiction.
             Sydney (N.S.W.)—Fiction.
Dewey Number: A823.3

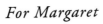

For Margaret

In June 2010 Justice Daniel Belltree, first Aboriginal judge of the New South Wales Supreme Court, was called to preside over a hearing of the court in the city of Armidale. He left Sydney in his car, accompanied by his wife, Mary, and daughter-in-law, Jenny, taking the scenic route north through the Barrington Tops between Newcastle and Uralla known as Thunderbolt's Way. On a winding section the car left the road and rolled down a steep forested hillside. Belltree and his wife were killed. Jenny survived, but lost her sight.

After an extensive investigation the coroner found that the cause of the crash was driver error, and made recommendations for improving the road. He discounted suggestions that a second vehicle had been involved. Harry Belltree, son of the dead couple and husband of Jenny, himself a homicide detective, knows otherwise.

1

Amber Nordlund lies in a hammock slung beneath the big pandanus tree on the edge of the coral beach. She wears a long silk wrap that covers the ugly scars all down her left side. Through the filter of drugs and dark glasses she observes the others.

Over there on the terrace, Uncle Konrad is standing beside his guest, the Chinese businessman, taking a last look over the beach and lagoon. They strike a discordant note in their suits and ties. The businessman's rosy, sun-flushed face makes Konrad appear almost albino. His skin is unusually pale for an Australian, his hair white, his suit light grey. The businessman transfers his briefcase to his left hand and raises his right in a stiff wave, like Chairman Mao blessing the young people lying in the sun. Cousin Ryan responds, leaping to his feet and crying, 'Mr Deng! You're leaving with Dad?' and runs up to shake his hand. The other two, Ryan's girlfriend Tayla and his younger brother Hayden, look up briefly, give an indolent wave and flop back down again. Amber closes her eyes, listening to the waves lapping against the shore, rattling the coral.

'Amber, dear?'

Her heart shrivels. Karen Schaefer is striding across the grass towards her carrying a tray with her pills and the little cup of morphine syrup. She protests but it's no use. She does as she's told, gulps them down, lies back and drifts into sleep.

She is wakened briefly by the thumping sound of the helicopter rising above the trees. It circles the island, then heads away to the south. The sunbeds on the beach are empty now.

Amber wakes again, her scars itching madly. She should go into the sea—the salt water is supposed to soothe the irritation, but she hates the coral. You can't lie down on it or walk on it without reef shoes.

Voices, heightened by alcohol she guesses—Konrad's two sons and Tayla along with one of the local staff boys, Selwyn, carrying gear down to the boat at the water's edge, flippers and scuba tanks. They fool around at the boat, Ryan and Tayla splashing through the waves, flicking water at each other. She looks hardly old enough to be sleeping with him, and Hayden watches her every movement from beneath his beetle brow.

Amber rouses herself, trying to shake the fuzziness from her brain. She gets unsteadily to her feet, slips off the wrap and concentrates on walking down the coral slope without falling over.

'Going diving? Can I come?'

They turn and stare at her, Hayden frowning doubtfully and the girl staring wide-eyed at the livid burn marks which she hasn't seen exposed before.

Ryan, muscled, tanned and arrogant, says, 'Not a good idea, Amber.'

She looks at him, tilting up her chin. 'It'll do my skin good.'

'We only have four tanks ready. Selwyn has to come down to show us where the giant clam is.'

Tayla chips in, 'She can have mine, Ryan. I really don't feel like it today. I'd rather stay on the boat.'

Ryan shakes his head in irritation, then shrugs. 'Okay, Amber, your call. You dive with Hayden and I'll buddy Selwyn.' He raises an eyebrow at his brother, who gives a quick nod.

They climb aboard and begin to strap on the scuba gear as Selwyn steers out across the lagoon towards the line of white water at the reef. When they reach it they drop anchor and lower themselves into the water. Ryan makes a final adjustment to his facemask, then he and Selwyn disappear beneath the surface.

Amber is having second thoughts. The water stings and her breathing isn't right. She's aware of how sluggish her brain is. She's in the ocean, no longer cocooned. It's what she wanted, but now it frightens her.

Hayden touches her good arm and she nods. Down they go.

The pressure begins building in her ears as they swim downward, side by side, following the figures of Ryan and Selwyn below them. The water is slightly milky, giving an ethereal effect, as if they are swimming through a pale mist.

Gradually the pressure in her ears becomes uncomfortable. She swallows but it makes no difference. Soon the pain becomes intense and she has to stop. Hayden turns and looks at her and she shakes her head, pointing at her ears. He waits while she tries again to clear them, but it's hopeless. He points upward and they swim back up towards the dark outline of the boat, the pressure easing as she rises.

Hayden gestures to the anchor rope and holds up his hands with extended fingers. Ten, he'll return for her in ten minutes, to give her a chance to adjust. She nods agreement, takes hold of the rope and hangs there as he dives away.

It's like being suspended weightless five storeys above the ground on a misty, sun-dappled day, swaying gently back and forth. Beneath her she can see Hayden investigating a cave, while the other two—Ryan with the distinctive orange cylinder on his back—work their way along the coral cliff that forms the reef. From time to time small shoals of brightly coloured fish dart into view.

Something larger, a groper perhaps, glides out of a dark hollow. A turtle swims by.

Time passes, dreamlike. Ryan and Selwyn have reached the far end of the coral cliff where it breaks down at the gap in the reef. Through the gap is darkness, the sudden plunge into deep ocean. Out there are the sharks.

The constant swaying is unsettling, creating a feeling like seasickness. She sees Hayden rising up towards her now as the nausea grows. He reaches her and offers his hand, but she waves it away, certain now that she will be sick. She imagines her facemask filling with vomit, choking her. She takes one last look below and sees a solitary diver, the orange cylinder, no sign of Selwyn, and then panic grips her, she grabs at her inflator valve and rockets up to the surface, rips off her mask and throws up. Blinking, gasping, she sees Tayla on the boat, staring at her in astonishment.

Hayden, laughing, helps her climb aboard, then goes to the controls and starts the engine. 'Let's get you to dry land.'

'What about the other two?'

'They'll swim back.'

When they reach the shore Hayden escorts her to her room in the villa, and despite her protests calls Karen, who bustles in, ranting.

'Stupid! Anything could have happened! You should never have let her go, Hayden.'

Amber tunes out, takes a shower, and when she returns Karen has turned down the sheets on her bed and is waiting with more pills. They knock her out within minutes.

It's dark when Amber wakes, the villa silent. She fumbles for the light, feeling disoriented and sore all over. She desperately needs a drink of water, but the glass is empty. She tries to stand but her legs won't hold her and she sinks back and rings for the maid. The time on her bedside clock is 1:36 am.

She stretches out a hand to steady herself and feels dampness on the bedsheet. She stares at it, then lifts her fingers to her nose, sniffs and gags on the sickly smell of semen.

There is a knock at the door and Pascaline comes in. She looks worried.

'Come here, Pascaline.' Amber points to the damp stain. 'What happened?'

'I don't know, ma'am,' she whispers, but she looks terrified.

'Yes, you do.' Amber takes her hand. 'Tell me. Was it Selwyn?'

'No, no, no! Selwyn is a good boy.'

'Who then?'

Pascaline bursts into tears, and Amber waits. Finally she hears a mumbled name.

'Mr Ryan? Is that what you said?'

Another sobbing mumble.

'And Mr Hayden? Both of them? Together?'

'And Selwyn is missing, ma'am,' she wails.

2

Kelly Pool catches a cab to the airport and is directed to a small office and waiting room for Yalanji Airlines. Two other passengers arrive with large bags, and in turn each person and bag is weighed on the scales, then taken out to the small plane on the strip.

They take off, rising above Cairns and turning north over the harbour dotted with small craft. The suburbs fade away and now the vast dark green mantle of rainforest appears below. Out beyond the coastline the shimmering blue of the Coral Sea is streaked with the pale irruptions of the Great Barrier Reef.

After half an hour they begin their descent. Kelly sees a break in the forest, a dark river, the brown gash of an estuary and then large bare paddocks where cattle scatter as the plane roars overhead. They land on a dusty grass strip and taxi up to a small tin shack with a set of scales and a fuel bowser standing outside.

A waiting taxi takes the other two passengers away and Kelly is left in the shade of the shack's veranda. Eventually a truck comes swaying out of the trees on the far side of the strip and pulls up in front of her. On its side is written:

O'Brien Pest Exterminator
—snakes
—spiders
—mothers-in-law
—daughter's useless redhead boyfriend

A wizened nugget of a man gets out of the truck and shakes her hand. 'Gus O'Brien,' he growls, and throws her bag in the back. She gets in beside him and they lurch off.

'Goin' to the lodge, right?'

'Yes.' A dust-filled wind whips Kelly's red hair and she struggles to close the window. 'Maybe you can help me, Gus. I'm hoping to contact someone I think is working up here. Name of Harry?'

O'Brien grunts. 'Know a few Harrys.'

'Belltree, Harry Belltree. Mean anything?'

Another grunt. He doesn't seem to want to elaborate.

After a couple of kilometres they arrive at the end of the track, a sandy beach on the edge of the dark river she saw from the plane. They get out and O'Brien retrieves her bag, takes it down to a small aluminium boat tied up at the water's edge and helps her in. He pushes off, starts the outboard and they set off upstream.

Dense rainforest crowds the banks, broken only by the occasional glimpse of a fibro cottage in a clearing. Eventually he throttles down and turns in towards an opening in the trees with a few rotten timber stumps driven into the bank. A large brown log is lying nearby in the shadows.

'Harry stays here.'

She glimpses a mould-stained hut set back in a small paddock.

'Him and Marilyn.'

'Marilyn? He has a partner?' She feels a pang of disappointment.

'Could say that. That's Marilyn there.' O'Brien points at the log, which stirs.

'Oh my God.' Kelly has made out the ridges down its back, and the pair of eyes staring balefully at her. 'A crocodile.'

'Yeah, a saltie.'

'It's huge.'

'Nah, fourteen foot. The males are bigger. She's vicious, but. Took Wally's dog last week. This is her stretch of bank.'

'But how…how does Harry get to the house?'

'Lands at a different spot each time, so she doesn't know where to lie in wait.'

Crocodile roulette, Kelly thinks. Harry's suicidal. That figures.

At that moment Marilyn decides to lumber to the edge. She slides down the muddy slope into the water and disappears with barely a ripple. Kelly feels a flutter of panic.

'She's bigger than this boat, Gus! She's underneath us! She could tip us over, couldn't she?'

O'Brien shrugs and revs up the engine, turns the boat away. 'You want to see Harry now? Reckon he'll be up at the school.'

He becomes more talkative, pointing out birdlife on the river banks, an osprey and the flash of a blue little kingfisher catching shrimp. Then a stretch of shallow water, the ford where an Aboriginal boy was taken by a croc last year, a big male that was chased far out to sea before it disappeared. Then he probes, none too tactfully. Is she a sister? A girlfriend? An abandoned wife? Just an old friend, she says.

They reach a weir, and O'Brien takes the boat in to a jetty where they disembark and follow a track leading up to the gates of a compound of low buildings, spreading eaves. He leads the way in, Kelly's bag slung over his shoulder. They cross a courtyard, hearing the sound of children singing, and O'Brien shoves open the door of one of the buildings, a workshop of some kind, machine tools on benches, pulleys hanging from steel girders. At one of the benches a group of teenagers is clustered around an engine which a man appears to be dismantling. He looks up and Kelly barely recognises him—the hair grown out in long locks, the shaggy beard, the weathered features.

'Harry,' O'Brien says. 'Brought you a lady friend,' and half a dozen small black faces turn to stare.

He comes over, looking sombre, then a smile. 'Kelly. This is a surprise. How did you find me?'

They sit on a bench beneath a tree in the courtyard, awkward. She looks around, trying to imagine this strange place as Harry's home in the wilderness—Harry the broken-hearted hermit. Perhaps he isn't the man she knew; he certainly looks different.

'The paper has, um…resources. I traced an airline ticket in your name up to Cairns, so I flew up and found the boatyard where you were working. They told me you'd come up here.'

'Why?'

'It's Jenny, Harry.' She hesitates. 'She's missing, disappeared.'

He's very still, says nothing for a moment, as if adjusting to a different time and world. 'Go on.'

'Her sister Nicole got in touch with me last Tuesday and I went to see her. She was very worried. Ten days ago Jenny asked her to look after her baby while she went away for a few days…Nicole said you know about Abigail? Your daughter?'

'Yes, I spoke to Nicole a couple of times, earlier in the year. How is Abigail?'

'She's lovely, Harry, growing quite steadily now…anyway, Jenny left her with Nicole, which was kind of strange, because she hadn't let her out of her sight since she was born. Then, before she was due back, Jenny called Nicole and said she had to go away. She sounded distressed and Nicole was convinced that something bad had happened. She contacted me and asked if I knew how to reach you. She wants you to help find her.'

Harry frowns, shaking his head. 'If she wanted to be found she'd let you know. I'm the last person she'd call for.'

Silence.

'Has Nicole spoken to the police?'

'That was the worrying thing. While Nicole and her mother were debating whether to contact the police, the police came round to see them. They wanted to know where Jenny was, wouldn't say why. They need your help, Harry.'

She rummages in her bag for her pad and flicks the pages. 'Here, this was the name of the cop that called on them—Detective Sergeant Anders. Maybe you could speak to him.'

She shows Harry the note and he stares at it.

'There was a woman in uniform as well, who didn't say anything. They didn't get her name.'

'You have a phone?' he says, his voice suddenly sharp. 'See if you can get us on the afternoon flight from Cairns down to Sydney, will you?'

'But…I'm booked in at the lodge for a couple of days.'

He's gone, striding over to O'Brien, who's waiting at the gate. They talk, O'Brien nodding, checking his watch. Harry returns. 'Let's go.'

O'Brien stops the boat briefly at Harry's forlorn house for him to pick up a small backpack of belongings. As he returns to the boat Kelly takes a photo of him, thinking about a possible feature, 'The Lost Detective', for the *Times*' weekend colour magazine. Marilyn in the foreground showing her teeth would be good.

3

On the flight back to Sydney, Kelly says, 'You know the cop?'

'Jack Anders, yes.' Harry turns away and looks out over the clouds. 'He's in homicide.'

'Oh shit…But surely if something had happened to Jenny they would have said?'

'You'd think so.'

It's dark by the time they land and catch a cab to Nicole's house in North Sydney, Kelly phoning ahead to warn her.

They hear her feet running to the front door, it swings open and Nicole gawps for a moment. 'Harry! It *is* you! Thank God,' she says, and throws herself at him in a hug.

She leads them down to the living room, with its views out over the dark hills of Middle Harbour, sparkling now with house lights among the native bush.

'You found him, Kelly. Where?'

Kelly explains and Nicole says, 'You must be exhausted. Something to eat, a drink?'

Yes, please, Kelly thinks, but Harry says, 'Later. Just tell me what's happened, Nicole, from the beginning.'

'Well, you know about Abigail. After the doctors decided they couldn't wait any longer—Christmas Eve it was—they operated and she was born and the bullet in Jenny's stomach successfully removed. The two of them were kept in the neonatal ICU at Westmead for a month, then transferred to a private clinic in North Sydney, near our mum. When they were fit enough they moved in with her, and for a long while Jenny just wanted to stay there, in her old room, looking after Abigail.

'Then finally the Ash Island inquest was held and she was called to appear at the court—the beginning of spring, it was, early September. She was very anxious about it. For almost nine months she'd isolated herself from everything, focusing on Abigail, and now she was forced to confront it all again. If only you'd been there, Harry. It was a disaster. Frank Capp's sister appeared, in a wheelchair, and when they got to the part where Capp was killed, the sister went crazy, screaming threats and abuse at Jenny.

'She changed after that, stopped breastfeeding Abigail and started drinking. She told me she was waking up in the middle of the night reliving the crash, seeing Frank Capp's face staring through the car window as he ran them off the road, and she didn't know if it was her memory come back or a dream. I tried to help, talk to her. One day she asked me to go with her to your old house in Surry Hills, to pick up clothes and some of her stuff that was still there. When we got there she broke down in tears, asked me why all this had happened to her. I asked her if she wanted me to try to find you, but she just shook her head and said it was all too difficult, with Mum so bitter about what happened to her sister Meri, and blaming you.

'After a while I thought she pulled round a bit. She seemed more composed, more her old self. We went out together, a movie, a concert, and I thought she'd settled down.

'Then a couple of weeks ago she said she wanted to have a few days away on her own, and would I look after Abigail, to give Mum a break. I said that was fine, and she dropped the baby and her stuff off here—that was the ninth, Thursday. She said she'd rented a cottage in the Blue Mountains and would be back on the following Tuesday but on Monday she phoned me, sounding in a bit of a state. I asked her what was wrong and she said she was sorry, but something had come up and could I look after Abigail for a while longer. She wouldn't tell me why and she hung up. Then the following day the police came round looking for her.

'The detective, Anders, did all the talking. He asked for a list of Jenny's friends and associates, and I didn't know what to tell him. I gave him a few names, but I asked why, and he just said they had concerns for Jenny's safety and it was imperative I contact him if I got any word of her. It was maddening—he wouldn't tell me what was going on. He mentioned a man's name, asked me if I knew him. I made a note...' She pauses and goes over to the notepad beside the phone. 'Palfreyman, Terry Palfreyman. I'd never heard of him and told him so.'

'You've tried to contact her?'

'Of course. We call her mobile all the time, but there's no reply, and I've been to your place in Surry Hills. Mum had a key for emergencies, and I went in, but there was no sign of her. The policeman, Anders, had been there too—he'd left his card in the postbox with a note to Jenny to call him urgently.'

'And Abigail is here with you?'

'Yes. Oh, Harry, I'm sorry, of course you want to see her. Come on.'

They go downstairs and are joined by Nicole's two girls, Clare and Helen, who regard their uncle's transformation with some awe. They lead him to a cot in the corner of the next room. Harry goes over to it, and for a long moment father and daughter look at each other, studying each other's features for the first time. Then Harry lowers his hand and carefully strokes the baby's cheek, and she gives a little kick of her legs. He lifts her up and she reaches out to his face and clutches his beard. Clare captures the moment on her phone.

'She's bigger than I expected,' he says. 'Heavier.'

Nicole smiles. 'She's almost ten months, Harry, though she was fifteen weeks premature. She's doing really well, considering— weighs almost six and half kilos.'

Then Harry says, 'I need to speak to your mother, Nicole.'

'She won't see you, Harry. She blames you for Meri and for what happened to Jenny. She said…' Nicole looks down, embarrassed.

'Go on.'

'That you were a menace and a curse and she never wanted you to come near us again.'

'All the same, Jenny stayed all that time with your mother. I need to search her room, check her computer if it's still there. Did the police do that?'

'I don't know. I'll try to persuade her, first thing tomorrow. Will you stay here tonight?'

He looks down at his clothes, the worn jungle-green shirt and shorts, the scuffed boots, as if realising for the first time how incongruous he looks here in the city, the wild man from the bush. 'Thanks, no. I'll go to Surry Hills. I should find some fresh clothes there.'

4

He opens the front door of the little house at the end of the lane in Surry Hills, his parents' house until they died, then his and Jenny's. When he reaches for the light switch he hesitates—on or off? Either way it'll be a sign. He presses the switch and the lights come on. Someone has been paying the bills. Someone reluctant to make a final break.

He closes the door, drops his bag and looks around the living room, breathing in the smell of old timber and over a century of habitation. He remembers dancing here with Jenny in the dark, when she was blind and he made himself sightless, to be closer to her. The table in the corner is still there, but her computer is gone.

He continues through to the kitchen. Everything is clean, orderly. There is beer and a bottle of white wine in the fridge, an unopened packet of biscuits in a cupboard. He sits himself down at the round table and eats and drinks and tries to slow down. So strong is the presence of the house around him that it almost feels as if he's never been away, as if the past months in north Queensland have never happened.

He goes upstairs and hesitates again at the wardrobe and chest of drawers in their bedroom—cedar pieces as old as the house. Some of her clothes remain, but many are missing, clothes bought before she became pregnant. He imagines her opening the drawers and seeing their colours for the first time. Picturing her here is intensely painful. She's all around him. What's happened to her?

5

Angophora Way, Frenchs Forest, in Sydney's northern suburbs. Large gardens, large houses, large trees and no one around. Harry sits in Nicole's car while she crosses the street to a solid brick house overarched by a huge Sydney red gum. He waits. After half an hour the front door opens and her mother Bronwyn appears with a yellow Labrador on a lead. It is Felecia, Jenny's seeing-eye dog, now retired. Bronwyn pointedly avoids looking in the direction of the car and they walk away down the street as Harry's phone rings.

'Mum's taken Jenny's dog for a walk, Harry. It's okay for you to come in if you want.'

Nicole closes the door behind him as he steps inside. He remembers the house when Jenny and Nicole's father was alive, a large genial man with a booming voice, generous with the gin. Now it's deathly quiet.

'All right?'

'Mum won't speak to you, but she said you can check Jenny's room. She said the police were in there for ten minutes or so when they called, but didn't remove anything as far as she knows. Apparently Felecia kept a close eye on them.'

They go upstairs to the bedroom Jenny had as a girl. There is a cot now standing in the corner, and a moist baby smell in the air. 'It seems Jenny went back to your house several times after I took her there to get her clothes. She brought stuff back here.' Nicole points at the pinboard above Jenny's table, covered with notes and old photographs. 'Mum asked her what she was doing and she said she had just collected a few family mementos.'

It was more than that, Harry thinks, more like the material for a family history. There is a picture of his father in school uniform, standing grinning with the white couple who brought him up, whom Harry called his grandparents. Another monochrome snap, faded and creased, that Harry hasn't seen before, of a young Aboriginal woman. And a photocopy of the picture of his mother and father before they were married, university students on the 1965 Freedom Ride across inland New South Wales, which hung in his father's study in the attic of the Surry Hills house. A scanner sits on the end of the table, but no computer.

'Yes,' Nicole says, 'Mum said Jenny had a laptop that she took away with her to the Blue Mountains.'

Harry takes photos of the pinboard, then searches drawers and the wardrobe, nothing significant. He picks up an empty wastebasket. 'The garbage, when is that collected?'

'Tuesdays, I think. Anyway, it's over a week since Jenny left, so it'll be gone. Except perhaps the recycling bin—that's only collected every second week.'

They go downstairs and out to the back of the house where the colour-coded bins stand. The recycling bin is almost full, and Harry starts to empty it, layer by layer—newspapers, wine bottles, plastic containers—until he reaches a swatch of torn A4 pages at the bottom. He recognises Jenny's handwriting on some, scribbled notes of dates, train times, a shopping list. Among them he pieces together three torn-up pages of printouts from her computer: one for a brand of baby clothes, another for a company dealing in bitcoins and the third a receipt for the purchase of a single share in Nordlund Resources Limited.

6

Kelly bustles up to her desk on the third floor, throws down her bag, puts the coffee mug beside her computer and starts to go through her emails.

'You're back early.' Hannah, her trainee assistant at the next desk, has returned to her seat, also nursing a coffee. 'I thought you were taking a week off.'

'Hmm, got bored. What's going on?'

Hannah briefs her on the latest office rumours and the research she's been doing for one of the other crime reporters.

'Have we heard of someone called Terry Palfreyman?' Kelly asks. 'Will you take a look?'

'The body in the Blue Mountains,' Hannah says immediately. 'His name was released while you were away. Fifty-four-year-old white male stabbed to death in a cottage on the edge of Blackheath. The body was found last Tuesday, remember? We talked about it the day you left.'

'Ah, yes, of course.'

'Why, you heard something?'

'Maybe. Do we have a picture?'

Hannah brings it up on her screen and Kelly downloads it to her phone, a blotchy lined face with an angry frown. Kelly says, 'If they ever find my body I hope they use a more flattering picture of me. What do we know?'

'Sounds as if he had a lady friend. The police are anxious to speak to a white woman, mid-thirties, slim build, 165 centimetres, who was seen in his company in Blackheath.'

'Name?'

'No.'

'Who's been following this?'

'Brendon, I think.'

Kelly calls up the report that Brendon filed, then goes over to his desk. He's one of the veterans, feet up on his desk taking a call, arguing with someone. She waits till he slams the phone down.

'Kelly, hi. Take a seat. Thought you were on holiday.'

'I came back. I wanted to ask you about Terry Palfreyman.'

'Who?'

'The murder in Blackheath last week.'

'Oh, him, yeah. The troll.'

'Eh?'

'A serial pest. One of those obsessed people who turn up at company shareholder meetings and ask curly questions about executive salaries and unethical work practices. Our business desk knew about him. Bit of a character. Sometimes he'd turn up in fancy dress or stark naked. He'd been arrested as a public nuisance a couple of times.'

'So he made enemies.'

'Lots. Heavy drinker, argumentative, prone to getting into fights with people. Probably went too far and got stabbed.'

'What about the woman the police are looking for?'

'No idea. A witness?' He shrugs. 'Maybe she did it.'

'Did you go up there to look around?'

21

'No chance. That was the day Slaughter Park broke. All hands on deck.'

'Slaughter Park?'

'Jesus, where have you been?' He laughs and reaches down to a drawer under his desk and pulls out a copy of the paper. Kelly glimpses a pile of identical copies beneath it.

She reads the front-page headline, *Slaughter Park*, byline *Brendon Pyle, senior crime reporter*. The report begins: *Police have revealed the discovery of multiple human body parts scattered in Slater Park, in inner west Sydney.*

'Oh, Slater Park,' Kelly says. 'I get it.'

'Slaughter was my tag.' Brendon taps the headline. 'Now everybody's using it. Even the police commissioner, by mistake, at the last briefing.'

One detective, who asked not to be named, described the dismembered corpses as 'fresh', and the carnage as the most gruesome crime scene he had witnessed in many years on the force.

'Christ,' Kelly murmurs. 'How many bodies were there?'

'Two, it turned out. Chopped up and the bits suspended from ribbons tied to the branches of trees.'

'Ribbons?'

'Pink ribbons, yeah. The victims were two girls who'd attended evening classes at the Slater Park Art School the previous night. The police haven't a clue. It's caused panic in the inner west. Wasn't this on the news where you were?'

His phone begins to ring.

'Well…congratulations, Brendon. I'll get up to speed.'

'Luck of the draw, Kelly,' he says smugly. 'So if you want to follow up on the Blackheath business, be my guest.'

'I'll do that.'

'Talk to Lou Reid in business. He'll tell you more about Palfreyman.' He snatches up the phone and turns away.

Kelly looks at him with a smile. Brendon, the oldest reporter left at the *Times*, was in need of a break. Good on you, she thinks.

She takes the stairs up to the next floor where Reid has a desk over by the glass curtain wall looking across Pyrmont Bay to the towers of the CBD.

'Yeah, Terry was a character. We'll miss him. Thing is, for all his stupid antics, he often had a good point to make.'

'What kind of companies did he target?'

'Banks and resources companies mainly—Rio Tinto, Xstrata, BHP, NRL—particularly NRL. He'd been some kind of mining engineer in the past, had a company that went bust and he got bitter.'

'NRL, that's Nordlund Resources?'

'Right, his favourite target. He'd worked for them at one stage. They had their AGM a couple of weeks ago and Terry was there. He kept his clothes on this time. You can download the video and see him.'

'The company releases a video of the meeting?'

'Yes, the bigger companies do that.'

Kelly goes back to her desk thinking, Nordlund, Nordlund. The big mining company. Ash Island all over again. What have you got yourself into, Jenny?

She tries to phone Harry, but he's not answering. She leaves a message.

7

Harry calls police headquarters at Parramatta and asks to be put through to Detective Sergeant Anders, who answers immediately.

'Harry! Where are you, mate?'

'In Sydney, Jack. We need to talk.'

'Sure, sure. Come in and see me. Soon as you like.'

'An hour?

It takes all of that for the cab to make its way out through heavy traffic to western Sydney, and Anders is waiting on the far side of the barrier in the lobby of the glass tower when he arrives. Harry's pass doesn't work and Anders signs him through.

'Coffee, mate?'

He follows Anders to the kiosk in the waiting area and watches him join a knot of uniforms and office workers at the counter. It's strange coming back, seeing them as if through a screen. He feels that he's no longer the person who used to come here every morning.

Anders returns with two paper cups and they go over to the lifts. Detached, Harry watches Anders press the button for the eighth floor. There are others in the lift and no one speaks.

When they emerge they walk through the rogues' gallery lined with old press cuttings and photographs of famous murders from the past and arrive at the main office area of the homicide squad, ranks of deserted desks and computers.

'Everyone's out?'

'Yeah, busy, busy. Slaughter Park, yeah?' Anders leads him to one of the meeting rooms. Deb Velasco is there, detective inspector, studying a computer screen. She gets to her feet. 'Harry. Long time.'

'Hi, Deb. Looking good.'

She gives him a warm smile, but her eyes are examining him, assessing. 'Take a seat. What've you been up to?'

He mentions Cairns, the far north, the school.

'Interesting. I've never been up there. Did you get hit by that cyclone?'

'It missed us, fortunately. Deb, what's this about Jenny?'

They look at each other for a moment, then she nods. 'We're going to have to record this, Harry.' She reaches forward to a console and presses a switch.

'Is she in trouble?'

'Detective Inspector Deb Velasco and Detective Sergeant Jack Anders interviewing Harry Belltree. Harry, when did you last see your wife, Jenny Belltree?'

No mention of his rank. He has no standing anymore. He lifts his hands, exasperated. 'The eleventh of December last year, at Westmead Hospital, intensive care.'

'Go on.'

'She was twenty-two weeks pregnant and had Frank Capp's bullet inside her and the doctors didn't know if they could save either of them. She told me it was all my fault and she didn't want to see me again. I complied.'

'Really? You just walked out and haven't seen her since?'

'Yes.' He feels that sudden nausea that hits him whenever he thinks of this. When he speaks again he has to clear his throat. 'I thought she was right—I was responsible for what happened and I believed that they would be much safer without me.'

Deb nods. 'Right. I'm sorry. Difficult for you. Did you have any kind of contact with her after that?'

'I got daily reports from her sister Nicole on their progress up until the end of January, when the baby had been safely delivered and they were both well on the way to recovery. Then I decided to leave Sydney. After that I phoned Nicole a couple of times to hear how things were going. I never spoke to Jenny.'

'Tell me again where you were exactly up north.'

'Why?'

'Just do it, Harry, for the record.'

He tells her: first Cairns, then up in the Daintree Rainforest. She insists on dates, addresses, employer contact details, and he begins to wonder if he's infringed the terms of his leave. He asks her, and she shakes her head. 'No, Harry. Nothing like that. Did you travel further afield while you were up there?'

'Out onto the reef a few times.'

'How about the Northern Territory?'

'Eh? No, nothing like that.'

'You made monthly payments into Jenny's bank account. Did she ever acknowledge those?'

Anders lifts an eyebrow and pointedly studies his notebook. Harry stares at Deb and she stares right back. Why is she telling him that they've accessed her bank account? Is she trying to warn him or just piss him off?

'No, she didn't.'

'And when did you return to Sydney?'

'Last night.'

'Why?'

'Nicole was worried about Jenny, especially after Jack here called on her and wouldn't explain why. She hoped I could find out what was going on. So what is going on, Deb?'

'We believe Jenny can help us with our enquiries into the suspicious death of a man at Blackheath in the Blue Mountains on Sunday or Monday of last week.'

'Have you released her name as a person of interest?'

'Not yet. We will if we have to.'

They've got a lead on her, he thinks, and don't want to spook her. He says, 'You don't sound worried about her safety, Deb. How do you know she isn't a victim too?'

'All the more reason to find her as quickly as possible.'

'She may be dead.' He hears the crack in his voice and tries to hold himself together. 'Who's the victim?'

'A man called Terry Palfreyman. Heard of him?'

'No. Who is he?'

She turns to the computer and taps the keyboard, then turns the screen towards Harry. 'This is a picture of him. You sure you don't know him?'

He studies the picture, shakes his head. 'No. And he lived in Blackheath?'

She doesn't answer that. Instead she says, 'So when you were up north, did you go over to Darwin?'

'Darwin? No.'

'It's not far from Cairns, is it?'

He laughs. 'Only two or three thousand kilometres. What are you going on about, Deb?'

She looks annoyed. 'Do you know anyone who lives in Darwin?'

'No.'

'Does Jenny? Think before you answer, Harry.'

'I've never heard her mention anyone living up there. Why?'

She frowns, checks her watch.

'Listen,' Harry says, 'I know Jenny better than anyone. If you'll just give me the whole picture I may be able to make sense of it for you.'

Neither of them will meet his eyes.

'For God's sake,' he says, 'you can't seriously have Jenny down as a suspect! There's no way.'

'But she's done it before, Harry,' Deb says softly. 'She killed Frank Capp to save you. Maybe Palfreyman was a threat to her and her baby.'

'In what way?'

She shrugs.

'Deb, please, let me in. Get me back into homicide and I'll work with you, I'll keep nothing back.'

They look at him as if he's joking. Deb says, 'I'm sorry, Harry, that's impossible. This has been a formal interview. Is there anything else we should know?'

He sinks back in his chair. 'No.'

Deb presses the console switch again and gets to her feet. 'I'll see you out, Harry. Thanks, Jack.'

'Sure.' Anders shakes his hand, looking apologetic, and mutters, 'Tough, mate. Chin up.'

Deb is silent as they walk to the lift. It's empty and she stabs at several floor numbers. The doors close and she says, 'I'm sorry, Harry, my hands are tied. We've been told we can only talk to you as a potential witness.'

The doors open and close at the next floor.

Harry says, 'I'll speak to Bob Marshall.'

'He isn't our boss anymore. There's been a lot of changes since you went away—new state government, two new deputy commissioners, and we have a new head of homicide, Superintendent Blake. You know Dick?'

Harry shakes his head. Another floor comes and goes as they make their slow descent.

'Bob's retired?'

'Moved to North Ryde, head of road safety division.'

'Hell.'

Next stop ground floor. Deb turns to him and says, 'This is a bad time, Harry. Maybe later, when we've got some answers, we can talk again, catch up properly, have a drink.'

The doors open and as he steps out she adds quietly, 'We have grounds for believing that Jenny's still alive.'

The doors close and she is gone.

8

Kelly sits at her computer watching the film of the recent NRL annual general meeting. The camera pans across an auditorium filled with shareholders and turns towards the stage on which board members are seated behind a long table. Behind them a large screen glows with the title of the event. Each board member has a microphone, laptop and name plate, and one of their places is empty.

A portentous voice announces, 'Ladies and gentlemen, the chairman of Nordlund Resources Limited, the Right Honourable Warren Dalkeith AO,' and there is a solid round of applause as the member sitting next to the central lectern gets to his feet to address the gathering. He is a familiar figure, a former premier of the state of New South Wales, the silver hair and ruddy complexion, the statesmanlike poise modified by a cheeky grin, as if to say *we're all good mates here, out for a day's sport*. He welcomes the shareholders and introduces the people on the stage, apologising for the one missing board member, Amber Nordlund, prevented from attending due to ill health. Then he sets out the order of business and hands over to the company CEO to present the annual report.

Konrad Nordlund is a very different character. He speaks in a low, emotionless monotone, making no attempt to engage his audience. His manner seems to imply indifference, or even contempt. When he sits down again there is a moment's silence before uncertain clapping breaks out.

After the board presentations comes question time and Dalkeith steps up to the lectern again, beaming, inviting the questioners by name, as if he's back on the floor of parliament at question time sparring with old rivals.

'Mr Palfreyman!' he calls and the camera swings to the unkempt figure in the audience who gets stiffly to his feet and speaks in a flat north of England accent that sounds out of place in this room.

'I should like to ask the CEO if this company has adopted the iniquitous practice of postponing payment of bills from small suppliers and subcontractors for sixty, ninety, even a hundred and twenty days, which in these times of dropping coal prices and shrinking markets is having the effect of driving many viable small businesses into bankruptcy.'

Dalkeith turns to Nordlund, who doesn't bother to get to his feet, but leans forward to his microphone and says flatly, 'This company follows general industry practice.'

The camera returns to Palfreyman, who seems on the point of saying more, but then slumps back down onto his seat.

Kelly pauses the video, looking at the people sitting around Palfreyman. There is a woman, three places along in the row behind, who looks very like Jenny Belltree.

9

Harry tries Bob Marshall's old mobile number, hoping it still works.

'Harry? Is that you?'

'Yes, Bob. I'm back.'

'About bloody time, mate.'

'Can I see you?'

'Come to my office in an hour. We'll have a sandwich and a chat. Know where I am?'

It's an anonymous office building set back in a compound filled with patrol cars. The officer on the reception desk tells him that Superintendent Marshall is expecting him and gives him a pass and directions to the third floor.

Harry is shocked by how much older Bob looks, diminished, as if only the uniform is holding him together. 'Welcome to my domain, son,' Bob says with a grim smile, gesturing at the large poster on the wall behind his desk: *The Five Rules of Road Safety.* 'Where the hell have you been?'

'Up north, Cape Tribulation.'

'Done you good by the looks of it. Maybe I should try it.'

'Been rough, has it?'

'Oh,' Bob sighs, waves him to a seat. 'Politics, you wouldn't believe. It's a relief to go out and talk to the school kiddies. But that's not what you're here for, is it? Jenny, right?'

'Yes.'

'What do you know?'

'Her sister Nicole got a message to me, that Jenny hasn't been seen since the thirteenth, and the cops—Jack Anders—were looking for her.'

'You've spoken to Jack?'

'Just came from there. He and Deb interviewed me as a possible witness. They suspect Jenny is involved in the death of a man called Terry Palfreyman in the Blue Mountains.'

Bob nods. 'Did they tell you anything else?'

'They asked me some strange questions about Darwin—had I been there, did Jenny know anyone there. Didn't explain why.'

'Hmm.' Bob reaches behind him to a platter of sandwiches and puts it on the table between them, peels off the plastic wrap. 'Have a bite to eat. Beer?'

Harry looks at him in surprise. Bob had an iron rule about drinking on duty.

'Who gives a fuck.' Bob reaches into a small refrigerator beneath his desk and brings out two cans. 'Strike Force Redgum traced a cash withdrawal yesterday from an ATM in central Darwin using Jenny's credit card. Doesn't mean Jenny used it of course. They're waiting for CCTV images.'

'How do you know?'

'I may be in the cold outer limits of the galaxy out here, mate, but I still have a few connections to the throbbing heart.'

'Anything else?'

Bob doesn't reply. He opens his can, then reaches down and slowly selects a sandwich. He says, 'Had any contact with Jenny in the last nine months, Harry?'

He shakes his head.

Bob goes on, 'Must've been bloody hard for her, the operations, the trauma, family torn apart, coping with a frail baby. I was worried, called in to see her a few times. She put on a brave front, like always, but I could see the strain in her eyes, her posture. I was concerned.' He takes a bite and chews thoughtfully. 'Then all of a sudden she walks out, leaves her baby with her sister and goes off for a weekend in the Blue Mountains—alone, she tells her family. Seems odd, yes?'

'Absolutely. And gets herself mixed up in a murder. It's crazy, insane...' Harry stops. 'No, I don't mean...'

'Well, that's one possibility, I suppose, that all that accumulated stress caused her to snap and lash out and kill a complete stranger who maybe made an inappropriate or threatening approach.'

'No, not Jenny. That's not possible.'

'Nine months is a long time, Harry. A lot can change in a person in that time.'

'Don't tell me she'd killed once before. Deb gave me that line.'

'She's thinking what a jury would think. But there are other ways of looking at it.'

'Go on.'

'Jenny's prints and DNA were found all over the victim's cottage—the living room, the kitchen, the *bathroom*, the *bedroom*. And on the murder weapon, a carving knife from the kitchen of the house next door, which Jenny had rented for a week. The knife was sticking in his chest, and there were bloody footprints leading from the body to the other house, a pair of Jenny's bloodied shoes inside. Palfreyman had been drinking a bottle of red wine that was bought on the afternoon of the thirteenth from the local bottle shop by Jenny using her credit card. The girl there remembers quite well, because Jenny was with Palfreyman, who was a regular there— a heavy vodka drinker—and there was something different about him that day. He'd had a haircut and was wearing aftershave, and instead of his usual grumpy monosyllables he was cheerful, even flirtatious—that was the word she used, flirtatious. Want to see?'

Reluctantly Harry gets up to watch as Bob taps at his computer, opening up the police e@gle.i database and finding the clip from the bottle shop security camera. And there is Jenny, looking smart in a jacket and skirt he hasn't seen before, being ushered into the store by a rather clumsy older man. The camera shows them examining a rack of red wines from which they select a bottle and go to the counter, where the man—Palfreyman—hails the girl behind the till, then reaches out for another bottle, vodka this time. Harry bites his lip as Palfreyman puts his arm round Jenny's shoulder as she opens her purse and pays for both. It feels shocking and voyeuristic to be watching this, and he wants to cry out to her, *Jenny, turn around, I'm here.* As they walk towards the door Palfreyman staggers against the wall and Jenny takes his arm and leads him out.

'A Brokenwood 2013 Nebbiolo,' Bob says. 'Forty bucks. Not bad, eh? That was the last sighting of the pair of them. So...' Bob resumes his seat and selects another sandwich, '...what was going on? Have they just met by chance? A casual encounter? There's another statement from a waitress in a café nearby where they had breakfast together that morning. Again she remarks about how happy and friendly they seemed, a regular couple.

'Or did they know each other from before? Had they perhaps *arranged* to be staying in neighbouring cottages up there, secluded in the bush on the edge of town, old mates reconnecting? You got any thoughts on that, Harry? Not old schoolfriends—he's too old for that—but maybe someone she met through her legal work? While you were in the army, perhaps? He did have a record of using lawyers, but I don't know if they've checked if he was ever a client of Jenny's firm. No doubt they'll get around to that. So were they lovers? Was it a deadly lovers' quarrel? They'd certainly been drinking pretty heavily—the pathology results show he had a blood-alcohol reading of point two three when he died, and he hadn't been drinking alone.'

Harry wants to tell Bob to shut the fuck up, but of course he can't. He has to sit and listen as Bob forces him to confront all of the painful possibilities.

'No,' he says at last. 'Jenny has better taste than that.'

Bob chuckles. 'Point taken. He's not much of a catch. But maybe he had something else she wanted.'

'And you're going to tell me what it was.' Harry drains his can and Bob reaches into his secret refrigerator and pops him another.

'You can find most of it on the web. Born in Pontefract, Yorkshire, England, 1960. Degree in mechanical engineering at Manchester University, worked on the North Sea oil rigs, married Sheila 1987. In 1990 got a job on the Saudi oilfields, then came to Australia in 1993 to work on Bass Strait. In 1995 he moved to the Hunter Valley coalfields and in 1998 set up his own engineering company, Palfreyman Engineering, designing a revolutionary hydraulic stone duster machine for underground mines. In 2000 he went into partnership with Nordlund Resources Limited to produce and market his machine. Four years later the partnership collapsed and entered a protracted period of legal disputes. Palfreyman ran out of money, went bankrupt, wife Sheila divorced him and returned to England, and he was left a bitter and obsessed man. He was arrested in 2009 for setting fire to a Nordlund maintenance depot in the Hunter Valley, and served eighteen months in jail.'

'Nordlund,' Harry says.

'Yes, Nordlund. I'm not sure if Strike Force Redgum has realised the significance of that yet.'

'But...that's crazy, Bob. The whole point of Jenny insisting I stay away from her was because she was terrified I would endanger her and her family again by getting mixed up with people like the Nordlunds. She would never have walked into a situation like that.'

'And yet it seems that's exactly what she did do, Harry.'

He's enjoying this, much more fun than talking to schoolkids about the five rules of road safety. But it's bruising Harry, who feels he's become mentally unfit for it, having tried to avoid hard thinking for so long.

'Why?'

Bob shrugs. 'I have no idea.'

Harry shakes his head, struggling with confusion, while Bob just sits there, munching, watching him.

'Apart from the credit card, have they found any other trace of Jenny after the murder?'

'Not as far as I know. They don't seem to have found any CCTV sightings so far.'

'What can I do, Bob?'

Bob shrugs. 'Not a thing. Wait and see.'

'Yeah. Well, thanks, thanks for filling me in.'

'I've told you nothing, Harry, nothing about Jenny, because I know nothing. All right? We've just had a chat about old times and a sandwich and you asked me about what's happened and I wasn't able to tell you anything more than I read in the papers. Got it?'

'Sure.'

'They're tapping your phone and tracking your movements for sure, and now they'll probably tap my phone too, if they're not already doing it. So it'd be best if you didn't come back here again.'

'Right.'

As they get to their feet Bob reaches into a desk drawer and pulls out something wrapped in a plastic bag and hands it to Harry. 'You can call me on the programmed number, son. They won't trace it.'

Bob escorts him down to the lobby, they shake hands and Bob says loudly, 'Sorry I couldn't help, Harry. Just be patient. All the best.'

10

Harry stands outside the road safety division offices feeling humiliated and helpless. And angry with himself. What bloody use is he? No car, no gun, no computer, and a phone that's bugged. He switches the phone back on to call for a cab and it immediately begins to ring. Kelly Pool.

'Harry! I've been trying to call you. I—'

'Kelly,' he says sharply. 'I told you I've got nothing to say to you. I know no more than you do.'

'Yes, but—'

'Look, I can give you five minutes, that's all.'

'O-kay.'

He hears the hesitation in her voice, wondering what's going on. 'In an hour. Meet me at Di Bella on Holt Street in Surry Hills. Five minutes, that's all.'

'Whatever you say, Harry.'

He rings off and calls the taxi. Once inside he opens Bob's package. It's an encrypted Blackphone, supposedly immune to police tracking.

He arrives ten minutes late and sees her sitting inside with a cup of coffee in front of her. He takes a seat at her table with his back to the window, leans forward and says softly, 'Sorry about that. Don't look, but they're sitting in that blue Falcon across the street, with a camera and a long-range mic.'

'What?' She has to lean close to hear what he's saying over the loud music. 'Who are?'

'Homicide cops. They're hoping I'll give them a lead to Jenny. My phone's bugged, that's why I had to speak to you like that.'

'Jesus, Harry. What are we going to do?'

'We're going to have an argument, then I'm going to get up and storm out of here and go back to my place around the corner, and you'll head back to your office. Sometime later I'll leave my phone at home and come and meet you wherever you like. Have you been up to Blackheath?'

'Not yet. I was going to suggest we did that.'

'Good. I haven't got wheels.'

'I'll pick you up below Central station, four-thirty?'

'Great.'

There's a lull in the music and he jumps to his feet. 'No, Kelly, no way! Just leave me alone for fuck's sake!'

People turn to stare as he jerks his chair away and marches out, scowling.

11

Harry hangs back in a corner, watching the crowds pouring into the station, looking for any sign of plain-clothes police. Kelly's late, and when her car appears he jumps in beside her and they speed away. Traffic is heavy along Parramatta Road and they make slow progress, Kelly glancing frequently at the rear-view mirror.

'You've had a rough day then,' she says.

'Kind of. Look, Kelly, I appreciate you doing this, but you're a newspaper reporter and you have your job to do, and maybe this isn't a good idea.'

'Yes, I do have my job, Harry, and I'm going to do it to the best of my ability, and this is going to be a big story. But I owe you a great deal—my life, in fact—and I'm not going to do anything that embarrasses you or endangers Jenny. I think it's in both our interests to work on it together.'

He looks over at her, the energy, the determination, the mess of red hair, and he feels better. 'I hope you're right. What have you got?'

'There's a Nordlund connection. The murder victim claimed he was screwed by Konrad Nordlund over a business deal a few years back.'

'Yes.'

'You know? That Jenny went along to the Nordlund AGM early this month?'

Harry remembers the receipt for a single share in NRL. 'No, I didn't know that.'

So, as they crawl out onto the Great Western Highway through western Sydney, they tell each other what they've discovered.

It's after seven by the time they climb up into the Blue Mountains and pass through Katoomba. The highway swings north by the national park. Far out to the west the sun is setting over the Megalong Valley. They reach Medlow Bath and finally Blackheath. Kelly has the address of the crime scene and they turn off the main road at the edge of the town and follow a heavily tree-lined lane. The houses become less frequent and then disappear. She turns onto an unsealed track and comes to a stop. Up ahead two small cottages hide in the gloaming beneath dark trees.

Kelly says, 'As I understand it, the house at the end of the road is the one that Palfreyman was living in. It's a weekender owned by a former friend who's planning to have it refurbished. The one next to it is also a weekender, owned by a Sydney family and rented by Jenny two weeks ago, on the sixth of October, for seven days starting on the ninth. Palfreyman's body was discovered on Tuesday last, the fourteenth, by the local butcher, who was owed money by Palfreyman and stopped by and found the front door open. The last sighting of either of them in the town was five pm on Monday the thirteenth, at the bottle shop where they bought wine and vodka.'

'Where did you learn all this?'

'One of our reporters has a cousin on the force in Katoomba. She was sent here door-knocking on the Tuesday.' She lets off the handbrake and drives to the end of the track, turns the car around and they get out. Both of the end cottages have police tape and warning notices on them. Kelly gets a flashlight from the glove box and they go over to Palfreyman's place, walking around the outside, peering in through the windows. At the front door Harry uses his bump keys to open the lock. They duck under the tape, closing the door behind them. It takes a moment to adjust to the deep gloom inside. They smell chemicals. To one side of the small hallway an open door leads into the living room and they go in, then pause. Chaos, cushions thrown off chairs, a bookcase tipped over and paperbacks scattered across the floor. They move forward into the room, checking the numbered plastic markers left behind by the crime scene team, and Harry indicates an armchair. He takes the torch from Kelly and shows her the dark stain of blood on the floor in front of the chair.

'I'm guessing he was sitting or standing here when he was stabbed. He fell forward and lay here and bled…you see the way the blood is smeared? I would guess that the killer stood here, on this side, struck with their right hand, and would have been sprayed with blood. A deliberate and determined attack.' He shakes his head. 'Jenny didn't do this.'

From this position the markers make a pattern spreading out across the room, back to the hall door. Harry examines each one, pointing out bloodstains and a footprint. They follow them across to a bedroom, which has also been turned over. Everywhere they look the surfaces are smeared with powders, white powder on dark surfaces and black on light.

Kelly says, 'The way everything's been thrown around—did they have a fight?'

'No, it's too systematic. And at least some of it was done after the murder—see how those books are lying on top of the bloodstains?'

'Why then?'

'Searching for something? Or maybe to make it look like a violent home invasion.'

'Maybe it *was* a violent home invasion.'

'Maybe, but why did Jenny disappear?' He looks through the window at the dense scrub, imagines her body lying out there in the dark. 'Did your contact mention whether they searched the surrounding bushland?'

'Yeah, they had several teams searching the bush and police rescue checking the trails along the escarpment.'

Harry nods. 'Let's take a look at her place then.'

They leave, locking the front door behind them. At the back of Jenny's cottage they find a new plywood panel screwed into place over a window opening. Beside the front door is a burglar alarm box with a warning sticker. Harry ignores it and opens the front door. No alarm sounds, and they move inside. It looks as if all traces of Jenny have been removed—no clothes in the bedroom, no toiletries in the bathroom, no foodstuffs in the kitchen. In the small bedroom at the rear, Harry crouches beneath the plywood panel and finds fragments of broken glass in the pile of the carpet. In the kitchen, hallway and bedroom there are more plastic markers next to what looks like the faint traces of bloody footprints.

When they get back to Kelly's car Harry suggests they go into town. On the way he phones Bob Marshall on the Blackphone.

'Harry?'

'Bob, I'm at Blackheath. Two things. What do the crime scene reports say about a broken window in the bedroom of the house where Jenny was staying? And were there any other wounds on Palfreyman's body, any defensive wounds?'

'I'll get back to you tomorrow.'

'Thanks.'

They reach the main street and Kelly says, 'Where to?'

Harry nods at a hotel standing on the most prominent corner. 'The pub.'

At the bar they order drinks and chat to the barman. Harry shows his old police ID.

'You lot were here Tuesday.'

'Sure, just a follow-up.'

'Not arrested anybody?'

'Not yet.'

'Found the lady?'

Harry shakes his head.

'She seemed all right. But I suppose you can never tell.'

'How did they seem when they were in here?'

'Well, he was happy as a pig in mud. She was paying, see? Terry was always short of cash.'

'Why would she do that?'

'That's what we wondered.'

'So he was all over her?'

'You could say that.'

'And how did she seem?'

'She looked happy enough.'

He turns away to serve another customer and Kelly puts her hand on Harry's arm. 'She had some reason, Harry. He was no George Clooney.'

12

Kelly drives them back to Sydney, to Harry's house, and asks if she can come in to use the bathroom. 'That beer at the pub,' she laughs.

They go inside and Harry checks his phone. There's a text message from Nicole to call her, which he does.

'Harry, I've found something you might be interested in. When Jenny was—'

He cuts her off. 'I'll come over, Nicole. Half an hour.' He hangs up.

When Kelly returns he tells her about the call. 'I'll get a cab,' he says.

'I'll take you. I want to know what she's found.'

When they get to Nicole's house she scolds Harry for his lousy telephone manner, and is shocked when he tells her that their phones are probably bugged.

'I'll make some arrangements so we can keep in touch,' he says, 'but in the meantime we'll just have to be careful what we say. So what have you got?'

Nicole has remembered that when Jenny and the baby stayed

overnight with her one weekend, Jenny had forgotten to bring her own laptop and had spent some time using Nicole's computer. She has checked back through its history of web searches and found the record of Jenny's use that day. She shows them. 'I just thought it was weird.'

Harry scrolls through a long list. Every item concerns Amber Nordlund—news items, business directories, genealogy, social media references.

Harry checks the date: Sunday morning, September the twenty-first.

'Looks a bit obsessive,' Kelly says.

'Yes.' Harry is trying to think of a reason for this. Jenny hardly knew Amber, only met her once, at the big homestead, Kramfors, she had inherited after her father died in a plane crash when she was fifteen. She had seemed an angry, damaged soul, an environmental activist alienated from her family and especially her uncle Konrad. Why should Jenny be interested in her now?

'Two days later she bought a single share in Nordlund Resources,' Harry says, 'as a result of which she was able to attend their shareholders' meeting a week later. Was Amber there?'

'Yes!' Kelly cries. 'I mean no, but she was meant to be. She's on the board, and at the start of the meeting the chairman apologised for her absence on health grounds. I'll show you.'

She logs on to the NRL website and calls up the video of their AGM, Warren Dalkeith's introduction and apologies, Amber's empty seat, then fast-forwarding to question time and Terry Palfreyman. 'That's Jenny, isn't it, just along there.'

Harry and Nicole stare at the image. She says, 'Yes, I think it is.'

Then Harry says, 'If Jenny went there looking for Amber, then… why? And did she find her? Or was she trying to get Palfreyman to help her?'

They're silent for a moment, thinking, and then Nicole says, 'I wonder if they were friends on Facebook.'

Harry says, 'Jenny wasn't on Facebook, was she?'

'Not when she was blind—she didn't think there was much point because she couldn't see the images. But when she got out of hospital, being able to see again…one day she saw me watching a video clip that someone had sent me on Facebook, and she asked me how it worked, and I showed her. We set up an account for her. I don't know how much she used it—she did send pictures of Abigail and Felecia to the girls from time to time. They've been trying to contact her since she disappeared, but there's been nothing.'

'It would be good if we could get into her account,' Harry says. 'The police will have tried.'

Nicole says, 'Actually…I think I kept a record of her password when we set it up. But where did I put it?'

She searches a drawer, checks her phone and computer and eventually finds the scribbled note in a box of paperclips, rubber bands and pencils. They watch as she logs on to Facebook as Jenny, and scrolls through her messages.

'So the first is on the third of August, that's just after the Ash Island inquest ended, and it's to Amber Nordlund.'

Just wanted to say a big thank you for your support at the inquest. I thought I was doing all right until I had to go through that. And Kylie's threats. It really shook me up.

They all leaned in to read Amber's immediate reply: *We supported each other, the walking wounded. You've got to put all that shit out of your head. Focus on the good things. Amazingly we survived, and you got your sight back and a wonderful baby. Have they got you on medication? I don't know how I would have survived without the pills.*

Jenny: *No pills, I'm breastfeeding. But you're right. We've got to focus on the positives. What are your plans?*

Amber: *The doctors have to give me the final okay on the skin grafts, then who knows. Konrad is planning a family trip to Vanuatu next month. I don't want to go with them but I may have no choice.*

I'm pretty helpless. I'm really sorry about you and Harry. I thought he was a good bloke and I think you're very brave to leave him and bring the baby up on your own. I hate to think I was responsible for what happened to you both, getting you involved.

There's a break for five days, then Amber again: *You okay? Been thinking about you. The doc's cleared me, so that's something. How you going?*

Jenny: *Not good. I can't stop thinking about Kylie screaming at me, 'I'm gunna have your baby killed, see how you feel.' Frankly I'm terrified. I can't sleep, can't eat. I don't know what to do. The police can't suggest anything more than getting an AVO against her, but that won't stop her. She has friends, horrible friends. I saw them waiting outside the courtroom. Can you suggest anything?*

Amber: *There's only one person I know could scare her off. His name's Nathaniel Horn.*

Jenny: *The lawyer?*

Amber: *That's him. Our family lawyer. He has bigger and badder and more powerful friends than anyone else. Want me to ask him?*

Jenny: *I'd need a long spoon.*

Amber: *What?*

Jenny: *To sup with the devil.*

Amber: *Know what you mean. He'd take that as a compliment. Well?*

Jenny: *I'm desperate. OK.*

Amber: *What's your phone number?*

Harry groans. 'What next?'

'There's a gap…maybe they were using their phones. There's a brief exchange on September twelve.'

Amber: *Hi, this is the view from my window. Jealous? One day you and I will come to Maturiki on our own. We've been here a week now and I do nothing except sleep and take pills. You won't believe that my nurse is Karen Schaefer. I told Konrad that I didn't want her near me but he just laughed. Back in Sydney next week for company shareholders meeting end of month. Want to meet up for lunch next Thursday?*

Jenny: *Great. I need your advice re the devil. Where?*

Amber: *Bastoni's on Clarence Street, noon, see you then. PS They read my emails and Facebook while I'm asleep. So fuck off Hayden.*

'That's it,' Nicole says. 'Not a word from either of them after that.'

'Karen Schaefer,' Kelly says. 'This is the nightmare all over again.'

Nicole doesn't understand and Kelly tells her about Karen Schaefer and her husband Craig, the quiet unassuming couple in the background doing Konrad Nordlund's dirty work. 'They nearly got me killed.'

Harry says nothing, preoccupied, and when Kelly turns to him and asks him what they should do, he says finally, 'Better talk to the devil.' He scrolls through the numbers on his phone and hits one. A woman's voice answers.

'This is Nathaniel Horn's number. How may I help you?'

'My name is Harry Belltree. I'd like to make an appointment to see Mr Horn.'

'Can you tell me what it's concerning?'

'It's about my wife, Jenny Belltree, and Amber Nordlund.'

'Is it an urgent matter?'

'Yes, very.'

'One moment, please.'

There is a long pause, then she comes back. 'Mr Horn can see you now. His offices are in the Gipps Tower, twenty-third floor.'

'It'll take me half an hour to get there.'

'I'll inform him.'

He rings off and tells the other two.

'It's almost midnight,' Kelly says. 'Doesn't he ever go home?'

'The devil never sleeps.'

13

Kelly drives Harry to the Gipps Tower, and when he steps out of the lift on the twenty-third floor his eyes automatically turn to the tenant doorway to the right. Its former sign, *Bluereef Financial Services*, has gone, replaced by another, *Boulos Georgiadis Accountants*. He wonders if Boulos and Georgiadis know about the killing of Sandy Kristich and Benji Lavulo in those rooms. He turns the other way and presses a bell on Nathaniel Horn's door. It clicks open and he steps into a dimly lit corridor. A door opens at the far end and he sees the tall, angular figure of Horn, shirtsleeves rolled up, collar open and tie loosened.

'Mr Belltree, come in.'

Harry steps into an office crowded with files and stacks of documents, the devil's playground. 'Thank you for seeing me so late.'

Horn shrugs, as if time means nothing. He takes a seat behind his desk, indicating a chair for Harry. 'No longer *Detective* Belltree, I understand. I've been expecting you. Concerning your wife and Amber Nordlund, you said.'

'Yes. Jenny, my wife, is…'

He hesitates, wondering how to put it, and Horn finishes the sentence for him. 'Wanted by the police in connection with the murder of Terry Palfreyman.'

'How do you know that?'

'I hear many things. Have you any idea where she is?'

'No.'

'Then how can I help you?'

'I believe that she was in contact with Amber Nordlund during August and September, during which time she told Amber of her fears concerning threats made by the sister of a client of yours, Frank Capp.'

'Half-sister, ex-client,' Horn corrects him. 'Yes, I attended the inquest and witnessed Kylie McVea's outburst.'

'Amber advised her that you might have sufficient influence over Kylie to get her to back off. Did Jenny come to see you? Did she ask for your help?'

Horn sits back in his chair, considering Harry. 'I understand that you and Jenny were estranged.'

'Yes.'

'When were you last in contact with her?'

'Last December.'

'And Amber? When did you last communicate with her?'

'The same, last December.'

'Then how do you know what they were saying to each other? Do you have access to their email accounts? Phone messages?'

'No. But Jenny's sister has been able to access Jenny's Facebook account, read their correspondence.'

'Ah, interesting. Do you have a transcript?'

'I could get one, but I can remember it pretty well.'

'When was their last exchange?'

'The twelfth of September. Amber was on Maturiki Island. She said she would be returning to Sydney shortly and would contact Jenny when she got here.'

'Nothing after that?'

'No, nothing.'

Horn nods, picks up a pen and strokes it, as if it might provide some enlightenment. 'I did meet your wife recently, on the first of October. She attended the annual shareholders' meeting of Nordlund Resources at the Menzies Hotel that morning. I recognised her and was surprised to see her there. I spoke with her when the meeting closed. She told me that she had hoped to see Amber and I explained that Amber was still very unwell with the after-effects of the injuries she sustained last December. I wasn't able to tell your wife how to contact her. She then told me that Amber had advised her to speak to me on a personal matter, and we arranged to meet the following day, here in my office.

'As you say, she was concerned about Kylie McVea's threats and wanted me to influence her. I agreed to try. Ah…' Horn gives a chilly smile, seeing the look of doubt on Harry's face, '…you're wondering why I would do that. Well, I had an ulterior motive. The previous day, after the AGM, at the board members' lunch, Konrad Nordlund took me aside and told me that his niece was missing. She had returned from Maturiki to Sydney two weeks previously and vanished. Her family was unable to contact her by phone or email and had tried all her known contacts. Mr Nordlund instructed me to engage private detectives to look for her. I did so, and in addition I made your wife an offer—if she could help us find Amber I would remove any threat from Kylie McVea and waive my fee. And now you're giving me that look again.'

'I'm wondering why you're telling me this.'

'Of course you are. You have to understand how ill Amber is. Her physical injuries last December were severe enough—burns, fractures, concussion—but the psychological damage was equally serious. She suffers from trauma-induced psychosis, and was diagnosed with schizophrenia. She's subject to hallucinations and delusions and has suffered violent episodes. She has been hospitalised for extended periods for both physical and psychological conditions and requires substantial medication. Last month, when she was deemed fit enough to travel, her family took her to their island in Vanuatu for a complete rest, and unfortunately there was an incident when she went swimming and almost drowned. She flew home to Sydney with her nurse, evaded her at the airport and disappeared. The authorities were alerted and, as I said, private detectives were engaged, but they have not been successful.

'I think we have to assume that, if she is still alive, Amber is being sheltered by someone. We understand that she used to be involved with political fringe groups and we've tried to contact them, but they've not been helpful. It seems likely that Amber suffers from an irrational belief that her family are trying to harm her, and she will persuade her friends not to cooperate.

'And that's why I enlisted Jenny's help. I think it likely that only a personal friend will be able to reach her.'

'And Jenny agreed to your proposal?'

'She was reluctant at first. I know, probably because of what Amber has told her, that she doesn't have a high opinion of the Nordlunds. But I believe I was able to persuade her how vital it is for Amber to get medical help. And Jenny is very worried about the threat to her child.'

'Have you done anything about that?'

'I've made a preliminary...approach. If Jenny is able to locate Amber I shall follow it up with a firm intervention. But I've heard nothing further from your wife, nothing at all.'

'So you can't help me to find her?'

'I'm afraid not. We have a strange dilemma—two missing women, who were looking for each other. But now you come to me, another former friend of Amber, and from what I hear an even closer one than Jenny was. And so I can put to you the same proposition I put to your wife—help us to find Amber and we will help you.'

'How?'

'The police believe that your wife killed Terry Palfreyman. When they find her, and they will, she will need all the help she can get. I can offer you that help.'

'She's innocent. The facts will speak for themselves.'

Horn laughs. 'You're a policeman, Harry. You know that isn't true. Justice isn't a science. It's not a mathematical equation. It is an argument between two contentious and contradictory hypotheses about what may or may not have occurred. And a convincing hypothesis, one that will persuade a jury, depends on the ability to influence, to *shape* the available data. That's what I'm good at— shaping a convincing truth. That is exactly what Jenny will need. I think you understand that very well. I think you know that if you don't get in there and shape the truth the way you want it shaped, others will shape it their way. And this isn't some scumbag lowlife we're talking about, this is your wife, who I think you still care for. Am I right?'

Harry nods.

'Yes, I thought so. And the Nordlunds are equally concerned about Amber. It is essential we find these two women before worse things happen. And we can do that more effectively by cooperating.'

'What can you tell me about Palfreyman?'

'Ah, Palfreyman.' Horn gives a dismissive flick of his fingers. 'Once he was one of those towers of files that you see around you. An interminable problem.' He shakes his head. 'A talented engineer, innovative, energetic, enthusiastic, but a hopeless businessman. He had a company based on one principal invention which was useful in underground coalmining. I'm told it was a genuine break- through, but it required more money for production and marketing than he had or the banks would lend him. So he approached Martin Nordlund, who agreed to invest in the project, and then when he was killed in his plane crash, his brother Konrad took over.

Now Konrad *is* a businessman, a very successful one. I admire him greatly. He's a tiger in that jungle out there, and he had Palfreyman for breakfast. Palfreyman, who knew every detail of his machines, didn't pay the same attention to his business matters. Eventually Konrad decided to dispense with him. Instead of being sensible and settling on the terms he was offered, Palfreyman became angry and stubborn, and tried to fight back. Konrad tore him to pieces. Other people—banks, creditors—saw which way the wind was blowing and moved in for the kill. Palfreyman lost everything. At our final court session the judge told Konrad that he was the most ruthless and unconscionable litigator he had ever encountered. Konrad asked him if he would put that in writing, as he would like to frame it and hang it on his office wall.'

Horn laughs again, that dry, humourless laugh. 'Palfreyman became one of those sad, bitter old men you see sitting outside parliament with a placard, or trying to disrupt shareholders' meetings. He came to all the NRL AGMs—he still had a couple of their shares—and was there on the first of October, and I can only imagine that he must have latched onto your wife at that meeting, as a possible ally, perhaps? I don't know. How else would she have become caught up with him?'

'Did Amber know Palfreyman?'

'That I don't know.'

'I'd like to see the investigators' reports.'

Horn reaches into a desk drawer and slides a folder across to Harry. 'That's a copy for your use.'

'And I'd like to speak to Konrad Nordlund.'

Horn is startled. 'Not possible. He's on an extended overseas business trip. He's a very busy man.'

'Amber's nurse, then—I'll need to talk to her.'

'I'm afraid that too is not possible.'

'Why not?'

'She's indisposed. Anyway, she wouldn't be able to help you.'

'I want to speak to someone who was on the island with Amber. Someone she might have confided in. Who else was there?'

'Hmm.' Horn looks doubtful. 'I'll think about it. Let you know.' He looks pointedly at his watch. 'Time I was off. If anything else occurs to you give me a ring.'

Horn walks Harry to the lift. As they wait for it he says, 'How are your police colleagues treating you these days? Do they keep you up to date?'

Harry shakes his head. 'They're telling me nothing. You're probably better informed than I am.'

This seems to please Horn.

Harry tells Kelly of his meeting as she drives him back to Surry Hills.

'So you're going to work for Nathaniel Horn?' She shakes her head. 'I never thought I'd see that day.'

'I suppose I am.'

'The devil's disciple, eh?'

'Don't let's get carried away, Kelly.'

'What's he really after?'

'I think they're genuinely worried about Amber, and I don't think it's family affection. I think they're afraid that she may cause them trouble of some kind. Horn got uncomfortable when I mentioned Maturiki Island. Maybe something happened there, or she got her hands on something she shouldn't have? We'll see whether he'll let me talk to someone who was there. My bet is he won't. You've got a contact over there, haven't you?'

'In Port Vila, yes. I'll get onto him.'

They have arrived at the lane in Surry Hills. She says, 'Have you got a photocopier here? We could make me a copy of that file he gave you.'

They go inside. He offers her a drink, pours them both a glass of scotch and takes her up to the old photocopier in his father's study in the attic.

'This is fantastic!' she says. 'Just as he left it? His papers, his law books. This should be in a museum.'

Actually, looking around, Harry realises that it isn't as his father left it. For a start, it's all much neater and more organised now. He goes over to the desk beneath the window and sees his father's diaries stacked in date order to one side. His in- and out-trays, previously a shamble of papers, are now straightened and tagged with post-it notes annotated with comments in Jenny's handwriting. She's been up here, systematically going through it all, and he remembers how frustrated she'd been, when she was blind, that this was exactly what she couldn't do. But why would she do it now, when she'd decided she wanted nothing more to do with Harry or with any further investigation into his parents' murder?

'Oh, this is interesting. Is this him as a young man? And that looks like Charlie Perkins and Jim Spigelman beside him.'

Harry takes the photograph from her hand. 'That was in 1965. They were going on the Freedom Ride. Where did you find this?'

'On that shelf.'

The photograph used to be in a frame, hung over there on the wall. He looks around and sees the empty frame. Why did Jenny take it out? Then he remembers the copy pinned to the wall in her bedroom at her mother's house. To photocopy it.

'Yes,' he says, 'this room is his life. They moved here in 1980, when I was a toddler. I remember having to climb that last flight of stairs on my hands and knees to get up here, because it was so steep.'

They get to work, photocopying the investigators' report. The atmosphere is unavoidably intimate in the confined space beneath the sloping attic ceiling. He hadn't noticed Kelly's perfume until now. He thinks how long it's been since he's been this close to a woman.

They finish the last page and he pats them straight and says he'll get an envelope, but she puts her hand on his arm to stop him, and when he turns to her she moves close and presses her mouth to his.

They stand for a moment, motionless, then she says softly, 'I could stay tonight, if you want me to.'

He doesn't speak. She looks at his face, steps back. 'Oh well.' A careless shrug. 'I thought it would cheer you up.'

'Yes...yes, it did. Thank you, Kelly. I'm flattered.'

She bites her lip and turns away. 'See you tomorrow then.'

At the front door he says, 'There's a white van parked out there on the street. It's been there since I got back. I think they're watching us. Maybe this place is bugged too.'

'Well, I nearly made their night.' She walks away.

14

A few hours later, in that dead time in the middle of the night when this part of the city has gone to sleep, Detective Inspector Deb Velasco stands apart in the shadows of Slater Park, trying to imagine how this has been done and what it means. Over there, beneath the giant fig tree, the ghostly white figures of crime scene officers are working in a pool of light, a photographer moving among them. How could this have happened again? Just eight days later, beneath the same tree, more ghoulish fruit has been found suspended from its branches by pink ribbons. Just one victim this time, identified from prints taken from the fingers of her dismembered hands: Christie Florian, thirty-three years old, with a record of soliciting, drug possession and attempted blackmail. Her usual territory was Kings Cross, where police are now trying to establish if she was abducted and brought to the park.

Deb's boss, Detective Superintendent Dick Blake, has just left after instructing her to take charge of Strike Force Spider, investigating the Slater Park murders, the previous team leader having fallen ill. 'These are crimes against women, Deb,' Blake said. 'So get the bastard.' He looked worried, as well he might. This will reflect badly on all of them, a second slaughter beneath the same tree.

She leaves the crime scene in the charge of one of her detectives and returns to her car. On her computer she taps in her password and opens up e@gle.i to get some background on the first Slater Park murders, traversing the data quickly. It makes discouraging reading. After forensics failed to find any useful traces at the crime scene and a search of CCTV cameras in the neighbourhood was also unsuccessful, they pinned their hopes on the ribbons—pink satin, Chinese manufacture, widely distributed across the city. A huge search for a male customer through CCTV images and purchase records at retail outlets yielded nothing. A female buyer then, or an online sale. The search is continuing, with less and less likelihood of success.

Deb turns to the pathologist's report on the first murders, and when she's read it and reviewed the images she calls the morgue at Glebe and asks for Dr Rebecca Jardine. The pathologist comes on the line, a familiar Canadian voice.

'Hi Deb,' she says, 'I'm ready for you now.'

When Deb gets there she's taken through to the forensic pathology suite and into Rebecca's office, where the pathologist waves her to a seat in front of the big TV screen and taps the keyboard of her computer to bring up the first of the CT scans. An external image first in vivid colour, of a human leg, then the skin melts away revealing flesh and muscle, which in turn dissolves into bones.

'This is interesting,' Rebecca says. 'Quite different from the first victims.'

'How?'

'They were butchered on site, crudely, with something like an axe or machete. Look.'

Rebecca brings up images from the first murders, splintered and cracked bones, then returns to the new scans. 'Not this time. See the clean slice through the bone?'

She rotates the image on the screen, showing what she means, then zooms in to see the marks in close-up. 'She's been sectioned with a machine saw, like they have in abattoirs.'

'What about a hand-held chainsaw, or a circular saw?'

'No. Too regular. I reckon she was cut up off-site and brought in in pieces.'

Deb tries to picture it, some maniac in a shed, just a few hours ago, doing his horrific business.

15

At her desk the next morning, Kelly stares at the photocopied report in front of her and wonders if it isn't time to drop this whole Harry Belltree business and move on to something new. All it's brought her is pain and misery. Well, it's brought her here, to a well-paid job on her own crime desk in the best newspaper in the city, but apart from that...

She tells herself to grow up, picks up her phone and punches in the Vanuatu code and the number for Brad's Hamburger Bar in Port Vila harbour.

'Morning, Brad.'

'Kelly sweetheart! I was just thinking of you last night. When are you going to finally make up your mind to come over here and live a life of tropical languor as my squeeze?'

Kelly laughs. 'Languor, eh? By day two you'd have me in the back kitchen scrubbing dishes.'

'You should think about it. So how can I help you, love?'

'Maturiki Island again. The Nordlund family went up there for a holiday early September. Amber Nordlund was with them, but sometime around the middle of September she had an accident of some kind—they say she nearly drowned—and returned to Sydney on the fourteenth with her nurse, Karen Schaefer. At Sydney Airport Amber ran off while Schaefer was at the baggage carousel, and hasn't been seen since. I'm interested in finding out what happened and any background, like who else was on Maturiki.'

She gives Brad the flight details listed in the investigators' report and he promises to get on to it straight away. He seems to know everyone in Port Vila—reporters, police, government officials, market traders, travel agents—who all drop in to his bar.

Kelly hangs up and sits there, tapping her pen, itching with frustration.

16

Out of the window, across the street, early shoppers are trudging into the Trái Cây Ngon Hơn Minimarket. Mr Công Thành is rattling up the shutter on his money transfer office. And the lights are going on in the Viện Tram My internet café.

The woman waits and watches. Most of the faces are familiar to her now.

At seven-thirty she gets to her feet and goes down the narrow stairs to the ground floor and makes her way through the fruit and vegetable shop. Mrs Ngô is serving a customer and gives a toothy smile and a cheerful 'Xin chào, Scarlett!' and carries on with her work.

Scarlett crosses the street and opens the door of the internet café. She says chào to young Carly Viện, who has been trying to put curls in her straight black hair. Curly Carly. She orders a coffee and a tomato and cheese roll for breakfast and goes to her usual computer at the back of the store. She taps away, and the message *Welcome to Facebook* comes up. She logs in and checks her messages. As usual, Clare and Helen have sent a report of their doings. Today the picture takes her breath away. At first she doesn't recognise the bearded man holding Abigail. Then she does. The girls have sent a message: *Harry has come back to help you, Jenny. Please please get in touch!!! XXX*

Scarlett closes the page and wipes the tears from her eyes as Carly comes over with her coffee and roll.

17

Harry is eating toast in his kitchen when the unfamiliar tone of the Blackphone sounds. He takes it outside into the little courtyard.

'Hi, Bob.'

'Morning. Your two questions. One, nothing special about the broken window—no bloodstains, DNA or prints. Two, Palfreyman's autopsy found no defensive wounds, only the single stab wound that killed him. How are you going?'

Harry hesitates, then decides to tell him about his visit to Horn.

Bob growls his disapproval. 'What's the old fox up to?'

'I think they're just desperate to get hold of Amber.'

'Maybe so, but why involve you? They could be trying to set you up for something, Harry.'

It's possible. He's been set up before. 'Like somebody's done to Jenny?'

Bob gives a neutral grunt. 'On the subject of Jenny, her card's been used again.'

'Really? Where this time?'

'Still Darwin. It was used to book a ticket on a Greyhound bus south to Adelaide. By the time they found out, the bus was long gone and already passed through Alice Springs. They've alerted the South Australian police, who'll be waiting in Adelaide, but she could get off along the way, at Coober Pedy or Port Augusta. Or maybe she got off before Alice, at Katherine, and went west to Broome, or at Tennant Creek and headed east to Queensland and the Pacific Coast. Lot of alternatives to check, and four different state forces to liaise with. Could keep them busy for a while.'

'Right.' Harry picks up the doubt in Bob's voice. 'You don't buy it?'

'You know Jenny better than anyone, Harry. She's a bright girl.'

'Yes.'

'On the run, trying to hide. Would she be stupid enough to use her own credit card?'

'No.'

'You'd already worked that out?'

'I had my doubts. Unless she was very short of cash.'

'Quite, and that is a possibility. They've accessed her bank account and she did withdraw cash the morning after the murder, from a bank in Sydney, but there wasn't a huge balance, just $800. That won't get her very far. Still, Deb knows Jenny too, and she must be asking herself the same questions. Deb's sharp, Harry. She'll be thinking of all the possibilities. If somebody else is laying a false trail all over the bloody country, where the hell is Jenny?'

'I have no idea, Bob. I really don't know.'

'Well, we'd better work it out before homicide do. Listen, we should meet up and talk this through. How about a drink tonight?'

'Sure.'

'Have you been back to Crucifixion Creek lately? It's been completely flattened. They're building a new development there, Phoenix Square. First stage has just opened, and they say it's worth a look.'

Harry doesn't welcome the idea of returning to that place. What does Bob want to do, chew over old times, old cases? But he agrees to meet him there that evening.

18

Harry walks briskly towards the city centre, and along the way buys a copy of the *Times* and makes a call on a public pay phone. When he reaches the twin spires of St Mary's Cathedral he turns down into the parkland of the Domain and along the tree-lined avenue towards the Art Gallery of New South Wales, where people are sitting on the front steps waiting for it to open. He buys a coffee at the Pavilion kiosk and sits, reading the paper. The front page is dominated by the discovery of a new murder victim in Slater Park. Another young woman. The *Times* reporter Brendon Pyle reveals that she has a police record for soliciting and drug possession. He speculates that she may have been picked up at one of her usual haunts in Kings Cross and taken to Slater Park by the murderer. The park is now deserted, he reports, the art school closed down, the dog-walkers and picnickers gone. Panic is spreading through the surrounding suburbs. Shops and cafés are experiencing a forty per cent drop in trade.

The people on the steps are getting to their feet, passing beneath the banners hanging over the portico, and Harry finishes his coffee and makes his way across to join them. Inside he switches his old mobile off and puts it into the backpack, which he hands in at the cloakroom counter, keeping the Blackphone in his pocket. Then he turns and leaves, walking across the Domain and into the CBD. At a branch of his bank he checks the balance of an old joint savings account that he and Jenny opened when they married. He hasn't used it in years. He gets a copy of recent transactions. There's only one within the past five years, a cash withdrawal of $8130, leaving just $100 in the account. The timing is interesting: two months ago, soon after the Ash Island inquest finished. Jenny must have been making plans.

Harry catches a bus out to Glebe and walks along Glebe Point Road until he finds the address he's looking for, an office above a Tibetan restaurant. From the street he can see the posters in the office windows above: *Sustain Our Earth, Sustain Our Environment.* He climbs a steep flight of stairs to a small office lined with filing cabinets and more posters. A young woman is fiddling with a photocopier. She straightens up. 'Hi. Bloody machines. Can I help you?'

Harry says that he's interested in Sustain. She explains that they are an environmental activist group, currently mounting campaigns in the coalfields of New South Wales and Queensland and in the old-growth forests of Tasmania. She offers him a sheaf of pamphlets.

'I met a couple of people who told me about you,' Harry says. 'Amber Nordlund and her partner, Luke Santini. Do you know them?'

'Umm...I know the names.' She goes to a computer and types. 'Oh, yes, I remember—they joined up last year, came to a couple of meetings. Only...doesn't look as if they renewed their subscriptions this year. She was nice. I think he was a bit...'

'Prickly?'

'Yes!' She laughs. 'But she was okay.'

'Yes. It was her really that I wanted to get in touch with again.'

70

'Ah, I see. Well, we have an address here, Kramfors Homestead near Gloucester, north of Newcastle.'

'Yes, but I believe she's not there anymore.'

'Really? Well, I'm afraid I can't help. That's all we have.'

'How about other friends of theirs? Anyone I might try?'

'Hang on.'

The girl consults the list of contacts on her phone, then calls a number. Harry listens to her half of the conversation, obviously leading nowhere. Eventually she rings off and gives him an apologetic shrug.

Harry says, 'How about a list of your members? I could try contacting them.'

'What?' The girl's manner abruptly changes. 'I couldn't possibly give you that. It's confidential.'

'But surely…'

'You're not from the police, are you? My God, you are, aren't you?'

'No, no. I just want to contact Amber.'

'I think you'd better go.'

'Couldn't I give you a hand with the photocopier?'

'Just get out!'

Harry raises his hands and leaves. When he gets outside he makes a call on the Blackphone, then makes his way back along Glebe Point Road towards the campus of Sydney University.

It's nine months since he came here with Amber, and he follows the same route, across the quadrangle and into a maze of corridors and stairs to the door marked with the name of her uncle, the other Nordlund brother, Professor Bernard Nordlund, who opens the door as soon as he knocks.

'Mr Belltree, come in, come in. Can I offer you a coffee?'

'No, I'm fine, thanks.'

They sit, facing each other across a table piled with papers in the small book-lined room, and Bernard regards Harry with a vague,

71

quizzical smile. 'How interesting to hear from you again. How can I help you?'

'I'm trying to get in touch with Amber, Professor Nordlund.'

'Bernard, please. Ah, yes, we're very concerned about Amber. No one's heard from her for several weeks now. Why are you after her?'

'My wife, Jenny, was in touch with her on social media until early September. Now she too is missing.'

'But that's terrible. Are the police aware of this? Could they be together?'

'It's possible. I'm anxious to find both of them and help them if I can. Has Nathaniel Horn spoken to you about this?'

'Horn? The lawyer? No. He represents my brother Konrad's side of the family, not mine. You've probably gathered from Amber that we've been a rather dysfunctional family since our parents died. For a time our older brother Martin—Amber's father—held things together, ran the Nordlund companies in a fair and proper manner. But then he died tragically, twelve years ago. You may have heard about it.'

'Flight VH-MDX,' Harry says. 'That Martin was piloting when it crashed in the forests around Cackleberry Mountain. Yes, I spoke to the local police sergeant who told me search parties still go out looking for it.'

'I rather wish they wouldn't. After all this time the remains of the plane and its two occupants will be completely swallowed up by vines and undergrowth, and it's probably best they should be left in peace. But anyway, as I was saying, things fell apart after Martin died. I was never cut out to be a businessman, and Konrad quickly got his hands on all the family companies, and hasn't looked back. As an economic historian I can only look on in wonder. He probably has much in common with that character up there...' He points to a small portrait on the wall of a stern-looking moustached Victorian. 'Sir Henry Pottinger, who negotiated the Treaty of Nanking and

72

became the first governor of Hong Kong. The Chinese gentleman facing him in that other portrait tried to stand up to him. Lin Zexu, a favourite character of mine. A very able and intelligent man who stood against the tide of history, and was swept away, as I would be if I tried to stand up to Konrad.'

Harry says, 'After we saw you last, Amber told me that Konrad raped her not long after her father died, and that her son Dylan is the result.'

Bernard sighs. 'Ah, she told you about that, did she? Yes, she told me also, and I tried to persuade her to go with me to the police, but she refused. So no, Mr Horn works for Konrad, not me, and I'm not sure how I can help you. I haven't heard from Amber for some months. You know she's had great difficulties recovering from her injuries?'

'Yes. I remember how much faith she put in you, Bernard, and I wondered if she might have spoken to you about friends and contacts she had.'

'Oh…' he strokes his rosy cheek, pondering, 'no, no, I don't think she did. Latterly we spoke more about family matters, her dispute with Konrad about the future of the Cackleberry Estate, that sort of thing.'

'Yes. She was very passionate about environmental issues, wasn't she? The impact of the coal industry? Did you meet her partner, Luke Santini?'

'Yes, we had lunch together one day. I got the impression she was very taken with him, but I think she could see that I wasn't much impressed. A bit flaky, I thought, that phoney American accent, and rather full of himself.'

'Yes, you've got it.'

'But of course he was killed at the time Amber was so badly hurt, wasn't he? I shouldn't speak ill of the dead. All very tragic.'

'He was involved in environmental protest groups—something in Australia called Sustain, and an American outfit called Burning

Rage. Did she talk about that? I'd like to speak to the people she knew there.'

'I see, yes. But I don't think we discussed anything of that kind. Amber regarded me, quite rightly, as irrevocably stuck in the past. I really know nothing at all about Burning Rage and so on.' He frowns for a moment in thought. 'But I might know someone who does. A young university colleague. His name is…what was it?' He stares up at the ceiling, waiting for inspiration. 'Ramsey, that's it. Ramsey Awad, in the Department of Environmental something or other. He's made a study of environmental protest movements. Got a large government grant recently. I was jealous. Shall I try him?' He reaches for the phone on his desk, thumbs through a directory, finds a number and dials. There is a slightly awkward exchange as Bernard has to remind Awad who he is and where they met, then he explains what he wants, listens, nods his head and rings off.

'A stroke of luck. Ramsey can see you now, Harry. I'll show you the way.'

He gets to his feet and opens the office door, gives directions to Fisher Library. 'Now, Harry, please let's keep in touch. Let me know if you hear anything about Amber, will you?'

Harry finds Awad waiting for him in the library lobby. The young man leads him to a seat, checks his watch and says, 'I've got a lecture in twenty minutes, but I'll try to help.' He has a soft American accent—Californian, Harry guesses. 'I do know something of Burning Rage—I worked on them as a case study when I was at Caltech. So what's your interest?'

'I'm trying to trace someone who's missing, name of Amber Nordlund. She was the girlfriend of a man called Luke Santini, who I believe had some connection with them.'

'Oh.' Awad looks surprised. 'Santini was her boyfriend? Like… lover?'

'Yes, I assume so.'

'Here in Australia?'

'Yes. They were involved with environmental groups over here and I'm hoping that someone may know where she is.'

'As far as I know, Burning Rage hasn't been active in Australia. In fact I'm not aware of it being active in the States anymore either. But I have heard of Luke Santini. What has he told you?'

'Nothing—he died last December, I'm afraid.'

'Oh really. How come?'

'He was killed by a bomb.'

'Oh, boy…This isn't my current research area, but maybe I should do some work on it. Well, Burning Rage was a group that believed in direct action—violent action—to achieve environmental aims. Their method was to target influential individuals in the fossil fuels industries—oil executives, coalmine owners, shale gas company executives, that kind of thing. Their speciality was blowing up or burning down their vacation homes in wilderness areas. They hit the headlines in 2006 when they blew up a holiday mansion in the Catskills belonging to the chairman of an Appalachian strip mining company. Unfortunately, his wife and two small children and a maid were in the place at the time. Overnight Burning Rage became notorious. People called them the Green Baader-Meinhof and the FBI started a major manhunt.

'Turned out there were three ringleaders—one was shot dead by the cops, one was brought to trial and sentenced to ninety-nine years, and the third disappeared. His name was Sol Fleischer, a native of New York and most probably the architect of the Catskills bombing. The FBI widened the search for associates, one of whom was Fleischer's lover, an Australian citizen by the name of Luke Santini.'

'Fleischer was male?'

'Right. Santini was questioned at length by the Feds, but in the end they let him go. Fleischer was never found—some said he'd gone to Canada, or Mexico, or Europe. Nobody really knew.'

'Could he have come here, with Santini?'

'Anything's possible. It'd be very interesting if he did.'

'Anything else you can remember about Fleischer?'

Awad ponders. 'I'll take another look at my old research... I remember there was a rumour that he was HIV positive, and needed medication. Who knows if it was true.' He checks his watch. 'Look, I have to go, but I'll give you my contact details and let you know if I find out anything else.'

19

Harry walks down Broadway towards Central station and finds an internet café full of backpackers. He takes the last free computer and spends an hour checking websites, making notes, downloading a picture of Sol Fleischer, which he forwards to Bob with a query asking if it would be possible to identify this man. When he's finished he gets cash from an ATM and catches a bus out to Petersham, where he walks to Ricsi's backstreet shoe repair shop, making sure he isn't being followed.

As usual Ricsi says little, leading Harry into the little room behind the counter. His complexion looks greyer than usual, his feet shuffling, and Harry asks if he's okay.

'Just getting old, mate. Thinking about getting out of the business. Better get what you need from me while there's time.'

Harry settles for half a dozen untraceable phones and a pistol. All Ricsi has is a small Smith & Wesson J-Frame and Harry takes it and a box of .38 Special rounds.

'Where can I get a cheap used car around here, Ricsi?'

Ricsi gives him the name of a local yard where he picks out a ten-year-old Subaru and heads out of the city, north and west, until the suburban streets give way to paddocks, small farms and stands of gum. He stops to check the maps he printed off at the internet café and turns off the main road onto deserted unsealed back lanes. It feels good to be out doing something, almost like being back on the force but without the regulations and report-writing.

He comes at last to a sign nailed to a tree in a grove of sad-looking ironbarks: *Doggylands Dog Breeders, Boarding Kennels— K. McVea proprietor.* The sign has been decorated with bullet holes. In the distance he can hear the howling of dogs. He turns onto a rutted track, the howling turning into frenzied barking as the dogs hear his approach. Chain-link fenced pens appear on either side. He sees greyhounds, pit bulls, staffies, racing back and forth.

He comes to a stop in a rough yard. To one side is a large agricultural shed from which the sound of a radio is just audible over the barking. On the other side sits a timber house with verandas beneath an ancient pepper tree, its branches drooping onto the rust-streaked tin roof.

As Harry gets out of his car a figure emerges from the shed, a big, heavily built man in a check shirt, muddy jeans and boots, red beard, head shaved except for a long pigtail down his back, carrying a shovel.

'Yes, mate. After a pup?'

'I'm after Mrs McVea. She around?'

'Who's askin'?'

'Tell her Harry Belltree would like a word.'

The man turns towards the house and bellows, 'MUM!' Then, to Harry, 'Tell her y'self.'

While they wait Harry points at the only dog in the pens that isn't running around, a spaniel sitting on its haunches in the mud, quivering. Its long hair is matted with dirt and faeces and one ear appears to be torn. 'What's wrong with that one?'

'Nuthin'. She's boardin' for three months, havin' a great time.'

78

Harry peers through the wire at it. Its eyes are staring blankly, as if from shell-shock.

There's a screech as the screen door at the front of the house opens and a woman in a motorised wheelchair trundles out onto the ramp. 'Whassa matter, Gavin?'

She stares at Harry as he walks over and climbs the veranda steps, followed closely by Gavin.

'Do I know you?'

'I'm Harry Belltree, Kylie. I'd like a word.'

'You've got a fuckin' nerve. Gavin, call Khalil. Tell him to bring his shottie.'

Gavin pulls out his phone.

Harry says, 'Just a quiet word, Kylie. I want you to stop threatening my wife.'

'Want what you like. She killed my brother. She hit 'im with a fuckin' axe. She's gotta pay, bigtime.'

'Your brother was going to kill me—that's why Jenny had to hit him. He'd just killed her aunty and he was about to kill me. She had no choice.'

'He was my brother! He looked after me when I was a little 'un, when no one else did. He protected me!'

'It was him put you in that wheelchair, Kylie. You know what sort of man he was.'

A ute is skidding to a stop in the yard, and another man, heavily developed shoulders and arms covered in tats, gets out of the cabin with a shotgun in his hand.

Kylie roars, 'I know what sort of man you are, Belltree, a fuckin' trumped-up abbo, that's what you are. And your Jenny's a stuck-up abbo-lovin' bitch and she's goin' to pay. Khalil! You and Gavin kick this piece of shit off our property.'

Harry raises his hands. 'Take it easy, Kylie.'

Khalil is advancing towards him with shotgun raised, an angry scowl on his face. 'Git away from the lady.'

Harry turns back to Kylie. 'Your brother killed my mother and father, but now he's dead. I have no quarrel with you. It's time to move on. It's over, okay?'

Kylie leans forward and hisses, 'It's not over till I feed Jenny and her baby abbo brat to my dogs, matey. Now piss off.'

'You hurt either of them and you and your boys are dead, Kylie. I mean it.'

Harry turns to leave, and as he goes Gavin McVea feels impelled to step forward and punch Harry on the arm. 'Piss off, abbo.'

Harry hits him twice, two quick thumps to his soft belly. As he topples backwards into Khalil, Harry grabs the gun and keeps walking towards his car, Kylie shouting after him, 'You'll regret that, you abbo bastard. I've got friends, big friends. You'll see.'

Harry unloads the gun and throws it into the pen with the quivering dog. 'I'd learn to shoot if I were you, mate,' he says.

20

Kelly is typing up a story about a new government report on the ice epidemic, making heavy weather of it, when a call comes in from Brad in Vanuatu.

'I've put out a few feelers, Kelly, but it may take time. There was one mention of Maturiki in the Vanuatu *Daily Post* here recently might interest you. Fishermen in the waters between Pentecost and Maturiki brought up some human remains in their nets. Looks like a shark attack, and some of the people up there have claimed it's the work of a shark sorcerer.'

'A what?'

'There's an old belief in what they call *nakaimos*, sorcerers who can turn themselves into sharks and go hunting for swimmers.'

'Really?'

'Yeah, few years back three men up there were actually arrested and charged by police for a series of fatal shark attacks. The charges were dropped due to lack of evidence.'

'Do they know who the victim was?'

'I'm looking into it. I'll get back to you.'

Kelly thanks him and rings off. She is thinking that the most likely candidate for shark sorcerer that she knows is Karen Schaefer, the woman who brought Amber back from Maturiki. And thinking of Karen Schaefer, she remembers that she knows where she and her husband Craig were living ten months ago, before they took off in such a hurry to Vanuatu. Is she back there now? And is it possible that Amber didn't disappear at the airport as Karen has told everyone, but is now being held by the Schaefers? She picks up her phone again and rings Harry's Blackphone number, but it goes straight to messages. She leaves one, asking him to call her, then grabs her bag and tells Hannah that she's going out for a while.

She drives out to Riverside Park at Strathfield, where she saw the Schaefers last December. From here she followed them back to their house, a small suburban villa somewhere not far away. She tries now to retrace that route, and soon becomes uncertain. This is unfamiliar territory, and the streets all look much the same to her. She wishes she'd made a note of their address, but at the time everything developed in a rush.

Eventually she comes to a street on a shallow incline that seems familiar, and a house that might be the one. Previously the Schaefers left their little green car in the narrow driveway, but there's no car there now. She parks and walks over to the house, still uncertain. The last time she raided their garbage for information, and she wonders about trying that again—assuming it's the right house. She takes a deep breath and tries the front doorbell. Chimes echo faintly inside. No one answers. She goes to the front window and peers in, cupping her eyes to see into the dark interior.

'Excuse me, can I help you?'

Kelly spins around. A young woman is staring at her. She's dressed smartly, a bag slung over her shoulder, looking as if she's returning from work.

'Oh, I, er, I'm not sure if I've got the right house. I was looking for a couple called Schaefer, and I thought they lived here.'

'The Schaefers, yes. They were the last tenants here, before me. I never met them, but I know the name. You're a friend of theirs?'

'Yes, I was hoping to catch up with them. You don't have a forwarding address, do you?'

'No, I'm afraid not. I suppose the rental agency will. Actually, if you're going to see them you could do me a favour. I've got odd bits of mail that have come in for them.'

'Fine, yes, I'll take care of that.'

So Kelly waits while the woman goes inside and fetches a plastic bag full of mail and gives her details of the rental agency.

'I don't think there's anything important, but I didn't like to throw it away, and I didn't have their address to forward it.'

Kelly drives to the rental agency, but they have no new address for the Schaefers. She returns to the *Times* offices and takes her loot up to her desk, begins to go through it. Most of it is advertising circulars, giving an uninformative picture of the Schaefers' purchasing history. There's a reminder for an appointment for Craig Schaefer at an eye clinic and several monthly statements for their road e-tag account, all zero.

Disappointed, she looks through the items again. One of the leaflets makes her pause, from a kennels out in western Sydney. Did the Schaefers have a dog? And the name, McVea, rings a bell. Wasn't that the name of Frank Capp's half-sister, who caused so much fuss at the Ash Island inquest, threatening Jenny Belltree?

Kelly checks the kennels' website and confirms the name, Kylie McVea. Then she looks more closely at the leaflet. On the back, next to the map for locating the place, is a handwritten note: *Saturday 14th, 8:00 pm*. The Schaefers left in a hurry for Vanuatu on the fourth of December, a Wednesday. The fourteenth, ten days later, was a Saturday. What goes on at a kennels at 8:00 pm on a Saturday night? And what's the connection between Kylie McVea and the Schaefers?

21

The transformation is astonishing, disorienting. Standing on one of the perimeter streets, Harry works out that the multistorey car park over there is built directly on the site of the Crows' bikie compound. Beside it a broad flight of steps leads up to an elevated piazza burgeoning with palm trees, fountains, cafés and restaurants buzzing with activity. One side of the square is flanked by a vertical garden of lush plants climbing twenty metres up the side of a building within which a department store and fifty shop units are being fitted out. In the background cranes are working on the concrete frames of apartment towers rising into the evening sky.

Harry finds a free table and orders two glasses of wine. He waits, watching children clustered around a juggler and a pair of human statues, and thinks of the horrors buried beneath their feet. And he thinks of Kylie McVea. He gets out his phone and calls Nicole.

'Hi, Harry, how are you?'

'Good. How's Abigail?'

'Oh, she's fine. The girls are with her at the moment.'

'I'd like to ask a favour, Nicole. I wondered if I could sleep over at your place for a few nights, just to keep an eye on things.'

'An eye on things? Is there a problem? We're quite capable—'

'Of course, no, I didn't mean that. It's just, with Jenny away I feel responsible. I'd like to keep an eye on the baby.'

'Well…yes, of course. I'll make up the bed in the spare room.'

'There's a bed in Abigail's room, isn't there? I'd like to sleep there, if it's okay.'

Across the square Bob Marshall emerges from the car park entrance and strides towards him. He's changed out of his uniform, in shirtsleeves on the warm spring evening, and looks like any other big, amiable bloke approaching retirement age. Except perhaps for the way his eyes take in the people he passes, assessing, recording.

'I'll see you later then. Thanks, Nicole.'

'Harry. Got the first round in, I see.' Bob settles himself, takes a sip. 'Amazing, isn't it? Seems to have sprung out of the ground in no time. Chinese construction company, apparently. So, tell me about James Zuckermann.'

'Who?'

Bob gives him a quizzical look. 'You don't know the name?' He takes a folded sheet of paper out of his pocket and slides it across to Harry. It's a photocopy of a New South Wales drivers licence. The face is that of Sol Fleischer.

Harry nods. 'That's him. How did you find him?'

'They're trialling a new facial recognition system to pick up speeding drivers. That's the story anyway. Bloody good. Not a hundred per cent of course, but bloody good. Thing is, Zuckermann has no police record…'

'So?'

'…or tax file number, or Medicare number. Apart from this drivers licence, obtained eight years ago, there appears to be no record of him. There was a James Zuckermann born on the same day in Queensland, thirty-seven years ago, but he died of SIDS at seven months.' Bob stabs a thick finger at the piece of paper. 'This James Zuckermann is a ghost. So, what do you know about him?'

Harry says, 'The picture I sent you was of an American citizen called Sol Fleischer, wanted by the FBI on multiple murder charges.' He tells Ramsey Awad's story. 'He was the lover of Luke Santini, who died on Ash Island, remember? And who was the boyfriend of Amber Nordlund, who was badly burned trying to rescue him.'

'And you're looking for Amber.' Bob takes a thoughtful sip of his drink. 'Jeez, Harry, you always had a nose for trouble, didn't you?'

'And I'm looking for Amber because she may know what's happened to Jenny.'

'Yes, Jenny...Seems they've got a picture from the ATM in Darwin. Female, baseball cap, big dark glasses. Might be her, might not. They reckon probably not.'

He takes another sheet of paper from his pocket. Harry unfolds it and stares at the image, and a chill grips his heart.

'No, it's not her. It's somebody else with her credit card.'

'They're trying to track the woman with CCTV images. It'll take time.'

'I've been trying to prepare myself, Bob. For when they find her body.'

'We're not there yet, mate. Not by a long shot. You know what I think? Sooner or later she's going to run out of cash and hope and she's going to ask herself who's the one person on earth can help her. And then she's going to try to contact you.'

Harry shakes his head. 'If she's still alive...She's stubborn, Bob. Told me to get out of her life.'

'Post-traumatic shock, mate. That's all.' He drains his glass and waves the waiter over. 'I'm not driving, so I'll have another. How about you?'

'The five rules of road safety. Caught the train.'

'Good. Let's get a bottle and a pizza. Yes, the five rules. I must say it's comforted me a little, stuck out there, to watch them in homicide chasing their tails over this Slaughter Park business. You should see the emails, Harry, the messages from the commissioner, the police minister—blind panic. And they haven't got a clue.'

'Early days.'

'No, I mean literally, they haven't got a clue—no forensics.'

'How do you mean?'

'No fingerprints, no footprints, no DNA, no traces at all. Even the dogs couldn't sense him. I tell you, there's another ghost, a real scary one too.' Bob sits back with a smug smile. 'Bloody frustrating for my successor, Dick Blake. He's a tech man, our Dick. Digital Dick. Three women dead and his flashy gear can't tell him a damn thing. He's put Deb in charge of Strike Force Spider now. I wish her luck.'

The bottle arrives and Bob pours. 'So, are we going after Zuckermann?'

Harry thinks. 'If he turns out to be Sol Fleischer you'll have no choice but to arrest him, and then he may clam up. Let me take a look around first.'

'It's your game, Harry.'

22

It's almost ten when Harry reaches Nicole's house. She greets him with a kiss on the cheek.

'The girls are asleep. Wasn't sure if you were eating with us. Made enough for you. I can warm it up.' She sounds mellow, her words slightly slurred.

'Oh, I'm sorry. I should have made that clear. I just want a bed, to keep an eye on Abigail.'

'Okay. Drink?'

They sit in the lounge room overlooking the valley, and Harry realises that he's in Greg's favourite armchair. He doesn't tell Nicole that he's been to Crucifixion Creek in case it brings back bad memories of how her husband died.

'God, these murders, Harry, aren't they shocking? I actually went to the Slater Park Art School for two years until I decided to change to graphic design. I loved it there. I can't bear to think of those girls, those students, what he did to them. Have you heard anything—about Jenny, I mean?'

'Nothing new. Tell me, did she ask you for money before she went away?'

'Yes, she said she was short of cash, and I gave her a thousand dollars.'

'Ah. I'll pay you back.'

'Don't be silly.' She stares out into the darkness, sighs. 'Those poor girls…' Then, dropping her voice, 'Do you think Jenny's dead, Harry? Tell me truthfully.'

'No,' he lies. 'The police are confident she's alive.'

She seems inclined to keep drinking, but Harry says he's tired and she rouses herself to take him to the room where Abigail is asleep.

'I keep the night-light on,' she whispers. 'Isn't she beautiful?'

He looks down at the strange little sleeping face. 'Yes. Yes, she is.'

'That bed is pretty small for you. Are you sure you wouldn't prefer to sleep in one of the other rooms? There is a baby monitor.'

'No, this is fine. If you could just tell me what I need to know.'

'Well, she's still in nappies, and has a bit of nappy rash, but I try to avoid changing her at night because it interrupts her sleep, unless she gets really uncomfortable.' She takes him through the baby gear, the change table and mat, the nappy wipes, the spare teats of the right size, the toy Abigail likes. 'I'm getting her off a bottle at night now, and she's pretty good, but if you need to give her a little feed the bottles are in the fridge next door, and this is the thermostatic bottle warmer. You know how to test the milk temperature? No?' She laughs. 'This is all alien territory to you, isn't it, Harry? You look like you're training on some new weapons course. You'll soon get the hang.'

'Yeah. So if she cries I warm up a bottle and stick it in her mouth.'

'No, you pick her up and cradle her in your left arm and put the bottle to her mouth tilting it up so the teat is full and she doesn't just suck air. When she's had enough you burp her.'

'Jesus.'

The lesson comes to an end and Nicole leaves him to take a shower and go to bed, but only after he's gone around the house checking doors and windows. When he lies down he feels tired and worn, acutely conscious of the fragile little thing lying in the cot next to him.

The fragile little thing wakes him an hour later, with an alarming grunting sound that quickly develops into a whimper. Harry leaps out of the narrow bed and picks her up, holding her awkwardly to his chest and rocking her. But this seems to make things worse and soon Abigail's whimper has turned into a howl. Nicole hurries in and takes the baby, who gradually calms down. 'Colic probably,' Nicole says, 'and an unfamiliar person. Poor thing has had to get used to so many changes.'

She hands the baby back to Harry. 'Just relax. She's not a hand grenade. Let her feel you're confident. Let her get to know you.'

By dawn Harry and his daughter have come to know each other quite well. Neither have had much sleep. Nicole comes into the nursery with a mug of tea.

'I heard some of it,' she says, 'but thought I'd leave you to it. Immersion training. You look buggered.'

'Yeah, she won on points.'

She takes Abigail from him and immediately the baby falls into a deep sleep.

'She just needs to get used to you, Harry.'

The rest of the household comes awake—Helen, Nicole's younger daughter, excited because today is her tenth birthday. The breakfast table is piled with cards and presents. Harry, half-asleep, is mortified because he's forgotten; Jenny always took care of that.

They sit around the table, the girls shrieking over the surprise presents, the wonderful cards. Then Helen says, 'Who's Scarlett?' She shows the card to her mother, who shakes her head. 'Súng Vàng? No idea.'

Harry says, 'Can I have a look?'

It's a standard commercial birthday card with an image of balloons and candles. Inside, in careful, childlike printing, the message reads: *Many happy returns, Helen! With heaps of love from your friends Scarlett and Súng Vàng, XXX*

Harry is suddenly very awake. *Scarlett*…it was the name that Jenny had wished for herself as a girl. At the time of Ash Island, when she needed to hide, she suggested that name as an alias. *Gone with the Wind.*

Nicole notices Harry's expression and says to Helen, 'Weren't they your friends at primary? Anyway, what did Gran send you?'

While Helen unwraps the largest parcel, Harry slips away to the computer in the little office space Nicole uses on the floor above. Although the words Súng Vàng sound Vietnamese, they don't appear to be people's names. They translate as *Golden Gun.* He runs them through Google and finds an entry in a business directory for a restaurant called Súng Vàng in the inner west suburb of Marrickville.

23

Something's going on over there, on the far side of the office floor. Brendon Pyle's desk—there's a cluster of people around it, cries of 'Oh my God!', 'You've got to be joking!'

Kelly gets to her feet and joins a stream of others heading for the sensation, whatever it is. The news works its way through the crowd. The Slaughter Park killer has sent a message to Brendon. A confession.

They part for Brendon, who emerges holding a sheet of paper and an envelope by the tips of his fingers and makes his way to the nearest photocopy machine. 'Kelly!' He's energised, eyes bright, ten years younger. 'Come and look at this!'

The others return to their workstations, chattering among themselves, while Kelly goes to his side, watches him copying the two things, front and back, several copies, together with a coil of blonde hair which he tips out of the envelope.

'Have you been following the reaction after the third killing?' he gloats. 'It's been on CNN, Al Jazeera, the BBC. And they're all calling it Slaughter Park! Now with this...' He hands her a copy of the letter. 'I tell you, this is going to be Jack the Ripper on steroids.'

The letter was left overnight outside the front door of the *Times* offices, marked *For the personal attention of Brendon Pyle*. It has been typed on what appears to be an old typewriter, with some letters barely visible.

> *My dear Sir,*
> *You have been so good as to write about my experiments so long delayed. Much time has passed but I am now returned to complete the scientific marvel I so long anticipated. Miss Florian was so good as to assist me in my latest attempt but alas without success. Many more trials will be necessary but I shall prevail.*
> *Your humble servant,*
> *Cador Penberthy*

'Wow,' Kelly says, but she's thinking, this is crap.

Catherine Meiklejohn is hurrying towards them. 'Brendon? Is this true?'

'Absolutely, Catherine.'

'You've called the police?'

'Sure. Dicky Blake, head of homicide, on his personal mobile. He's on his way.'

Brendon, Kelly thinks, calm down.

'Aren't you...' the senior editor is looking at the jumble of documents and hair on the photocopier, '...contaminating the evidence?'

'No, no. I'm being careful, Catherine. I know what I'm doing. But we need a record, right? For tomorrow's front page.'

He begins to gather everything together as someone shouts, 'The police have arrived downstairs. They're coming up.'

Meiklejohn tells him to take his trophies to a meeting room and she goes to meet the officers. Kelly watches them arrive, a tall man and a woman she recognises from Crucifixion Creek—Deb Velasco, looking tired and a lot less confident than last year.

Kelly sits at her desk and types in *Cador Penberthy*. It doesn't take long to find him: a Cornish tin miner who emigrated to Australia in 1886. In 1892 he was charged with the murder of a woman whom he had decapitated. Police found him watching the body because, he explained, he wanted to see if she would be able to find her head again. To help her, he had tied a pink ribbon to her hair and laid it out within reach of her outstretched hand. Instead of hanging, Penberthy was committed to the recently opened Slater Park Hospital for the Insane, now the Slater Park Art School. He died in the influenza epidemic of 1919.

24

This length of Illawarra Road is filled with Vietnamese businesses—hair salons, butchers, pharmacies. They all have bright, colourful signs and shopfronts, all except the Súng Vàng Restaurant, which sits, darkened and unwelcoming, beneath the offices of Huynh, Trinh and McPherson, Solicitors. Harry can see two figures inside sitting at a table. He goes in.

They scowl at him suspiciously, two Vietnamese tough guys—black leather jackets, jeans, scars. 'We're closed.'

'Oh, that's too bad. I was hoping to find Scarlett here.'

'You a cop?'

'No.'

'You look like a cop.'

'No, I'm her friend. She sent me a message.'

One of the men gets to his feet and walks to the front door and locks it. The other waves Harry to the back counter where there's light from the kitchen. He pats Harry down, examines the name on his drivers licence, takes out a phone and photographs his face.

The man says something in Vietnamese to the other, disappears into the kitchen. They wait, Harry and the man at the front door, standing there silently for ten minutes. Then the other man re-appears, waves to Harry. 'Come.'

They go through the kitchen to the back door. A laneway leads along the rear of the shops, and they weave around bins, a builders' skip, a delivery van, then turn down a gap between shops to emerge onto the main street. They cross, and the guide leads Harry into a fruit and vegetable store where a small elderly Vietnamese woman in an apron scrutinises him carefully.

'You Harry?'

'Yes, I'm Harry.'

'Okay.' She nods to the guide, who turns and leaves. 'Follow me.'

She pushes through the plastic strips in the doorway at the back and leads Harry into a dark lobby from which a stair rises to the next floor. As he makes for it, the woman growls after him, 'You better look after her damn good, mister.'

Another woman is waiting in a doorway on the dark landing at the top of the stairs—young, possibly Eurasian, straight black hair in a fringe, narrow glasses. She steps back into the room to let him in and closes the door behind him. There is no one else there and he turns as she removes the glasses and he recognises her. It is Jenny.

25

It's so strange to see him. For three and a half years—forty-two long months—she had been blind. Then for a few brief turbulent days she had been able to see his face again, and then he was gone. Her eyes explore his features, retrieving him, and then he's coming to her, calling her name, wrapping his arms around her, and for the first time in an age she lets go, gives a great sigh, and presses herself against him.

They cling to each other for a long while. He whispers, 'Jenny, Jenny, I thought I'd lost you.'

She finds she can't speak. They separate and she takes his hand and leads him to the small threadbare couch where they sit close together. Finally he says, 'How did you find this place?'

'I figured, if I was going to stay in Sydney it was either this or the burka.'

'You've planned it for a while, haven't you?'

'Yes, from the time of the inquest. When I heard Frank Capp's sister threatening me and Abigail I realised how wrong I'd been to think that by banishing you I could keep her safe. Now look at me.

I can't protect her—just to be near her puts her life in danger. I'm petrified that they'll go to Nicole's house and take her.'

Harry says, 'I'm sleeping there nights, next to the cot, to be on the safe side.'

'You're staying with Nicole?'

She feels a mixture of relief and alarm, remembering how Nicole had a habit of stealing her boyfriends when they were young. Harry nods, understanding what's going through her head. 'Don't worry.'

She manages a little smile. 'Anyway, I decided to make a plan, just in case. I put some cash aside, found this room to let, and worked out how I could straighten and dye my hair and look Asian. I approached Mrs Ngô and told her that I had a violent husband. I had left him and fallen in love with another man called Harry, and together we'd had a child. Now my husband wanted to kill me. He was a policeman, a bad man with contacts and influence, and I was terrified. Mrs Ngô took pity on me. I paid her to hold the room for me until I was ready to come with my child. In the event, though, things happened so fast I couldn't get Abigail, and then I decided she'd be safer without me, at least until things quietened down. You see, Harry, I really am in trouble, not just from Kylie McVea. The police think I murdered someone. They're hunting for me.'

'I know. They came to see Nicole and your mother the day after Palfreyman was killed.'

'So you know about him?'

'I know what the police are saying. Do you have a friend in Darwin?'

'Yes, her name's Nora. We were at university together. She married an engineer, went up to the Northern Territory. We kept in touch. She agreed to help me.'

'They're trying to track her. They've got pictures of her at the ATM and the bus station. She should get rid of the sunglasses and cap, the T-shirt.'

'I'll get a message to her.'

'I'll do it, if you give me her phone number. She's got your credit card?'

'Yes.'

'She'll have to destroy that as well. So, tell me about Terry Palfreyman.'

'Oh, he just barged into my life. I was looking for Amber—Amber Nordlund.' Jenny stares at the old dead fireplace in the wall in front of the couch, thinking how crazily, how impossibly, one thing has led to another.

26

Amber and I spent quite a lot of time together at the time of the inquest. We just seemed to hit it off. So much shared recent history—there was you, Harry, and both of us damaged by Ash Island. And we felt protective towards each other, me with the baby and Amber with that creepy Karen Schaefer, her nurse or chaperone or jailer, whatever she was, hovering in the background. There was a kind of helplessness about Amber, as if she couldn't resist any longer what was happening to her, the doctors, the skin graft operations, the drugs, and the Nordlund family machine. So we became co-conspirators, texting, meeting secretly. At some stage she suggested that their family lawyer, Nathaniel Horn, might be able to help me with Kylie McVea. Horn had been Frank Capp's lawyer, but the Nordlunds were his bread and butter and jam, she said, and she thought she could persuade him to warn Kylie off. Of course I was grateful. Right then, after Kylie's vicious threats, I was more than grateful. Then Amber told me that the Nordlunds were taking her to this Pacific island they owned, to recuperate, and she'd see me again in Sydney in September. We made a date but when it came round and she never showed up I was worried. I did some work on the web and found she was on the board of Nordlund Resources, and they were having their annual shareholders' meeting on the first of October, so I bought a share and went along. But she wasn't there. Medical reasons, they said. Nathaniel Horn was at the meeting; he recognised me and came to speak to me and I mentioned Amber's proposal about his help. He told me to come and see him. As I was leaving the meeting another shareholder who had spoken there caught up with me outside. He said he'd heard Horn refer to me as Mrs Belltree and said he had important information for me. My immediate impression of Terry Palfreyman was that he was mad and I should run a mile. I was right, of course, but then he said, 'You know this is all about what happened to Judge Belltree on the twenty-sixth of June 2010, don't you?' and so I had to find out what he knew.

He wooed me, Harry. I knew he was doing it, and I went along with it because I was convinced he knew something really big. He said he had evidence, documents, and I had to find out. And when I heard his life story I felt sorry for him. He'd worked with the Nordlunds, and when Konrad took over he treated Terry terribly— I was able to check some of it online, and by talking to lawyers I knew in litigation and tort, who'd heard of the case. Konrad Nordlund destroyed Terry, his marriage, his company, his resources. He left him a pauper, and when I checked and found this was true I felt a kind of admiration for poor old Terry, who was still somehow on his feet, punching, maybe only at shadows. And he said he had a dossier, the truth about the Nordlunds, and why your father had to die. How could I resist that?

Once he realised I was hooked, he started playing hard to get, the reluctant suitor. He insisted on meetings that led nowhere, and I saw that he just liked being seen places with me at his side. He smartened up a bit, shaved, got his hair cut, sort of. And of course I paid the bills because he was flat broke. Eventually I told him I'd had enough, either he told me exactly what he knew or he wouldn't see me again.

And that's when he told me that he had proof that Konrad Nordlund murdered his brother Martin, by sabotaging the plane he was piloting the night he died, in order to take control of the family businesses. And that your father had to die because he knew that Konrad had done this.

I know, I can see the expression on your face. I felt the same way—that this was the conspiracy fantasy of an unhinged obsessive—and I told him it was rubbish. What proof could he possibly have?

It was at the house he was living in at Blackheath in the Blue Mountains, he said, and he would show it to me there. When I said that I wasn't interested, he asked me if I was aware that your father had been present at the meeting in the Sydney offices of solicitors McKensey, Schwarz and Comfrey on the ninth of August 2002, at which Martin Nordlund and his solicitor Norman Comfrey were also present? And that it was immediately following that meeting that Martin and Comfrey took their fatal flight up to Cackleberry Mountain?

That made me think. Did your father know the Nordlunds back then? How were they involved? I thought that at least I might be able to check this part of Terry's story. So I went back to our house and up to your father's study in the attic and started looking. I found his old pocket appointment diaries, and sure enough, there on the ninth of August of that year he'd written: *3:30 Norman Comfrey.* If Terry hadn't told me his story the entry would have meant nothing to me, but here was at least some sort of vindication of what he was saying. But what did it mean?

I decided that the only way I could pin him down was to go to Blackheath and stay with him until he told me everything he knew. There was no way I was going to stay in his house, but I found that the cottage next door did holiday lettings and I booked it for a week.

When I got there he started playing his games again, prevaricating, avoiding straight answers, launching into long, rambling diatribes against Konrad Nordlund. I think he was just very lonely. He'd alienated everybody else, and now he had a captive audience. And he was drinking a lot, and I was picking up the bills. In vino veritas, he kept telling me—in wine is truth.

Finally, on the Saturday, I lost patience. I told him I was going to leave if he didn't tell me exactly what he knew, and in the end he came out with it, that he had a sworn statement from a witness proving Konrad's guilt. I said, if that was the case, why hadn't he gone to the police with it? He said he had a reputation and the police wouldn't listen to him. He did try to speak to Bernard Nordlund, but Bernard said Terry was just a troublemaker and he wouldn't meet him. He had managed to interest an independent member of the New South Wales parliament, who was hot on corruption issues, but in the end he'd refused to see him too. But they would listen to me, and that was what he wanted from me, to be his advocate.

I said I would have to examine this evidence. He was very secretive about it, said it was hidden in his house, said we must have a meal first, and a drink, so we walked into town and I bought him both. Then I challenged him, who was this witness? He was becoming more voluble as he got more drunk, and he was showing off. He said, you don't believe me? Then he leaned close to me and whispered in my ear. He said, early on the morning after the plane disappeared, Konrad sent out two men from their estate in Cackleberry Valley to search for it. And they found the plane.

Yes, I was stunned too. Every time I was about to walk out on Terry he came up with some fantastic new thing. They found the plane, the two men dead inside. It was in a very difficult location, he said, inside a deep ravine, and all they could do was try to identify the spot and return for help. Terry's witness was one of the two men—he didn't know who the other man was. When they got back to the homestead, they reported to Konrad, who was very pleased with them, told them he'd reward them. But Terry's witness had seen something out there in the forest that made him realise there'd been foul play, and he got cold feet and fled. He never told a soul until Terry found him, but he'd felt increasingly guilty over the years, when he heard that everyone believed that the plane had never been found. So he made a full statement to Terry, a signed confession. That was the evidence Terry had been promising me. Okay, I said, let me see it, and Terry said he'd need to go back to his house first and retrieve it from its hiding place, and get it ready for me. So we separated, and he went home, while I walked out to the Govetts Leap lookout. It was late afternoon, the weather fine and I sat and tried to decide if Terry really had something important or was completely mad. I wanted it to be true, because I hoped that it would somehow solve all our problems. Little did I know that my problems were about to get a whole lot worse.

I walked back through town and took the bush road out to the cottages. Terry had had almost an hour to get ready for me, and it was getting dark. When I got there I saw a car parked outside his house, which was odd. As I reached the house I heard a scream, and looked through the front window. There was a light on inside, and I could see Terry on his knees on the floor, his face contorted with pain, and a tall man standing over him, doing something to him. The man was wearing gloves and those white disposable over-alls that crime scene officers wear, you know, covering everything. He looked so weird, kind of ghostly and very scary.

I was horrified and reached for my phone to call for help, but just as I lifted it to my ear, a second man suddenly appeared on the other side of the window right in front of me. We stared straight at each other through the glass, and then I screamed and turned and bolted. I ran to my house, fumbling with the keys in the front door, when he came bursting out of Terry's house and charged towards me. I turned and fled, into the trees, and they both came after me, shouting, crashing through the undergrowth. It was dark in the bush, and I stumbled and ran on, and hid in a patch of scrub, and they couldn't find me. Eventually they gave up. After a while I saw the headlights of their car move off along the lane and disappear. I waited and waited, but didn't dare to go back in case one of them was still waiting for me. I knew I had to get out in case they brought back more people to search for me, so I made my way to Blackheath station and got a train back to Sydney. And I've been hiding ever since.

Oh, Harry, it's been a nightmare.

27

Harry holds her. She's trembling from the memories, and he waits until she's calmer. Then he says gently, 'But you didn't call for help? You didn't ring the police?'

'How could I, Harry? They were the police.'

'*What?*'

'When the man looked through the window at me we recognised each other immediately. I'd seen him before, in hospital after Ash Island. He came with Ross Bramley one day, a sort of official sympathy visit. I can't remember his name. He was higher in rank than Ross, his superior officer at Newcastle.'

'What, Superintendent Gibb? Kevin Colquhoun? Ken Fogarty?'

'That's it, Fogarty. Ross had a nickname for him—Foggy. Ross came into the room first and told me that I should feel honoured, Foggy was coming to see me. He arrived shortly afterwards. He brought flowers for me.'

'Detective Chief Inspector Fogarty? This is crazy, Jenny. How could that be?'

'It's all crazy, Harry. All just crazy. But it was him all right. And he recognised me. That's why I haven't dared to go back to Nicole, or collect Abigail. Thank God I'd made preparations here.'

Harry, stunned, picks up the Blackphone and texts Bob Marshall: *Ken Fogarty Newcastle police—where is he now?*

He turns back to Jenny. 'You're sure Palfreyman was alive when you looked through the window?'

'Yes, he was struggling, mouthing off.'

'He was found with a knife in his chest, from the kitchen of the house you were renting, with your prints and DNA all over it.'

She looks shocked. 'I...I remember using it at lunchtime to make a salad. I got interrupted, just left it on the worktop, I think—didn't wash it up.'

'So the men must have got into your house—there was a broken window at the back—and staged a crime scene, with you as Terry's murderer.'

They sit in silence, trying to picture it.

'Poor Terry,' she whispers. 'I wonder, maybe if I hadn't turned up they would have let him go.'

'No, he'd seen their faces. They had to kill him.'

'And if they didn't find his secret evidence, they probably think I've got it.'

They fall silent, holding each other, thinking of the implications.

After a while Jenny says, 'Do you know if Amber's all right? I've been worried about her.'

'Nobody knows where she is. Apparently she flew back from Vanuatu with Karen Schaefer on the fifteenth of last month, and disappeared at the airport. I've been trying to find her, thinking you might be with her, or she might know where you were. What I don't understand is what she was doing with Schaefer and the Nordlunds in the first place, after all the animosity between them.'

'She had such a hard time after Ash Island, devastated by Luke Santini's death, terribly burned by the explosion. They gave her morphine for the pain, and I think she just gave up and let her uncle take over. I wish I could reach her.'

'I've tried to contact people she and Luke might have been friends with in the environmental movement, without success so far.' He tells her about Luke's former partner Sol Fleischer and the possible link to James Zuckermann. 'I haven't checked out the address on his drivers licence yet. I was going to go this morning until I read your birthday message to Helen.'

'We should go now.'

Harry says, 'Not you, Jen. I'll try it later.'

'No, Harry, I'm going crazy here. We'll just be careful, and if he does know where Amber is, she's more likely to respond to me.'

He concedes and they go downstairs, where Mrs Ngô calls them a cab. She beams at Jenny. 'At last you look happy now, Scarlett,' she says, and they hug.

The taxi takes them to the address, Mont Street, a narrow thoroughfare lined with old terraces in variously dilapidated condition, running from Waterloo into Redfern. There is a ruined couch sitting in front of number thirty-two, on which sits a haggard-looking man with a huge black Rottweiler on one side, and a small bird in a cage on the other. As they get out of the cab and check the door number the man watches them with pink staring eyes. The dog, at least sixty kilograms, does the same.

The man says, 'Help you?'

'We're looking for Mr Zuckermann,' Jenny says, trying to sound as unlike a police officer as possible.

'Jim?'

'Yes, Jim.'

'Attic,' the man says, losing interest.

'Thanks.'

They make to go inside but are met with several young men rushing out of the house, clutching backpacks. They wait as more appear.

'Students,' the man says. 'Chinese. Four to a room.' He gives a croaky laugh and puts a rolled cigarette of some kind in his mouth and lights it.

Harry and Jenny go into the dark interior; there is a smell of Asian food and rising damp. They climb the stairs. Harry counts five rooms—sixteen students, assuming Mr Sunshine at the front door has one to himself. At the top of the final flight a single door faces them. A tiny brass nameplate has a card with *Zuckermann* hand-printed on it. Harry taps on the door.

They hear the scrape of a chair inside, then a muffled voice. 'Who is it?'

A woman's voice.

Jenny puts her mouth to the keyhole and whispers, 'Amber? Is that you? It's Jenny.'

There's a hesitation, then the scrape of a bolt, and the door opens on a chain. Amber's pale face appears in the gap. 'Jenny? Are you alone?'

'Harry's with me. It's just the two of us. No one else knows we're here.'

The door closes, the chain rattles, the door opens again and Jenny and Harry step quickly inside. Jenny and Amber embrace while Harry looks around the cramped room. A small table with a jug of water, two old wooden chairs, a clothes rack, a wash hand basin, a bed beneath the low sloping ceiling. It takes him a moment, his eyes adjusting to the dim light from the small grimy window, to make out the man lying in the bed, watching them.

Amber introduces them. 'Jenny, Harry, this is Jim. He was a good friend of Luke's, remember?'

It's clear that Jim is not well, barely able to raise a hand to give a little wave. 'Hi,' he says faintly. 'Welcome to the crack house.'

Amber laughs, pointing to the cracked walls. She goes over and sits on the edge of the bed, taking hold of his hand.

It is suffocatingly hot in the room, a big electric heater next to the bed. As they draw closer Harry sees what look like open sores around Zuckermann's mouth. 'Is Jim seeing a doctor?'

'Yes,' Amber says brightly. 'We have a medical friend. Please, sit down.' She looks pretty rough herself, eyes large in a pale haggard face.

'I've been so worried about you,' Jenny says, drawing one of the chairs towards the bed. 'What happened?'

'Oh, family.' A brave, pained smile. 'Just had to get away from them all.'

'So where are you living?'

'Here. Jim and I look after each other.'

Now Harry sees an electric wok on the floor beside the table, a box of groceries beside it.

'Please,' Amber goes on, 'you can't tell anyone where I am. Promise?'

'Of course,' Jenny says, 'but can we get anything for you? Maybe we could take you out for lunch?'

'No, no. We prefer to stay here. I don't really go out, except to the newsagent on the corner for cigarettes.' She laughs, as if at her own eccentricity. 'Actually, you could do something.' She gets to her feet and goes to her handbag on the dressing table, finds a slip of paper inside. 'If you wouldn't mind getting Jim's prescription.' Then her face drops. 'Oh…no. Sorry. Can't do that.'

'Why not?'

'Um, no money. Sorry, stupid, run out of cash.' She looks on the point of bursting into tears.

Jenny goes to her, puts her arms around her. 'Don't be silly. We'll get it. And while we're at it we'll get any supplies you need. Just tell us what.'

'Well…maybe one or two basics…' Amber haltingly begins to recite a list that Harry jots down in his notebook.

'No problem,' he says.

'That's so good of you. I'm afraid we're just a bit desperate at the moment.'

Jenny says, 'Is there no one we can contact? How about your uncle—Bernard?'

Amber shakes her head. 'There's no one I can trust. They even took Dylan, my little boy, away from me, sent him to boarding school. They said it upset him to see me.' She begins to weep.

'That's terrible. What about a phone? We should keep in touch.'

Amber gives a despairing shrug. 'I swapped it with one of the Chinese students for the wok.'

Harry takes all the cash out of his wallet and puts it on the table. 'We'll go to an ATM.'

'Oh no,' Amber protests faintly. 'We can't let you.'

'Don't be silly. We won't be long.'

'Thank you, thank you. The best pharmacy is on Elizabeth Street.' Amber gives directions. 'They know us. They've done this before.'

Done what? Harry wonders, as Amber lets them out and bolts the door behind them.

28

Kelly stares out of her car window at the sign with the bullet holes, hears the howl of dogs through the bush. She puts her foot down and moves on, then pulls in among the dog pens and gets out, trying to avoid getting mud on her shoes. The nearest pen contains a solitary dog who catches her eye and she steps carefully over to look more closely at it, bedraggled, quivering. 'You all right, girl?' Kelly asks, and the dog gives a little whimper.

Kelly looks around and sees Kylie McVea sitting in her wheelchair on the veranda of the house, watching her. 'Hello there,' Kelly calls, and goes towards her.

'Mrs McVea, my name is Kelly Pool. We've met before.'

Kylie has been reading a copy of *Australian Greyhound Weekly*. She lets it drop onto her lap and takes off her glasses, peers up at Kelly. 'Is that a fact?'

'Yes, at the inquest couple of months ago. I said hello then. I'm a reporter.'

Kylie frowns. 'Nothing to say.'

'I'm writing an article on the impact of violent crime on the families of victims, and I thought of your brother.'

Kylie's face reddens. 'My brother was not a violent man!' she shouts. 'The cops made all that up. They defamed him.'

'No, no,' Kelly says hastily. 'I meant, he was the *victim* of a violent crime.'

'Oh...yes, that's a fact.'

'And I remember at the inquest how deeply you were affected by his loss.'

'He was the most important person in my life.'

'Closer even than your husband?'

'My mongrel husband buggered off nineteen years ago.'

'Oh, right, so Frank was your mainstay.'

'He was like a father to my boy Gavin. He was the example he looked up to.'

Oh dear, Kelly thought. That I must see. 'How old is he, Kylie?'

'Twenty-one.'

'He must be a great consolation to you.'

'He is. Looks after his mum. Him and Amal and Khalil. My boys.'

'They live and work here, in the kennels?'

'Yeah, they do all the physical work. I look after the paperwork.'

'So you're a successful businesswoman.'

'Too right.'

'Would you like to show me around? I'd love to be able to give you a bit of a plug.'

So Kylie sets off down the ramp and shows Kelly the sheds, the howling dog pens and the fenced paddock for the breeding bitches.

'Twelve active bitches,' she says, 'and over there the new litters.'

Four pens each contain a bitch surrounded by squirming puppies, two of Rottweilers and one of greyhounds. The fourth one has a greyhound mother with unidentifiable puppies.

'That was a mistake,' Kylie says. 'Greyweilers.'

'Oh.' Kelly is taking pictures as she goes, and now she points to a cleared area in the bush off to one side, the ground heavily chewed up by wheels. 'What's that?'

'Just a car park.'

There must be room for thirty or forty vehicles, but there are none there now. She notices cables running through the trees towards an open area on the other side of the house, in which she can make out lighting poles, and what looks like an empty swimming pool. Nearby is a tall pile of timber, as if for a bonfire.

'I suppose you have big parties out here, do you?'

'What d'ya mean?'

'Oh, I just thought, your boys, this would be a great place to have their mates over for a Saturday night bush party.'

'No, nothing like that. We're very quiet here. You seen enough?'

Kylie leads the way back. When they reach her car, Kelly points to the solitary dog in the pen. 'What about this one?'

'Saw you lookin' at Sophie when you arrived. Owners abandoned her. She'll have to be put down.'

'That's too bad.'

'Yeah, shame. It's an unusual breed, a Danish spaniel.'

'I've never heard of that one.'

'Rare. But she'll have to go.'

'How do you put them down?'

'Quickly.' Kylie grins.

'I heard that farmers shoot their dogs.'

'Not worth the cost of a bullet, darlin'.'

Kelly reaches for the car doorhandle, then says, 'Maybe I could take Sophie off your hands.'

'Well, reckon you could. Cost you a few bucks, mind.'

'You said she wasn't worth the cost of a bullet.'

'I was just saying that. She's a valuable dog.'

'How much?'

114

'A hundred.'

'Fifty.'

They split the difference. Kylie hauls Sophie out by the scruff of the neck and throws her into the back of Kelly's car.

29

'What happened on Maturiki?' Jenny says.

They are waiting in the pharmacy for Jim's prescription. Shopping bags at their sides contain groceries and the phone Harry has bought for Amber.

'Something bad,' Harry says. 'That she doesn't want to talk about.'

'But how can we help her if we don't understand? She seems terrified of being discovered. I know exactly how she feels, cooped up in that little room, afraid to go out. You don't know what a relief it is just to do something normal, like this.'

They return to the house in Mont Street. The man on the front couch is talking to a young woman, who hurriedly stuffs something into her pocket. The man and his dog eye their bags as they go through the front door.

Amber is overjoyed to see them. She unpacks the bags, eagerly reeling off the list of things they've bought to the man in the bed, who seems barely conscious.

'And Jim's medicine?'

'Yes.' Harry takes it from his pocket and hands it to her. She fills a glass with water and takes it to the bed, where Jim struggles to sit up.

'I'll help,' Harry says, but she says no, quickly.

'I'm used to this. You can boil some water if you like, and we'll have coffee. They bought coffee, Jim.'

They sit, Jenny and Harry on the chairs, Amber on the edge of the bed, and sip their drinks. Harry says, 'How can we help you to sort this out, Amber? Your family are worried about you. Your uncle Konrad has hired private detectives to try to find you. His lawyer Nathaniel Horn even asked me to look for you.'

She looks at him, alarmed. 'You can't tell him where I am!'

'Okay, but won't you tell us what happened? We might be able to help.'

'There's nothing you can do. I don't want to talk about it.'

They leave, promising to come back in a couple of days.

As they get into their car, Harry's phone rings. Bob Marshall.

'Ken Fogarty's left Newcastle, moved back to state crime command in Sydney. Organised crime squad. Why? What's this about, Harry?'

'There's something I'd like to run by you, Bob. Can we meet?'

'I'm about to give a talk to five hundred schoolkids, out here in Parramatta. I could meet you afterwards. Same place as before? Say four o'clock?'

Harry rings off, explains to Jenny. 'I'll drop you back at Marrickville, then head out there.'

'Are you sure you can trust Bob, Harry?'

He nods. 'Reckon so.'

'Then I want to come with you. I'll stay in the car or keep out of the way. No one will recognise me.'

When they reach Phoenix Square Jenny is astonished. 'I came here a couple of times with Nicole to Greg's unit. I can't believe how it's changed.'

Harry points. 'His builder's workshop was somewhere under-neath that piazza up there with the palm trees. That's where I'm meeting Bob.'

He parks the car and they separate. Bob is already at a table outside the café, sitting in the sun. He's changed out of his uniform and looks buoyant after his session at the school. There are two glasses of beer on the table.

'How'd it go?' Harry asks.

'Great. Headmistress told me I had a knack of communicating with children.'

Harry thinks that's probably true. Uncle Bob. Harry wonders if it was a mistake involving him.

Bob says, 'So, what's the mystery about Detective Chief Inspector Fogarty?'

Harry runs his finger through the puddle of beer beside the glass. 'Formerly of the drug squad, along with his good mate Toby Wagstaff.'

'Was he now? I didn't know that. And?'

'I'd like to put a hypothetical to you,' Harry says.

Bob narrows his eyes at him, nods, leans forward. 'Go ahead.'

'Let's say that Jenny went to the annual shareholders' meeting of Nordlund Resources three weeks ago, in the hope of catching up with Amber Nordlund, one of the directors. She wasn't there, but Terry Palfreyman, serial pest, was. He followed her afterwards and tried to get her interested in his feud against Konrad Nordlund. She brushed him off until he let drop that he knew that Nordlund was responsible for my parents' death and Jenny's injuries. He claimed that he had evidence of some kind of conspiracy also involving the death of Konrad's brother Martin in an unsolved air crash back in 2002. It might just be his obsession with Nordlund, but Jenny felt she had to follow it up. He said he would show her the proof at the cottage he was living in out in Blackheath, and she decided to rent the adjoining house and go out there for a day or two and settle it, one way or the other.

'On the afternoon of Monday, October thirteenth, Palfreyman goes back to his house to retrieve his evidence from its hiding place. Jenny gives him an hour then walks over there, and sees a car parked outside. She looks through the window and sees two men in forensic suits, searching the house and trying to force information from Palfreyman. Suddenly one of the men appears at the window in front of Jenny and immediately they recognise each other. When she was in hospital after Ash Island, this man, a police officer in Newcastle, visited her there. Now he and the other man leave Palfreyman's house and chase after Jenny, who runs into the bush and hides. Sometime later she sees their car drive away. She goes to Blackheath station and gets a train back to Sydney and goes on the run because she knows that the man who saw her will kill her.

'The man was Detective Chief Inspector Fogarty.'

Bob sits back with a sigh. 'And Fogarty was a friend of Wagstaff, who tried to kill you here, on this spot, two years ago. Very neat. Very symmetrical. How long did it take you to dream that one up?'

Harry says nothing, stares at him.

'No,' Bob says slowly. 'Don't tell me *she* dreamed it up? You've heard from her?'

'You're a serving police officer, Bob. If I said yes you'd be duty-bound to report it and I'd be arrested quick smart. Like I said, it's a hypothetical.'

Bob shakes his head. 'All right, hypothetically, they didn't torture Palfreyman. He had no other injuries apart from Jenny's knife in his chest.'

Harry nods. 'So they didn't leave any marks. Anything else?'

'Anything else? These two men carry out a murder without leaving a single trace? The forensic evidence against Jenny is over-whelming, Harry. You know it is.'

'The Slaughter Park murderer isn't leaving any traces either.'

'Oh, so Fogarty's up for that too, is he?' Bob roars with laughter.

Harry feels his face flushing. 'These two guys were experts, Bob. They knew exactly how to rig a crime scene. Remember, it was done to me, in Newcastle—Logan McGilvray's death, my tyre marks, my murder weapon. And anyway, they did leave a trace at Blackheath—the broken window in Jenny's house. They were in a hurry and they needed to get in for her knife and to plant a trail of her bloody footprints.'

'You really believe this?'

'Yes, I do.'

Bob folds his arms, frowns. 'Well, I don't. Not without hearing it from her mouth. I'll know then if she's telling the truth.'

'She can't do that.'

'Forget the duty-bound business. If she's telling the truth, I won't betray her. If she isn't, then I'll arrest her on the spot. Tell her that.'

Harry says, 'That's a tough one, Bob. I'll put it to her. But if she decides not to speak to you, you've got to forget we had this conversation.'

'Fair enough.'

Harry takes out his phone and calls Jenny, explains Bob's proposal, advises against it. She replies immediately that she'll do it. He begins to explain where they are, but she stops him.

'I know, I'm sitting across the other side of the square watching you.'

Harry rings off and tells Bob she's coming.

'You carrying a gun, Harry?'

'Why?'

'You're thinking how you're going to stop me arresting her when she doesn't convince me.'

'True enough.'

120

'You're younger and fitter than me, but I'll make a fight of it, and security'll be here in seconds.'

Bob looks puzzled as a young woman with black hair and big dark glasses approaches their table, then gets to his feet as she takes the glasses off and he recognises her. 'Jenny. This is a surprise. You've been running rings around my friends in homicide.'

'I had no choice, Bob.'

She sits and he asks her to tell him what happened at Black-heath. She goes through it, and from time to time he interrupts with questions, demanding details.

'You say one of them was torturing Palfreyman. How?'

'I couldn't see clearly. I think he was twisting his arm.'

'Which arm?'

'Um…the left one.'

Bob takes out an iPad and taps away at it for a moment, pulling up a document. 'Pathology report,' he mutters. 'Victim had bruising to left hand, torn and inflamed tendons. All right, the man standing over Palfreyman, what did he look like?'

'I didn't see his face. He had his back to me.'

'Then how did you know he was a man?'

She thinks about that. 'His build—very tall. And the way he moved. I just immediately saw him as a man. I don't think I was wrong—No! I heard his voice, later, when they were searching for me in the bush. It was definitely a man.'

'Go on.'

When she gets to the part where Fogarty suddenly appears in the window in front of her, the hairs rise on Harry's neck.

'I had the phone in my hand,' she says. 'If I'd only thought I could have taken a photo of him. But I was frozen with shock. I knew that face, and he knew mine. I couldn't remember his name until Harry told me the senior officers he worked with in Newcastle. But I knew his face.'

'From that one visit to you in hospital, soon after you were hurt, full of painkillers and goodness knows what else.'

'Yes, I remember it very clearly. He was in uniform then.'

Bob shakes his head, takes out his phone and begins flicking at the screen, scrolling through images. After a search he shows her a picture of a police officer in uniform. 'This is him.'

She looks at it. 'No, it's not.'

Harry tenses, holds his breath. Then Bob flicks at his phone some more, shows her another image.

'No.'

A third time, and this time she says, 'Yes, that's the man. Ross Bramley called him Foggy.'

Bob shows the screen to Harry. It's Fogarty.

'Well, Jenny...' Bob says reluctantly. 'You're very convincing.'

'Do you believe me?'

'Yes, I do.'

Jenny takes a deep breath, reaches out for Harry's hand. He feels hers trembling.

Bob turns to Harry. 'So what the hell is Fogarty up to?'

'Trouble is, you get to think like Palfreyman, seeing conspiracies everywhere. Like, how Fogarty was in charge of Strike Force Ipswich to solve the Ash Island murders, which they didn't. Like, how Nordlund Resources security staff were running a drug racket that didn't get discovered. Like, how the person most threatened by Palfreyman was Konrad Nordlund.'

'You think Fogarty is in Nordlund's pocket?' Bob asks.

'I do,' Harry says.

'So how can we prove it?'

'I was hoping you might put tabs on him.'

Bob shakes his head. 'Not easy. If I try to target him directly he'll know. I'll have to think.'

'Me too.' Harry looks around. Two security men are moving through the crowd in the square. 'We've been here too long. Better

122

go. Could you get me Fogarty's details, Bob? Where he's living, private email, phone numbers, family set-up?'

'I'll see what I can do, mate. Good luck to you both.'

They leave Bob and head back to their car. On the way to Marrickville Jenny says, 'What do we do now?'

30

Kelly taps at her computer, frustrated. McVea was a dead end. All around her there is activity, new people enlisted to help Brendon on Slaughter Park—graphic reconstructions, profiles of the victims, rumours circulating among the Friends of Slater Park about previous odd goings-on. But the Palfreyman case is dead, not a word from the police. She wonders what she can do to resurrect it. And at that moment she gets a call from Harry.

She answers immediately. 'Hi. Is your phone safe?'

He says, 'Mine is, but…'

'We've all been given an encryption app, Harry. So this phone's safe too.'

'Good. What have you been doing?'

'Nothing interesting. All the excitement here is about Slaughter Park. How about you? Any news of Jenny?'

He says, 'You sure your phone is safe?'

'Absolutely. Nobody can unscramble this conversation, not the police, ASIO, nobody.'

'I've found her, Kelly, and she's told me what happened. She's been framed.'

'My God, Harry. How? What happened?'

He tells her about Jenny returning to Palfreyman's house and seeing him being assaulted.

'But...why doesn't she surrender to the police and tell them the truth?'

'Because the men *were* police. Do you remember Detective Chief Inspector Fogarty who used to give the press briefings at Ash Island? He's now in the organised crime squad here at Parramatta. He was one of the two killers. Jenny recognised him from Newcastle, and he recognised her.'

'That's...incredible. Is she quite sure?'

'Absolutely. She's completely convincing, and terrified.'

'This is dynamite, Harry. But the *Times* won't let me print this without corroboration.'

'Of course. I don't want you to print it, Kelly, I just want you to keep it in mind. What I'd like to do is stir the pot a bit.'

'How? I'd be happy to do a follow-up on the Palfreyman murder if I had any material to use, but at the moment the cops are keeping mum and I'm being told to forget it until they come up with something.'

'There may be a way. The cops have been monitoring Jenny's bank account, and have discovered that her credit card has been used recently in Darwin. If you printed that it might get them to talk to you. But there's something else. Palfreyman told Jenny that he had got a member of parliament interested in his case for a while, and I thought if you talked to him he might give you more material on Palfreyman. The thing is, everyone assumes he was a joke, an accident waiting to happen. But suppose he really was on to something, a corruption whistleblower who was silenced because he was a threat?'

'Yes, that would be interesting. Who was the MP?'

'We don't have a name, but he was an independent, and there aren't many of them. Male, and he has a reputation for pursuing corruption issues.'

'Okay, I'll follow that up. Poor Jenny. How is she coping?'

'It's tough.'

'Let me know if there's anything I can do.'

Kelly gets to work with renewed energy. In front of her on her desk she has two pictures of Sophie, before and after their extended visit to the vet to stitch up her ear, get rid of her parasites, inoculate and bath her and get a heap of medicines and special food. Kelly stares at the before picture and thinks again of Kylie McVea. There was something bad going on out there, but whatever it was, Palfreyman is what she needs to concentrate on now.

31

Harry rings Nathaniel Horn's number, gets put through to Horn, who is in court.

'Yes, Mr Belltree. Have you found Amber?'

'I have a lead, but I need to know what happened on Maturiki Island to make her run like that.'

'It's not relevant. Just tell me where she is. Her family will reward you handsomely, I assure you.'

'I need to talk to someone who was there, on Maturiki with her, to make sure I'm on the right track.'

Horn sighs, breaks off to speak to someone, then comes back on. 'I'll see what I can do.'

'Yeah, do that.'

32

It doesn't take Kelly long to identify the MP. Husam Roshed, repre-senting a western Sydney constituency, has a reputation as a scourge of corruption in the public service. Kelly has met him before, some years ago, but doesn't expect him to remember her.

'Of course I remember, Kelly. And I read all your articles in the *Times*. Always thought-provoking.'

Kelly feels herself being charmed, and liking it. He suggests she come to Parliament House and meets her there at the security point on Macquarie Street, shows her into one of the rooms nearby.

'This place has always been steeped in corruption. When Governor Macquarie told the British government that the new colony needed a hospital, they said go ahead, but we won't give you any money for it. So he paid for it with a drug deal—he gave the builder a monopoly on the import of rum. This room was part of the principal surgeon's house. So what sort of corruption are you interested in?'

Kelly is a little disconcerted by his dark eyes, his easy smile.

'Actually, I wanted to talk to you about the murder of Terry Palfreyman.'

He nods, a little wearily. 'Ah, Mr Palfreyman, yes.'

'You knew him?'

'Oh, yes, over a number of years. It began promisingly enough. He had recently lost his mining engineering business, but he had current knowledge of what was going on in the coalfields, and he pointed me in the direction of a corrupt deal between an official in the Department of Mineral Resources and one of the big mining companies. I raised questions in the house, there was an investigation and his information proved to be correct.

'From then on things went downhill. He became more and more erratic and obsessive. He tried to involve me in his feud with the company that bought out his business, but then he was charged with arson. I told him I couldn't help him. He ended up a crank, sitting outside here with a placard. It was a sad story. But I know nothing about his murder. How did you think I could help?'

'So he didn't tell you anything concrete? Anything that would provide a motive to kill him?'

'Oh, he made plenty of accusations, mainly against Nordlund Resources, beginning with commercial fraud and bullying, and becoming wilder and wilder. It culminated with some crazy conspiracy where Konrad Nordlund murdered his brother, and was even mixed up in the death of Justice Belltree—remember that business?'

'Yes, I do. But you didn't think there was anything in his claims?'

'Oh no, it was crazy stuff.'

'You see,' Kelly says, 'everybody seems to assume he was mad, stumbling around annoying everyone with his crazy stories, and his death was kind of inevitable, like the final act of a Greek tragedy. But suppose, among all the wild rantings, he had evidence that really did represent a danger to someone?'

'Do you have anything to support that?'

'Apparently the killers turned his house upside down, as if they were looking for something.'

'Is that so? You say "killers", plural? I thought they were looking for a woman?'

'Apparently a car with two men in it was seen coming from his street at that time.'

'The police have told you this?'

'No, I got it from asking around out there. The police have said very little, almost as if they don't want to talk about this case.'

'They're probably overwhelmed by the Slater Park murders— Konrad Nordlund again.'

'I'm sorry?'

'You didn't hear him this morning? On talkback radio, 2GB. He's been trying to put together a development proposal for Slater Park for years apparently, but the government can't make up its mind to sell the land because of objections from local groups. He claims it was a disaster waiting to happen. He also had a go at the incompetence of the police.'

'Really?'

'Funny to actually hear Nordlund speaking out. Usually he keeps in the background, away from the media. Gets others to front for him, as he did for the redevelopment of Crucifixion Creek. But you know all about that.'

'You mean through Ozdevco.'

'Exactly, Maram Mansur. I know Maram—we went to the same school. His family and mine came from the same village in the Bekaa Valley.'

'I did try to contact him, but he seems to have disappeared.'

'That'd be Maram—duck and run.' Roshed rubs his cheek, thinking. 'You know, for all his infuriating manner and crazy ideas, I always had the feeling that there might be a germ of truth in Palfreyman's theories about Konrad Nordlund.'

'Can I quote you on that?'

'As long as you're very careful how you put it. Maybe it's time he and Maram felt some heat.'

33

Harry gets into a lift in the Gipps Tower and presses the button for the twenty-third floor. As he rises through the atrium he thinks about Jenny. Having found each other again, the parting in Marrickville was particularly painful, all the more so for Jenny since she's desperate to be with her baby again. But they agreed that the only safe course was for her to stay on with Mrs Ngô until they can work out an alternative.

The lift doors open and he heads to Horn's office. The summons was a curt text: *Come to my office 4:30 pm today re our matter.*

The receptionist takes him through to a small windowless meeting room, offers him tea or coffee, which he declines. He waits in silence for a while until he hears someone else arriving. Then Horn opens the door and shows in a young man. He is wearing an expensive black suit, dazzling white shirt with cufflinks, and shiny black shoes with red shoelaces.

'Ah, Mr Belltree,' Horn says, 'I'd like you to meet Ryan Nordlund, Konrad's eldest son. Ryan was at Maturiki at the time Amber left, and has agreed to tell you what he can.'

They shake hands, sit, assessing each other. Ryan Nordlund smiles at the receptionist, asks for an espresso. Horn takes a seat at the head of the table, gestures at Harry. 'Go ahead.'

'Thank you. Can you tell me who else was on Maturiki Island while Amber was there?'

Ryan gives him names, sounding bored. He perks up a little when his coffee arrives.

Harry says, 'Did she say why she was leaving?'

Ryan shrugs. 'A whim, I think. A sudden impulse. She's like that.' His voice is expensive private school.

'There was no special reason for it? An argument? A fight?'

'No, no, nothing like that.'

'You said her uncle left for Sydney around then?'

'The previous day, with a business colleague.'

'How did they travel?'

'Chopper to Pentecost, then private jet to Sydney.' He says it with a casual smile, showing off.

'But Amber and Karen Schaefer took commercial flights from Pentecost to Port Vila, then Port Vila to Sydney. It took them all day.'

'So?'

'So why didn't they go the previous day with your father in the private jet?'

'Don't know. She probably didn't think of it. She doesn't really plan things out.'

'Did something happen between the time of your father's departure and Amber deciding to leave?'

'Nothing special.'

'A disagreement of some kind?'

'No, I've already told you, nothing like that. Amber has mood swings, up one minute, down the next. Impulsive. It's her illness. She's mentally ill.'

'She must have told someone the reason. Surely you were curious?'

Horn broke in. 'I think Ryan has answered you, Belltree. What's the point of these questions?'

'The point is that I've tracked down someone who I think has seen Amber since she got back to Sydney, but he's reluctant to talk to me. He believes that something happened to Amber on Maturiki and that she is frightened of her family. That's why she's gone into hiding. He won't talk to me because he's afraid I'll betray her to them. So I need to know the truth, so that I can reassure him.'

Horn shakes his head impatiently. 'Waste of time. Tell me how to contact him and I'll persuade him.'

'How?'

'I'll offer him money, Mr Belltree. It invariably works.'

'No, not this time.'

'Actually,' Ryan says, looking thoughtfully up at the ceiling, 'there was something, now I come to think of it. After Dad left in the chopper, Hayden, Tayla and I decided to go scuba diving out on the reef. Amber saw us and said she wanted to come too. I wasn't at all keen, because she was on medication, et cetera, but she insisted, said it would be good for her burns. So she came, only when she went into the water she had trouble with the pressure in her ears, and we had to leave her below the boat to give her a chance to equalise. While she was there some kind of fish came up towards her. She thought it was a shark, though I don't believe it was—they don't generally come inside the reef. Whatever, it scared the shit out of her and she got hysterical. Karen had to medicate her, and that night she had bad dreams. I think that must have been what triggered her decision to leave. But look, between us, Amber's off her head half the time, imagining things, frightened of her shadow. Not surprising really, given what she's been through. Well, you'd know all about that, wouldn't you, Harry?'

Horn says, 'Satisfied, Mr Belltree? Now let me have this man's details.'

'I'd like to speak to Karen Schaefer.'

'Not possible. Ryan has been good enough to answer your questions. Time to get this settled. Give me the man's details and I'll sort it out.'

'I don't have his details, but I think I can find him again.'

'Do that. Reassure him. Tell him Amber's family will pay generously to have her returned home.'

34

Harry returns to Nicole's house and another night with Abigail. She seems quieter, maybe getting used to him. He has three clear hours of sleep before she starts up. He's more relaxed about it this time, more comfortable with the routine, and she settles again quite quickly.

At breakfast Nicole, reading the paper, mouth full of toast, exclaims, 'Kelly's written an article about the Palfreyman murder.' She scans it, then gives it to Harry.

It focuses on the character of Terry Palfreyman, and the possibility that he wasn't simply a mad nuisance, but an informed whistleblower who represented a danger to certain powerful figures, unnamed. She quotes Husam Roshed to support this view. If correct, it suggests that the police, whose investigation seems to have led nowhere, have been looking in the wrong direction. She also reports an anonymous Blackheath source as saying that a car with two men in it was seen leaving Palfreyman's street at the time of the murder.

*

At her office desk, Kelly is also reading her article. There's always something different, more authoritative, about seeing her words printed in the paper or on the screen, with the smart typography and supporting photographs. The picture of Detective Inspector Velasco leading the case is particularly good. It's an old photo that Kelly took at the time of Crucifixion Creek, and Deb looks harassed, not quite on top of things. That should get her going.

Kelly's phone buzzes. The receptionist in the front lobby tells her that two police officers are here to see her. Kelly asks for their names and is told Deb Velasco and Jack Anders. She says she'll be right down.

They're in the lobby, looking impatient, and she takes them to a meeting room where she offers them coffee. Both shake their heads, then Deb slaps down a copy of the morning's paper and barks, 'If you had evidence relating to the Palfreyman murder you should have given it to us.'

Kelly doesn't reply, and after an awkward moment Anders, more conciliatory, says, 'Pitching in with stuff like this without first talking to us isn't going to make you any friends in the police service, Kelly.'

'I'm sorry about that, Jack, but I've spoken to you several times since the murder, and you've given me nothing, so I decided I'd have to do a bit of investigating for myself.'

Deb tries again. 'I want to know who told you about the car with two men in it.'

'I'm sorry, Inspector, I can't do that. The person is very nervous and worried about consequences, and only told me on the strict condition that I didn't tell anyone their name.'

Anders says, 'What time exactly did they see the car, Kelly?'

'It was dusk. The light wasn't good, but they definitely saw two men in a sedan leaving that street. They didn't get the number or make, I'm afraid. I felt they were a credible witness. Maybe when you've got the killers locked up they'll be willing to come forward.'

'And who are these "powerful interests" that Palfreyman threatened?' Deb says.

'Well, I think that wouldn't take a lot of imagination. Palfreyman was pretty outspoken about his theories, only nobody paid any attention. He had a longstanding feud with Nordlund Resources, of course—everyone knows that—but I certainly wouldn't suggest in any way, shape or form that Konrad Nordlund was involved. Particularly since he owns thirteen per cent of this newspaper.'

Jack Anders chuckles; Deb Velasco glares.

Kelly says, 'Have you spoken to Husam Roshed?'

'Not yet. He seems to be unavailable at present.'

'Oh, well, I think he would be worth talking to. He got very irritated with Palfreyman, but he does seem to feel that he had genuine information. Tell me, was Palfreyman's house turned over? Could his murderers have been searching for something?'

Both detectives stare at Kelly blankly.

'You see,' she says. 'That's all I've been getting from you—no comment. How about the mystery woman you wanted to interview? Any sightings of her?'

'No comment,' Anders says.

'This isn't some kind of police cover-up, is it?'

Deb Velasco gets abruptly to her feet. 'Come on, Jack. This is a waste of time.'

They aren't long gone, Kelly back at her desk, when she gets a call from the MP.

Roshed says, 'Excellent article, Kelly. Do you want to follow it up?'

'Of course.'

'I've booked a seat for you in the gallery at question time in parliament this afternoon, two-thirty. I'll be putting some questions to the minister. Should stir things up.'

'Great. I've just had two cops from homicide here questioning me about my sources. They want to speak to you.'

'Yes, I know. I'm keeping out of their way till this afternoon, then I'm all theirs.'

'Well, I'll look forward to question time then.'

When she hangs up Kelly thinks about how else she might follow up on the Palfreyman murder. She has already investigated Fogarty online and in the *Times* archives, and has checked a string of references to him in crime stories dating back to the 1990s, but found only one mention of anything dubious—a report from his time in the drug squad, of a claim by a small-time drug dealer that he had been framed by Fogarty. She asks Brendon Pyle if he remembers anything. He's not sure, promises to look into it, in a vague, preoccupied sort of way.

35

Harry pulls into a space in a rooftop car park behind Illawarra Road and walks down to Mrs Ngô's shop. He fills up a bag with fresh fruit and vegetables, then goes through to the back and up the stairs to Jenny's room. They embrace, Harry gives her the latest report on Abigail—her weight, her mood, the rash—and shows her Kelly's article in the *Times*. When they're ready Harry brings the car to the back entrance to the shop. Jenny gets in quickly with the bag of produce and they head to 32 Mont Street. The drug dealer is still sitting outside with his dog and little bird, which is chirping up at the sun. In the hallway one of the Chinese students is standing in a doorway eating his breakfast with chopsticks from a bowl. They say hello and he nods silently and watches them as they climb the stairs.

Amber is sitting by the open window, smoking, and a jar lid on the sill is full of butts. Zuckermann appears to be sleeping, and they pull the chairs over to the window to talk quietly with her. Outside a dazzling blue sky arcs over the jumbled tin roofs and backyards, the CBD towers in the background. Amber wears a short-sleeved top and the white scar tissue covering her left arm is covered with vivid pink scratch marks.

Everything's fine until Harry mentions seeing Ryan Nordlund with Nathaniel Horn. Amber stiffens in alarm. 'You didn't tell them anything, did you?'

'No. I said it was important that I understand what happened at Maturiki to make you leave so suddenly.'

'Ohhh...' Amber groans as if in physical pain. 'I told you to forget that. Why did you have to...'

She seems on the point of tears, and Jenny takes hold of her hand and says, 'We just want to help you. If Harry can get an idea of what frightened you so badly he can do something about it.'

Amber shakes her head, sniffs. 'Go on then, what did he have to say?'

'He said that you went scuba diving with them on the previous day, after Konrad left the island.'

'Well, that's true. What else?'

'That when you were in the water you saw a shark...'

'Ha!' Amber laughs bitterly. 'The only sharks out there were Ryan and Hayden.'

'So what happened?'

'I got sick, with the water pressure and stuff, that's all. So when we got back to the beach Karen told me off and stuffed me full of junk that knocked me out cold until late that night, when I woke up and discovered that Ryan and Hayden had come into my room and raped me while I'd been unconscious.'

Jenny gives a cry and wraps her arms around Amber, who begins to weep.

When she has recovered a little, Harry says gently, 'Amber, I'm sorry, but I have to ask. If you were unconscious, how do you know what happened?'

'They didn't clean up very well. Then I made my maid, Pascaline, tell me what had happened. She was terrified.'

'Dear God,' Jenny whispers.

Amber says, 'Like father like sons, eh, Harry? I told you about Uncle Konrad, didn't I, what he did to me?'

'Yes. Amber, I can fix this. Either we can go to the cops...' She starts shaking her head. 'Or I'll sort it out myself.'

But she still shakes her head. 'That isn't why I had to run, Harry. There was something else.'

'What?'

'When I was in the lagoon I watched them swimming down below me. Ryan was with Selwyn, one of our staff, Pascaline's brother. They were swimming towards the gap in the reef, with the deep water beyond. But there was only one stream of bubbles rising up from them, and Selwyn wasn't swimming. He was sort of limp, and Ryan was guiding him towards the gap. When Pascaline told me that night about Ryan and Hayden, she broke down and told me that Selwyn was missing, and I understood what I'd seen out at the reef. I'd seen Ryan stop Selwyn's air and take him out to the sharks in the deep water.'

Harry and Jenny exchange a look, stunned. 'Why would he do that?' Harry says softly.

'I asked Pascaline, and she said Selwyn had heard something he shouldn't have. I don't know what. But maybe there was no reason, and Ryan just felt like doing it. That's what he's like, Harry, an evil boy.

'So next morning I told them I was flying home, and when I wouldn't change my mind they insisted that Karen go with me. At Sydney I ran while she was getting the bags at the carousel, and caught a cab here. It was the only place I could think of. Luke brought me here once, and Jim and I got on well. I hoped he'd shelter me. Turned out he needed me as much as I needed him. I was shocked to find him so sick.'

She adds in a whisper, 'I think it's AIDS. But he refuses to go to hospital. He has no Medicare number, no money. He was in trouble in the States, and he's terrified they'll send him back there. But I'm afraid he's going to die if I don't do something.'

'I can just drop him off at a hospital, Amber. No ID. They'll look after him regardless.'

'Maybe…maybe later, if he keeps getting worse.'

Jenny says, 'How about you? Do you need a doctor? Prescriptions?'

'I've been careful with the medications—Karen gave me so many I couldn't think straight. I feel much better now. My main worry is money. I drew cash out of my account when I arrived back here, but Jim said that the Nordlunds could get their detectives to put a trace on my account, and track me down that way, so I haven't dared touch it since.'

Jenny says, 'Maybe I could draw the money out for you. Not in person, but if you give me your account details I could hack into the account and transfer money somewhere else, where we could access it safely.'

'Could you really do that?'

Jenny smiles. 'Oh, yes. But only if you're sure.'

'I'd be so grateful.'

'Tell me,' Jenny says, 'did you have any dealings with a man called Terry Palfreyman?'

'Yes.' Amber sounds suddenly cautious. 'Why do you ask?'

'I met him at the NRL shareholders' meeting when I went there to try to find you. He tried to interest me in his theories about the Nordlunds.'

'Terry's a little bit crazy, but he's not stupid—very bright, actually. I've known him for a long time. He worked with my dad on his invention and he used to come to our home at Kramfors quite often. He was fun, full of jokes and interesting ideas. But then Dad was killed and Konrad took over. He stole Terry's invention and ruined him. He's very angry about it. It's really consumed his life.'

Jenny says, 'I'm afraid he's dead, Amber—he was murdered in the cottage where he was living in the Blue Mountains. I was in the area at the time, in contact with him, and the police think I killed him. I'm on the run, Amber, just like you.'

Amber stares at her, shocked, and tears fill her eyes. 'Oh, Jenny…then it's my fault. It's all my fault.'

'How do you mean?'

Amber can't speak, gasping rapid shallow breaths as if she's having a panic attack, and Jenny takes her in her arms, trying to calm her. She relaxes a little, wipes her eyes on her sleeve. Jenny says, 'Of course it's not your fault, Amber.'

'Yes it is,' she whispers. 'After I was discharged from the clinic they took me back to Kramfors to recuperate. It was very quiet and I was left on my own a lot. I thought of my life, how everything changed that night my father's plane disappeared, how everything went wrong after that—just as it did for Terry. One day I went into Konrad's study. He was at Kramfors that day, visiting from Sydney, and he was outside somewhere, talking to the staff. I saw that he'd left the safe unlocked, and I went and took a look inside. There were legal documents, some American and Chinese currency. I was about to leave it when I noticed an envelope tucked at the back. The address was handwritten, and it was to your father, Harry, to Judge Belltree. I couldn't understand why that would be in Konrad's safe, but then I heard his voice somewhere nearby, and I snatched the envelope up and quickly left.

'When I got back to my room I opened the envelope. Inside was a letter from someone called Joseph Doyle, confirming an arrangement to meet the judge on the twenty-sixth of June, 2010.'

'The day he was killed,' Jenny says. 'The day of the crash.'

'Yes. And there was something else in the envelope—a faded Polaroid photograph. At first I couldn't make out what it was showing, just a tangle of shapes. But then I saw what looked like a piece of machinery half covered in branches. And on its side it had some painted letters, VH–MDX, the number of the plane Dad died in. I didn't know what to make of it at first, and then I remembered the name, Joseph Doyle. He was a worker on the estate when I was growing up, an Aboriginal man. And I remembered that he had disappeared around the time that Dad died—it caused quite a fuss, nobody knew where he'd gone. But why had he written to your father in 2010, Harry? And why was the letter in Konrad's safe? I had a bad feeling about it and wanted to tell someone, but I didn't know who. If you'd still been around I would have told you, but I had no idea where you were. Then I thought of Terry. I found his website and sent him a scan of the letter and the photograph and asked him what he thought. He got back to me, very excited. He said it was a breakthrough, and he'd be in touch, but I never heard from him again. I think he must have tried to use it against Konrad. That's why he's dead, I'm sure of it.'

She falls silent. After a moment Harry says, 'Where are the letter and photograph now, Amber? Do you have them here?'

'They're safe, Harry.'

'This is really important, Amber. I need to see them.'

'Yes, yes, I'll get them for you. As soon as it's safe I'll go home to Kramfors and get them, bring them back to Sydney to show you.'

Before he can press her, she bursts into tears. 'Oh God, the world has gone mad. You reach a point where you can't go on fighting anymore. There's just been too many blows…'

Jenny takes Amber, sobbing, in her arms again. She rocks her gently and thinks of Abigail, whom she should be holding. 'Yes,' she whispers.

Eventually they separate. Amber wipes her eyes

'I miss Kramfors and Cackleberry Valley, Harry,' she says. 'You should go back, to the eagle cave, remember? It's so beautiful up there. My favourite place. If anything happens to me, take Jenny there and think of me.'

145

At the door she gives Jenny her bank details and says, 'Transfer that money into an account that *you* control, Jenny. No one else, okay?'

When they reach the car, Jenny says, 'What a mess.'

'I know. Do you believe all that about the drowning and the rapes? She said herself that she was on so many drugs that she couldn't think straight.'

'The point is, *she* believes it, and the images in her head have terrorised her. I feel helpless, Harry. What can we do?'

36

Kelly makes her way into the press gallery of the Legislative Assembly of the New South Wales Parliament—the lower house. Onlookers are filing into seats in the other galleries that wrap around the chamber, which is packed for question time. She has seen this on TV, but now it seems more intimate, more claustrophobic than she had imagined. The formal horseshoe layout of the members' benches, the central table, the speaker on his elevated throne at the far end, the polished timber, make her think of a posh Victorian cattle pen. It is currently full of what appear to be feral schoolkids, shouting, pointing, shaking their fists at each other.

The speaker calls them to order, asks for questions. Husam Roshed, directly below Kelly, gets to his feet, and the speaker calls out, 'The member for Campsie.'

Roshed speaks in a vigorous, attacking tone that commands silence. 'Thank you, Mr Speaker. My question is directed to the minister for infrastructure and planning. In the light of the recent comments by businessman and property developer Konrad Nordlund on 2GB Radio regarding his secret negotiations to purchase

Slater Park from the New South Wales government, will the minister assure the house that no such agreement will be entered into without full debate and approval by this house?'

There is a murmur of interest around the chamber as the minister, a wiry, energetic woman, rises from the government front bench and paces to the central table. 'There have been many approaches to myself and my predecessors by people concerned with the future of Slater Park, in favour of either redevelopment or preservation of its present status. I am always open to suggestions, but I can assure the house that the best interests of the people of New South Wales will be uppermost in our deliberations.'

There are cries of 'Hear, hear', and Roshed gets to his feet again.

'Which tells us precisely nothing. Will the minister at least condemn the outrageous and tasteless attempt by Mr Nordlund to bring pressure upon her office using the tragic circumstances of the Slater Park murders?'

Loud groans from the government benches.

The minister replies, 'We all regret the recent tragic events in Slater Park, and offer our sincere condolences to the families of the victims,' ('Hear, hear!'), 'and our full support and encouragement to the police to bring their investigation to a speedy conclusion.' Then, with a sly smile towards Roshed, 'Surely the member for Campsie is not implying that the Slater Park murders are the work of a property developer?'

Howls of derisive laughter.

Roshed shouts above them, 'Why not? Is the minister aware that a long-time critic of Konrad Nordlund and his dubious business practices, Terry Palfreyman, was found murdered at the same time as the first of the Slater Park murders?'

The chamber explodes. 'Shame on you!' 'Withdraw!' 'Scumbag!'

Gradually the shouting and foot stamping subside enough for the speaker to make his voice heard. 'Order! Order! The member for Campsie will withdraw his scandalous remark.'

'I will not, sir. Perhaps the minister knows more about these shocking events than she wishes to tell us.'

More cries of outrage.

The speaker booms, 'I instruct the sergeant-at-arms to remove the member for Campsie from the chamber.'

Roshed smiles and walks calmly to the door by the speaker's chair, accompanied by a man in a tailcoat. Around him there are chants of 'Lock him up! Lock him up!'

'Well,' the woman sitting next to Kelly says, 'that was more interesting than I expected.'

37

Harry wakes abruptly, thinking it's Abigail crying, but it's the sound of his phone. The clock says 1:33 am.

'Harry, it's me, Kelly. Sorry to wake you but I thought you'd want to know. I've just had a call from an ambo friend who lets me know about interesting cases. He just called me from Slater Park. Another body.'

'Oh…hell.'

'Yeah. Thing is, he saw the body. No ID, but there were distinguishing marks—she had extensive scars on her left arm, like old burns. And I thought, remember Ash Island? Amber Nordlund?'

He's completely awake now. 'Thanks, Kelly. I'll see what I can find out.'

He wakes Nicole and tells her he's got to leave, drives fast through empty streets across the city to Mont Street. At number 32 he is about to hammer on the front door when he notices it is slightly open. He takes a breath, steps back, then pushes it with his elbow and walks in. All the doors are open in the darkened house, the rooms deserted, no drug man, no dog, no bird, no Chinese students. He races up the stairs and sees Zuckermann's half-open door. Zuckermann's pale face lies on the pillow, eyes closed, no sound of breathing. Harry has no latex gloves so uses a tissue to cover his fingertips as he feels for a pulse in Zuckermann's throat. Nothing. He's cold. No sign of Amber.

Back to the car. Harry puts his foot down, slams through corners, traffic lights. A police barrier is in place at the main entrance to Slater Park. The uniform at the barrier peers at him uncertainly. 'Sarge?'

'Yeah, Belltree. Harry Belltree. Homicide.'

'Kilometre down the main avenue, boss. Turn left. You'll see the cars.' The man waves him on and he drives through the park, the first time he's been here. Up ahead the dark silhouette of a building, bobbing torchlights, a T-junction. He turns left and sees the vehicles all lit up like a circus.

He pulls in under the dark mass of a huge Moreton Bay fig and makes his way over to the activity. People in white forensic overalls, pale blue gloves and overshoes, white facemasks, move in and out of the light. One of them stops in mid-stride and stares at him.

'Harry?' Deb's voice, incredulous above the hum of the generators. 'What the hell are you doing here?'

'Deb, I need to see the body.'

Deb turns to two uniforms hovering at the edge of the activity. 'You two! Escort this man off the site. Arrest him if he gives you any trouble.'

Harry shouts, 'Female, one point six metres, sixty-two kilograms, natural blonde, one childbirth, old burn marks down her left side aggravated by recent scratches.'

Deb turns to stare at him, waves the uniforms away, comes to Harry and pulls him aside. She tugs her facemask off. 'What?'

'Have you identified her?' Harry asks.

She shakes her head.

'Let me see her face.'

'There's no head, just a body.'

'Let me see her.'

Deb frowns. 'Come on then.' She turns and marches over to the focus of the dazzling lights.

Harry stares at the pale body, the brutal absence above the neck, a pink ribbon tied to her right hand. He kneels by her left side and sees the familiar scars and scratches. Gets to his feet and backs away.

'It's Amber Nordlund,' he says, his voice sounding hollow in his head.

'*What?*'

'Konrad Nordlund's niece, badly burned at Ash Island ten months ago.' He turns away, pulls out his phone, begins hurrying back to his car.

'Stop! Harry, stop!'

'Got to go, Deb.' He is frantically scrolling for Jenny's number.

'Hey!' Deb is calling to the two uniforms again, who hurry over. 'Arrest that man.'

The number is ringing as he pushes away one of the men who's trying to grab his right arm.

'Hello?' Jenny sounds groggy.

'Run, Jenny. Run!'

'Harry?'

The phone is snatched from him, hand twisted behind his back and handcuffed.

38

In a blur of sleep Jenny pulls on some clothes, hears banging downstairs, voices calling out. She grabs her phone, purse and goes to the
rear window. Down below, light from the house illuminates a man
standing in the backyard, waiting. She goes out onto the landing,
down half a flight and stops, listening. Two men are arguing in the
shop, one of them Mr Ngô, the other demanding something.

'Scarlett!' Mrs Ngô is standing at the foot of the stairs. 'Come
down quick.'

Jenny hurries down and Mrs Ngô leads her to the door of the
cupboard under the stairs. Inside she moves some boxes to expose a
trapdoor in the floor, heaves it open. There is a short flight of steps
down into darkness. Mrs Ngô thrusts a small torch into her hand.
'Cellars all connected underneath. Go to end of block, get out there
if you can.'

'Who is it?'

'Your angry husband, I think. Says he is police.'

Jenny goes down and the trapdoor closes behind her.

The space under the terrace is very low, filled with brick piers, bits of rubble, desiccated dead rats. She crouches and ducks, making her way beneath the shops until she comes to the end. Shining the torch beam about her she sees some stone steps leading up to a trapdoor, but when she pushes it doesn't budge.

She gives up, retraces her steps to the previous bay. More steps, and this time the trapdoor opens with a creak. She climbs out and finds herself at the back of the laundromat, five shops up from the greengrocer's. She walks through the public area at the front, the machines ghostly in the dark, unbolts the front door and looks cautiously outside. A car is pulled up outside the Ngôs', a blue light pulsing. She steps out quickly and hurries in the opposite direction, keeping close to the shopfronts. Behind her the laundromat alarm begins to howl.

She breaks into a run towards the lights of Marrickville Road up ahead. A taxi is slowing across the junction, coming to a stop. Three men are climbing in and she rushes up behind them and jumps in as the door begins to close.

39

'Get hold of someone from the Nordlund family to confirm the identity,' Deb says.

'Yes, boss.'

The body is being loaded into a vehicle.

'And we need to find her head.'

'Sure.' The officer points to dark figures tumbling out of two white vans just arrived. 'More on their way. What about the bloke?'

'The bloke? Oh, Belltree. Yes, get them to charge him with obstructing a police investigation. I won't see him till later. By then I want to know everything on his phone.'

At the Glebe morgue, Deb introduces herself to Konrad Nordlund, who has arrived in a chauffeur-driven Bentley. He seems withdrawn, his pale face a mask.

'This way, sir. Thanks for coming so promptly.' She shows him into a small viewing room. The body lies on a gurney, most of it covered by sheets.

'That's her?'

'You'll notice the scars on the left arm.'

'Yes, yes. But can I see her face?'

'I'm afraid not.'

'Why?'

'Her head was separated from her body, I'm afraid. We haven't recovered it yet.' They have made up the form of the head with folded towels beneath the sheet.

He frowns, as if mildly disgusted. 'Well...it could be her, yes.'

'Can you tell us where Amber was living?'

'No, I can't. She broke off contact with us—her family—over a month ago. We were concerned. We had no idea what had happened to her.'

'Did you contact the police?'

'We reported it, and I also made my own arrangements, hired private investigators. But they came up with nothing.'

'I'd like to talk to them. Who were they?'

'Let's make sure it's her first.'

'You are a blood relative, Mr Nordlund?'

'Blood? Yes, her father was my brother.'

'If we can have a DNA sample from you, we'll be able to confirm whether it's Amber.'

He nods and turns away.

After Nordlund has gone, Deb feels a sudden wave of giddiness and has to lean against the wall. Through a window she sees the first glimmer of dawn in the eastern sky. She's been on duty now for twenty-three hours, after ten punishing days since the first murders. Once, ten or twenty years ago, she would have taken it in her stride, but it's not so easy now. She decides to get a couple of hours' sleep before seeing Harry, and calls for a car.

She recognises the young woman behind the wheel, a driver she's had before. Deb envies her air of cheerful competence, and imagines her having an untroubled private life outside of all this mess, with someone unconnected with the police.

'Morning, ma'am.'

Deb gets into the front passenger seat, buckles up, sighs.

'Where to?'

'A drink and a bed,' Deb says wearily and closes her eyes.

She opens them with a start. The car is stationary, in an underground car park. 'What's this?'

'A drink and a bed. You nodded off and I didn't know where else to take you.'

'It's a hotel?'

'No, it's where I live.'

'Oh yes?'

'I drove you before. My name's Charity. You're welcome to put your head down here if you want.'

'Charity, with the nice smile.' Deb thinks of her own place, cold and unloved since she kicked her scumbag boyfriend out. 'Well... lead the way, Charity.'

They take a lift up to the apartment, clearly the setting of a well-ordered life. It's apparent that no one else lives here.

'Wine or scotch?'

'Scotch, thanks.' Deb sinks into a comfortable chair.

Two and a half hours later she jerks awake to the sound of her phone alarm. She is lying in a bed and at first has no recollection of how she got there. Sunlight shimmers on the blades of a venetian blind. Her clothes are lying on a chair nearby. She gets up and goes out to a bathroom, takes a shower, gets dressed.

In the dim light of the living room she makes out the pale shape of an arm. She's seen it before, that arm, angled just so. A dismembered limb. She takes a breath, feeling her heart begin to race. Then the arm moves, and she sees that it belongs to Charity, lying beneath a doona on the sofa.

Charity stirs, struggles upright. She looks rumpled, sleepy, vulnerable. 'Oh,' she says, 'I'll drive you.'

'No, I'll get a cab. Thanks. And thanks for looking after me last night.'

'It was a pleasure.'

As she goes to open the front door, Charity adds, 'Ma'am?'

'Yes?'

'You should take some time off. Why don't you come to the fair in Victoria Park today?'

'That would be nice, but...' Deb shrugs.

'You're entitled to a lunchbreak, aren't you? I'll look out for you.'

Deb takes the lift and steps out through a landscaped strip into a narrow street overshadowed by the block of flats. She wonders where the hell she is.

She follows the street out to a main road, solid with the morning traffic, and recognises the restaurant on the corner. King Street, Newtown. She walks for a while until she spots a cab.

40

She shows her ID at the police station, speaks to the duty sergeant.

'I've come to interview Harry Belltree.'

'Yes, ma'am. He's had a mug of tea and a sandwich. Want someone to sit in with you?'

'No, I'll do it on my own. Has he said anything?'

'Asked me if I'd let him know if there were any new reports of a murder or abduction in the city. None that I know of. There's a bloke from TIB here to see you.'

He shows her into a small office where the man from the TIB, the telecommunications interception branch at Potts Hill, is waiting for her, fiddling with an iPad. Harry's phone is on the desk in front of him.

Deb shakes hands. 'Morning. Anything?'

He picks up Harry's phone. 'This is an encrypted Blackphone, but I've got this.' He slides across a sheet of paper with a list of phone numbers, times and duration of calls. He taps at his iPad and points at the first number on the list.

'This phone is currently located at the offices of the *Times* newspaper in Darling Harbour.'

'Right.'

'The next is at number 27 Worthington Avenue, Hornsby. The address belongs to a Robert Marshall. A serving officer, I understand—a detective superintendent.'

'Okay.'

'Now this one is all over the place, in a vehicle moving around the city, currently on Southern Cross Drive heading for the airport... international terminal, looks like.'

Deb picks up her phone and gives instructions to intercept, then gets to her feet. 'Thanks for your help. Much appreciated.'

'No worries.'

She picks up Harry's phone. 'I'll return this to him and let him go. I'd like you to keep a close watch on it.'

'Sure.'

She goes back outside and gives Harry's phone to the sergeant. 'You can return this to him with the rest of his stuff when we let him go. I wouldn't mind a mug of tea and a sandwich myself.'

She's eating when Harry's brought into the interview room. He sits down quietly, watches her.

She finishes, wipes her mouth. 'They tell me you've had your breakfast.'

He nods. 'You're looking tired, Deb. Pushing yourself too hard.'

'Mm. So what's the story, Harry? What were you doing in Slater Park?'

'Got a tip-off that another body had turned up there, old burn scars on the left arm. I remembered Amber Nordlund's injuries at Ash Island and thought I'd better check.'

'Really? Just like that?'

'Just like that.'

'Where was Amber staying?'

Harry lowers his eyes, doesn't reply.

Deb leans forward. 'Where, Harry? Tell me or I swear I'll have you locked away for another month.'

'A boarding house at 32 Mont Street, Redfern. Little room at the top of the house. There's another body up there.'

Deb looks at him, says gently, 'Is it Jenny?'

Harry shakes his head. 'Man, late thirties, in the bed. He was very sick, maybe AIDS. But I doubt he died of that.'

'Who is he?'

'Called himself James Zuckermann, friend of Luke Santini— Ash Island again, remember? But Zuckermann may have been an American called Sol Fleischer, on the run from US authorities on arson and murder charges. Amber took refuge with him after something happened to her in Vanuatu. She claimed Nordlund's two sons raped her.'

Deb looks doubtful. 'Where does Jenny come in?'

'Jenny?'

'Yes, Jenny. After you recognised Amber's body you got straight on the phone. You were heard saying, "Run, Jenny, run." Was she hiding with Amber and Zuckermann?'

'No.'

'Then where is she? You've been helping her, Harry, haven't you? Sheltering a fugitive. I'll put you away for years.'

'Deb, you have to understand that Jenny didn't kill Palfreyman. She's been framed.'

'Oh, really? I think I may have heard this one before. About a thousand times.'

There's a knock on the door and an officer comes in, whispers something in Deb's ear. She nods, gets to her feet. 'Try to come up with something more original before I come back, Harry. Like the truth.'

She goes out to another interview room where two local area detectives are waiting with a third man, an Indian.

'This is Girish Jaggi, ma'am, of the Agarwal Taxi Consortium,'

161

one of the detectives says. 'And this is the phone you asked us to track down.' He hands Deb a mobile. 'We stopped Mr Jaggi's taxi at the international terminal and found the phone tucked into the back seat.'

Deb asks Jaggi to tell her about his shift.

'I came on at midnight,' he says. 'I took over from Kumar, who was exhausted, poor fellow.'

Deb interrupts him. 'About three am, where were you then?'

'Let me think…About two-thirty I picked up a couple from Star City Casino and took them to an address in Marrickville. Then I continued along Marrickville Road and at the junction with Illawarra Road I was flagged down by three men. They had been drinking, most certainly, quite rowdy and boisterous, I must say. As they were climbing into the cab this lady came out of nowhere and threw herself all over the two men who were in the back seat! They were amazingly surprised, I can tell you! Then they were delighted, because she was quite a young, attractive lady, and I think they must have thought their wishes had all come true. She had trouble getting them to behave, and I thought I might have to stop and eject them all, but the man in the front told them to calm down. He asked the lady where she was going, and she said, "Where are *you* going?" and he said, "Woollahra," and she said, "That will do." They all became quite jolly at that point, handing round a bottle, for which I had to reprimand them, and—'

'So you took her to Woollahra?'

'Well, no. I was about to explain. After fifteen minutes or so she suddenly demanded that I stop, and she got out, with some difficulty, because the men were very disappointed and tried to restrain her. But she ran away.'

'Where was this?'

'Waterloo, at Elizabeth Street.'

'You'll have all this on your taxi camera?'

'Yes, certainly.'

They retrieve the memory card and view the sequence with the three men. At first Deb is disappointed to see the images of a woman with straight, dark hair, but as the cab moves into a patch of bright light the woman turns her face towards the camera and Deb recognises Jenny.

Seven hours have passed since she left the cab. Deb orders detectives and forensics to the address in Mont Street, and a general alert for a woman of Jenny's description. Then she returns to Harry.

'All right, Harry. Time for the truth.'

He tells her Jenny's story, the encounter with Palfreyman at the shareholders' meeting, going to Blackheath, the car outside his cottage, the two intruders, her flight. He doesn't mention Fogarty.

'That's it?' Deb shakes her head. 'Hell, what's happened to you, Harry? Blinded by love? Grief? Her story makes no sense. If she witnessed the men in the house, why didn't she call us? Why didn't she run to the nearest cop shop?'

Harry leans across the table and whispers something.

'What?' She bends forward.

'Turn off the tape.'

She looks at him as if he's gone mad. In fact he does look manic. Haggard, damaged—this isn't the Harry she used to know.

He whispers again, 'Please.'

She folds her arms, decides to stop this and arrange a psychiatric assessment.

'I'm terminating this interview,' she says, and stands up. She calls for him to be taken back to the cells.

The duty sergeant is outside in the corridor, hurrying towards her. 'Ma'am, we've had a report from Mont Street. Body of a man.'

'Okay, I'd better get over there.'

'There's a car outside...'

For one brief second as she hurries out she allows herself to wonder if the driver will be Charity. But of course it isn't. She jumps in the back and gets to work on her phone.

41

Kelly joins a horde of journalists and camera crews outside the mansion on the harbour promontory of Vaucluse. Catherine Meiklejohn has sent her here. 'You've got a thing about Konrad Nordlund, haven't you, Kelly?' she said. 'He's giving a press conference outside the family home later this morning.' Kelly peers over the front wall at the windows of the upper floor of the house, wondering if Karen Schaefer's face might appear there.

Nordlund opens the front gate. He is in a pale grey suit. Behind him, in black, is his lawyer Nathaniel Horn. The press shuffles closer.

Nordlund unfolds a piece of paper and reads. 'Earlier this morning I was asked by police to attend the Glebe morgue to view the body of a young woman, murdered last night in Slater Park.'

Muffled exclamations from the journalists are stifled as Nordlund gives them a bleak stare.

'Although a final confirmation will not be available until later today, there is no doubt in my mind that the young woman was my niece Amber Nordlund.'

He pauses, the crowd stunned, utterly silent.

'I accuse Husam Roshed, the member of parliament for Campsie, of inciting this murderous violence against my family by his slanderous and malicious attack upon me yesterday under cover of parliamentary privilege. His appalling suggestion that I was in some way responsible for the Slater Park murders has rebounded in the most tragic way. Amber was the gentlest and most caring of people, adored by all her family and friends. Her murder is an obscenity which cannot go unpunished. I call upon Mr Roshed to resign immediately from public office and face the consequences of his inflammatory words.'

The crowd erupts as Nordlund turns away and Horn steps forward, raising his hand for silence. 'Mr Nordlund and his family are in deep shock, mourning the loss of their beloved Amber. We ask that you respect their privacy and leave them in peace. Thank you, that is all.'

He closes the gate and returns with Nordlund to the house. Kelly moves to the back of the commotion, feeling sick. She tries Roshed's number and leaves a message.

42

'Bruises on his arms. My guess would be that he was held down and smothered with the pillow.'

Rebecca Jardine, the pathologist, stands beside Deb in the doorway of the attic room as the crime scene team works inside.

'Time?'

'From the state of rigor I'd say similar to the girl in the park—around midnight.'

They return to the ground floor, where a detective approaches Deb.

'Neighbours say that the house is normally occupied by Chinese students, dozens of them, they say. No sign of any of them, nor of a man they call Ben who usually sits on the sofa outside with a dog and a bird in a cage selling drugs.'

'Clever bird,' Deb says. She feels a little light-headed. 'Okay. I'm going back to Strike Force Spider headquarters. You can reach me there.'

In the empty warehouse on the edge of Slater Park that serves as their major incident room, she examines the big map on the wall with today's updates marked. Col, the task force manager, stands by her side, pointing to the areas being given priority in the fingertip searches of the ground, which began at dawn. So far nothing has been discovered. It's all too familiar. A call comes through from the local police station, the psychiatrist they brought in at Deb's request to examine Harry.

'I've carried out my assessment, inspector,' the woman says, 'but I just wanted to confirm a few issues of fact. He says his wife is missing, is that right?'

'Yes, she is missing. We've been looking for her for eleven days now.'

'And she's wanted for murder?'

'Again, yes.'

'Oh, I thought…Well, he's obviously experiencing a major life crisis at the present time. The first impression he gives is that of calm control, but underneath he's in great distress. I think he's holding himself together with difficulty, and I'm concerned at the possibility of self-harm, or of violence against those he believes are obstructing him. I propose to section him.'

'I see. What will happen to him?'

'He'll be given another assessment at the hospital. If he's found to be mentally disordered, he'll be kept there for up to three days. If found to be mentally ill, they'll keep him until he can be assessed by the Mental Health Review Tribunal to determine a course of treatment.'

Deb thinks about this. 'He has a baby.'

'Yes. He told me his wife's sister is looking after it. I'll make sure she's notified. She seems to be the next of kin. His parents were killed in that crash, of course, and he says he doesn't have any other close relatives.'

'Right. Keep me up to date, could you?'

'Certainly. I'll go ahead then, shall I?'

Deb hesitates a moment, then says firmly, 'Yes, do that.'

43

People are coming into the incident room with rolls, drinks, take-away orders, and Deb feels suddenly hungry. She checks her watch, 1:15 pm. 'I'm going out for an hour, Col,' she says. 'Clear my head.'

'Good idea,' he says. 'Beautiful day outside, so they tell me.' Col is unshakeable, an anchor.

She calls a cab, which arrives at the gates of Slater Park as she gets there. As they approach Victoria Park she hears the amplified music, sees crowds converging. There are people and their dogs in fancy dress, jugglers, a group playing on a stage, stalls, the smell of hot food. Deb wanders around for a while, eyes searching, but sees no sign of Charity. There are so many people that it seems unlikely their paths will cross. She checks the faces as they pass, asking herself, *Are you Cador Penberthy?*

She stops at a stall and buys a hotdog with mustard and onions, moves away to find a quiet place to eat—and bumps into Charity.

'Hi, Deb. You made it. Isn't it a gorgeous day?'

She's wearing a light cotton summer dress, sandals, a ribbon in her hair—white, not pink, thank God.

'Day off?' Deb asks.

'Yes, today and tomorrow. When did you last have a day off?'

'What are you, my mother?'

Charity laughs, bright lipstick.

They wander, buy coffee, chat about Charity's family in Adelaide, what brought her to Sydney. Then Deb checks the time and says she'd better get back to work. Charity is meeting some friends to go to a movie. She says, 'Here, this is for you,' and hands Deb a small envelope.

'What's this? Shall I open it now?'

'Later. See you.' She turns and walks away. As she watches her disappear into the crowd, Deb remembers friends she once had, girls like Charity, and thinks how long it's been since she had friends, real friends.

Her phone rings and she listens to the message, heads back to the main road. On the way she opens Charity's envelope and finds a key inside and a small note: *Entry code 9609.*

She has a frustrating afternoon and evening, achieving nothing: keeping track of hourly updates from the team dealing with incoming calls from the public; a new report from forensics; briefings for the premier, the minister for infrastructure and planning and the press; meetings with senior officers; a session on the task force budget; reports on forty-two persons of interest. Her boss, Dick Blake, is supportive, but when they meet with the police commissioner she senses an attempt to distance himself from the investigation, although that may just be her growing paranoia. She also meets with Jack Anders, back from two days off, for an update on the Palfreyman case, and advises him to forget Greyhound buses in the outback and concentrate on Sydney. She gives him the details of the taxi driver and shows him a still from the cab video.

He looks at it doubtfully. 'You reckon that's her, Deb?'

'I'm sure of it. She jumped in the cab at the junction of Marrickville and Illawarra roads. Lots of Vietnamese around there. That's where she was hiding out—she'd dyed her hair, trying to blend in. Something spooked her, made her run. Maybe somebody recognised her.'

'At three am? Okay, I'll get onto it.'

At ten she packs it in and calls a cab. When the driver asks for the address she hesitates. *A drink and a bed.* She tells him Newtown, King Street. 'I'll tell you where to stop.'

She finds the apartment block in the back street and presses the bell. Charity's voice on the intercom. The door clicks and she goes inside to the lift.

The apartment door is open. A big smile from Charity that makes her heart lift. 'Sorry,' Deb says. 'Couldn't face home.'

The glass of whisky is ready, a rich smell of cooking in the air.

'Smells like you had a great dinner.'

'Goulash. I kept some for you.'

A hot meal, wine, a shower; she feels human again. She thinks of Harry in the mental hospital, wonders what he wanted to tell her with the recording machine turned off.

44

She wakes from a profound sleep, feeling enormously rested. The bed is wonderful, deep and soft. She turns and studies the head on the pillow at her side, the curls of blonde hair across the white cotton. She props herself up on one elbow, leans down and kisses the girl's neck, her shoulder. Then she gets up.

The hospital receptionist shakes her head. 'I'll have to check with Dr Lambert.' She picks up the phone and dials. After a brief conversation she rings off and turns back to Deb. 'Dr Lambert needs to speak to you. He's coming in.'

'Oh, is there a problem? Is Mr Belltree all right?' She has an image of Harry being found hanged in his cell.

'You'll have to wait for Dr Lambert to get here.'

'Where is he?'

The receptionist looks accusingly at her. 'On the green of the second hole.'

'Oh. He won't be pleased then.'

'I should say not.'

'Isn't there anyone else I could speak to?'

'Dr Lambert wants to talk to you himself. You can get a coffee over there if you want.'

Deb waits, thirty minutes, forty minutes, her earlier euphoria rapidly evaporating. Outside it's a fine Sunday morning and this part of the hospital has few visitors.

Finally a man marches in through the front doors and goes to the receptionist's window, looks at Deb. 'You're Inspector Velasco?'

'Yes. Dr Lambert? I'm sorry to—'

He turns away. 'Follow me.'

They go to an office, where Lambert takes the chair behind the desk, waves Deb to another seat. 'I had a long session with Harry last night. He told me things that I found frankly disturbing. You have him under arrest, I believe?'

'Yes, I—'

'He, a police officer, has crucial information about the identity of a murder victim, and comes to give this to you, and you arrest him for trespassing. Is that right?'

'And interfering with—'

'You are also hunting for his wife, I understand, on a murder charge?'

'She's a person of interest. We want to interview her, but so far—'

'And then you have Harry sectioned. This sounds like some kind of vendetta.'

'Dr Lambert, I don't know what Harry's told you, but you don't know the whole story. Please don't jump to conclusions.'

Lambert gazes at her for a moment, frowning. 'I knew his father, the judge. A fine man. A dreadful tragedy when he and Mary were killed. And now this. You don't have a problem with Harry's Aboriginal heritage, do you?'

Deb gets to her feet. 'Of course I don't, and I deeply resent the question. I want to speak to Harry now.'

'All right, all right, I apologise.' Lambert waves his hand for her to sit down, which she does reluctantly. 'I had to ask. Harry only told me those things when I pressed him, and there was obviously a lot more that he didn't tell me. He's had a hell of a trot, and I'd hate to think that his colleagues were undermining him.

'Anyway, the point is this—he's under great stress, but in the circumstances is handling it well. In my opinion he is not suffering from either a mental illness or mental disorder and is therefore not liable for admission under the terms of section C of the act.'

'I see. So what happens now?'

'The act says that where the second assessment contradicts the first, there must be a third assessment by an authorised medical officer. I have arranged for that later today. I believe Harry doesn't need a doctor—he needs a good lawyer. For that reason I don't think I should allow you to interview him in here.'

Deb says, 'Believe it or not, Dr Lambert, I am a friend of Harry's, and I do regret what he's going through. I think—I hope— that if he talks to me now, off the record, it will help me to get to the bottom of what's going on. I guarantee that I won't record our conversation or use his words against him.'

Lambert sits back in his chair, makes a steeple with his hands. 'Hmm. The thing is, inspector, he seems to believe that, despite all appearances to the contrary, you're on the side of the angels. I hope to God he's right.'

He lurches forward and picks up the phone. 'Ah, Agustina. Would you be so kind as to escort Inspector Velasco to see Mr Belltree? Thank you so much.'

Deb gets to her feet. 'Sorry about the golf.'

Lambert checks his watch. 'With any luck I'll catch them up on the tenth tee.'

45

'Ah, Deb.' Harry squints up at her against the bright sky. 'What have you got for me now? Straitjacket? Lobotomy?'

She sits down beside him on the bench. They are in an enclosed courtyard in the heart of the hospital. On the far side a young man is obsessively pounding a basketball against the wall.

'There are no recording devices here, Harry. What did you want to tell me?'

He looks at her, assessing. 'This isn't to go in your notebook, Deb. Or onto e@gle.i. It's strictly for you to think about.'

'Okay, okay. It's about how Jenny was framed, is that it?'

'Let me ask you something about Slater Park. The first two victims, the art students, they were butchered on the site where they were found, right? Blood everywhere?'

'Yes.'

'How about Christie Florian, the third victim?'

'No. She was killed and dismembered elsewhere. No blood.'

He nods. 'And Amber?'

'Same, no blood.'

'So why the difference?'

'Because we were active on the site, patrolling, searching.'

'You sealed the perimeter?'

'No, not completely. It's a huge site, sixty-two hectares surrounded by industrial, commercial and residential buildings, a school, streets. The perimeter is over four kilometres all up, and it's largely unfenced parkland. It fronts onto the river, too. After Christie we got approval to install a perimeter intrusion detection system—microwave units on poles 200 metres apart. But it's not easy—there are thick pockets of bush, adjoining structures with irregular shapes, all kinds of challenges. The system still isn't functioning properly.'

'So how did the killer bring those bodies in?'

'That's what we all want to know. Believe me, I've had every crazy idea thrown at me. The local historical society thinks there may be a tunnel from the old asylum to a nearby house that originally belonged to the senior doctor. Someone else suggested they were dropped from a helicopter.'

'Why not the easy way?'

'What's that?'

'Drive in with the body in the boot.'

'No way. Every vehicle has to be authorised and checked in at the main gate.'

'They're all searched?'

'Contractors' vans, trucks, yes.'

'What about police cars?'

'They're not searched, no—of course they're not. What are you getting at?'

He leans closer to her, lowers his voice. The other patient continues pounding his ball. 'The reason Jenny can't surrender to the police is that she recognised one of the two men inside Palfreyman's house. A police officer. And he recognised her. That's why she's on the run—if she surrenders he'll kill her.'

Deb sits back with a jolt. 'Who?'

'She was framed in a highly professional manner, Deb, just as I was in Newcastle, and by the same person. You remember the officer in charge of Strike Force Ipswich? Detective Chief Inspector Ken Fogarty?'

'Yes. He didn't like you, did he?'

'He's transferred back to Sydney now, state crime command, organised crime squad. That's who Jenny saw.'

Harry watches the incredulity cross Deb's face. She shakes her head. 'And...what? He's responsible for the Slater Park murders too? You're crazy...' She stops, corrects herself. 'Sorry, but where's the connection?'

'Konrad Nordlund. Palfreyman was a threat to Nordlund and had to be silenced. And Nordlund wants to get his hands on Slater Park. He's manoeuvring the state government into a position where it will be impossible to resist his demands that they sell.'

'But Harry, his own niece!'

'They hated each other. Amber was on the run from the Nordlunds, who were trying to find her. Now they have. It's perfect, Deb. It makes Nordlund the victim in all this.'

'No, no. I'm sorry, Harry. I know how hard this is for you, but you can't protect Jenny with a wild conspiracy theory that can't be proved or disproved.'

'Maybe it can. Get someone to check the police cars and their occupants that came into Slater Park on the nights the last two women were killed. Say you need the information for strike force records.'

She takes a deep breath, then gives a tight little smile. She's going to humour him. 'Okay, Harry, I'll do it. Then we'll see. Who else have you shared this idea with?'

Harry looks down, doesn't reply.

'Bob Marshall, right?'

Harry nods.

'And he swallowed it?'

'He believes me, yes.'

'I'm surprised.'

'I pointed out that Fogarty was a close friend of Toby Wagstaff when they were in the drug squad together.'

'Wagstaff...who was killed that night you were shot at Crucifixion Creek?'

'Right.'

'I never understood what really happened that night. It was all hushed up.'

'Yeah. But Bob knows what happened. He seemed to find that very significant. It was Wagstaff who shot me.'

Deb stares incredulously at him. 'You're kidding.'

'That's why it was hushed up.'

'Is that right?' She feels her sense of reality slipping away again, as it always seems to do these days when she talks to Harry. 'And you trust Bob?'

'Yes, don't you?'

'To tell the truth, Harry, I'm finding it increasingly hard to know who I trust these days.'

46

'I am a pariah,' Husam Roshed says with some relish. 'An outcast.'

'I'm sorry,' Kelly says. 'Things got a bit out of hand.'

'Oh, don't be sorry. They hate independents anyway. A Leb independent most of all. I've done them all a favour—given them a legitimate reason to ostracise me. The important thing is that my constituents love me for it. The feedback on the Nordlund business is very positive.'

Several people passing their table in the Lebanese café give him a friendly wave as if to emphasise the point.

'I was thinking about your constituents.' Kelly stirs her coffee, thick, sweet and black. 'You said your family knew Maram Mansur's. So you must also have come across Frank and Kylie Capp.'

'Who?'

'An Anglo family lived next door to the Mansurs. The father was never around and the mother ran off with some bloke, so the Mansurs took the two kids in. Frank was a wild boy, and he stole a car with his sister and smashed it up, crippled her.'

'Oh…yes, right, I do remember something about that. Why?'

'Frank Capp became a big man in the Crows outlaw motor-cycle gang at Crucifixion Creek. He hit the headlines last December when he was killed in a siege following the Ash Island business up in Newcastle. Kylie's still around—Kylie McVea now, still in a wheelchair. Her carer is a niece of Maram Mansur.'

'Is that right? Small world. Is this relevant to us?'

'Maybe not. I just hoped you might have some inside scuttle-butt on them.'

'I'm afraid not, but I can ask around. The Mansurs aren't very popular around here. Maram got too grand for people's taste.' Roshed picks up a slice of sticky pistachio baklava. 'What are people saying about Amber Nordlund's death? It's very weird, isn't it?'

'It's one more turn of the screw.' Kelly tries to find the right way of putting it. It's been her gripe with Brendon Pyle's approach to the story in the *Times*—all very forensic and factual. But people's reaction has been far more visceral than that. 'I hear it among the people at work, in cafés and in letters to the editor. People are spooked. Slater Park has become a kind of bogey place, an evil heart of dark-ness in the middle of the city. The mood seems to be to purge it, exorcise it, get rid of it.'

'Much the way they feel about me, I guess.' Roshed munches happily.

'It's a pity Palfreyman didn't leave anything incriminating about Slater Park,' Kelly says.

'As far as we know. Maybe your paper could apply to the infor-mation commissioner for records of Nordlund's dealings with the government.'

'That could take months, years. By then Ozdevco's bulldozers will have moved in.'

Kelly thinks about this as she travels back into the city on the train. Her phone vibrates in her pocket—it's Brad in Port Vila.

'I've found someone you should talk to, Kelly. The sister of the shark attack victim I told you about.'

'The victim's been identified?'

'Yeah. The Australian Federal Police have a post out here that helps the Vanuatu police with forensics and stuff. They identified the victim from DNA—Selwyn Tamata, from Pentecost Island. His sister is Pascaline Tamata. I've been told that Selwyn and Pascaline both worked out at Maturiki, and she's very cut up about his death.'

'You've spoken to her?'

'Nah, she's not on the phone. Figured we could go up there together, if you were interested.'

'Where did you get this from, Brad?'

'Cop friend in the Vanuatu police. He's seen the file and reckons she's not telling everything she knows.'

'Look, I'll get back to you, okay?'

'Sure. It'll need planning—there's only a couple of flights up there each week. Not many visitors. The high season is over now.'

'Thanks, Brad.'

She rings off. It seems like a lot of trouble for what may be nothing. She calls Harry's number to see what he thinks, but can't get through.

47

Deb rings the doorbell, waits, then hears the thump of a big man's feet approaching. Bob Marshall opens the door.

'Deb! This is a nice surprise.' The warmth of his welcome doesn't quite mask the initial disquiet on his face.

'Hi, Bob. Is this a good time?'

'Sure, sure, come in.'

'Should have phoned, but I was in the area and thought I'd take the chance to call in.'

A family home with a family no longer. Somehow it shows, clean enough but uncared-for, cardboard boxes filling one room. Bob leads her through to the kitchen with its view over a lush suburban plot. There are family photos on the fridge, faded now, of Betty, dead nine years, and the two boys both overseas.

'Coffee, Deb?'

She sits while he brews up a plunger of coffee and finds mugs, milk, sugar.

'Things must be buzzing in homicide,' he says. He looks keenly at her. 'Slater Park and all. Putting in the hours, I'll bet. You were always the most conscientious one, Deb.' He eyes her fingers. 'Course, you probably want a smoke. Let's go outside. It's a beautiful morning.'

They go out to a terrace beneath a pergola heavy with wisteria. Deb lights up.

Bob sits down with a sigh. 'Out with it then, Deb. This isn't a social call, is it? Are we on the record?'

'No. I've just come from Harry.' She tells him where.

He looks at her in astonishment. 'You sectioned him?'

'Not me, the doctor. He was in a very agitated state.'

'I can well imagine.'

Bob's still looking at her like an incredulous headmaster, making her squirm. She decides to fight back.

'He's gone off on a limb, keeping stuff from us, running his own one-man investigation. Or should I say two-man?'

'Careful, Deb. Harry did come to see me when he came back to Sydney, and he's kept in touch on and off. Nothing wrong in that, is there?'

'He's been hiding Jenny from us, Bob, obstructing a murder investigation.'

Bob looks mystified. 'He knows where she is, does he?'

Deb recognises that deceptive puzzled look. 'He did, and so did you.'

Bob holds her eye for a moment, then waves a hand at the smoke drifting up to the canopy of leaves. 'No. I met her once, but what was I supposed to do? I'm not in the loop, Deb. I only know what I read in the papers. You haven't named her as a person of interest, have you?'

'Bullshit. Harry confided in you, his crazy theory that she's been framed for Palfreyman's murder.'

Bob sighs again, as if the world's gone mad since he stopped running it. 'Look, why don't you tell me what's happened? How did you come to arrest him?'

She tells him about Harry's sudden appearance at Slater Park, their subsequent conversations.

'Hmm.' Bob nods. 'Quite a story. What do you think of it, his claims about Fogarty?'

'Rubbish. Pure desperation to protect Jenny, coupled with a bit of resentment about the way Fogarty gave him a hard time in Newcastle. There's not a shred of evidence to support it. The case against Jenny is overwhelming.' She sees the doubt on Bob's face and leans forward. 'Bob, sir, don't get tangled up in this. We all feel very sorry for Harry, but he's digging a deep hole for himself, and he'll drag you down into it. Everyone in homicide admires you, but there are others out there...'

'I know, I know.'

'I'll go back and talk to Harry again, try to get him to face reality. If the medics agree, we'll release him from hospital and I'll drop the charges against him. If he contacts you again try to persuade him to leave Sydney, start a new life.'

'Did you know Jenny, Deb? Do you really think she could kill Palfreyman?'

'She killed Frank Capp, didn't she? We're all capable of killing, Bob, once we convince ourselves that we have no alternative.'

He nods. 'True enough. Do you have any idea where she is?'

Deb gets out her phone and shows him the picture of Jenny. 'This was taken on a taxi cam in Marrickville. She jumped out fifteen minutes later in Waterloo. We're looking for her in both places.'

Deb returns to the strike force office, Sunday quiet, and asks an administrative officer to draw up a schedule of vehicles entering Slater Park on the nights of Christie Florian's and Amber Nordlund's murders, then checks the stream of new reports coming in.

Later that afternoon she gets a call from Dr Lambert.

'Inspector Velasco,' he says, cold. He still doesn't like me, she thinks. Christ's sake, we're supposed to be on the same side.

'Dr Lambert, hi. Any developments?'

'A third assessment of Harry Belltree has agreed with my opinion. We have no reason to hold him. He's all yours.'

'I'll be right over.'

She gets to the hospital, where Harry is waiting in a small room, staring stoically at a notice about sharps.

'You're free to go.'

He takes his time to focus on her. Nods. 'Right.'

She hands him back his property—keys, wallet, Blackphone.

'Your girlfriend at the *Times* has been trying to call you.'

'Not jealous are you, Deb?'

'No, I'm very pleased to say that isn't one of my problems.'

'Well…You're obviously wanting to give me some advice.'

'I've always admired you, Harry, and I'm sorry all this stuff has happened to you, but now you've got to save yourself. Go back up north, get on with your new life. There's nothing but disaster waiting for you here.'

He nods. 'Thanks, Deb. Just forget all that stuff I told you, okay?'

'Sure. It's forgotten.'

'Have you got Jenny?'

She hesitates. 'No. She jumped into a taxi in Marrickville and hasn't been seen since. We will find her, Harry.'

'Tell me, was there a police car there in Marrickville when she ran?'

'Forget it, Harry. Move on.'

He nods. Gets to his feet, stretches. 'A new life, then.'

'Best thing.'

48

Harry gets into the taxi, calls Nicole, asks if she's heard from Jenny. Nothing. He asks about the baby—everything's fine—then rings Kelly's number.

'Harry, you okay? I haven't been able to reach you. It was Amber, then, at Slater Park.'

'Yes. It was her.' He tells her what happened with Deb.

'That's ridiculous. That Velasco woman's a menace. What about Jenny?'

'I don't know. As soon as I saw it was Amber I called Jenny and she ran. I haven't heard from her since. I have no idea where she is.'

'Oh, Harry. I'm sorry.'

'Did you have something for me?'

'Yes, it was the Maturiki business. I got on to my friend in Port Vila, and he's come back with information about a shark attack victim who worked for the Nordlunds. He thought I should talk to the victim's sister, who also worked out there.'

Harry thinks of Amber's story of the scuba dive, which had seemed so unlikely. 'That's interesting. You going?'

'I'm not sure if it's worth it. What do you think?'

'Could be.'

'There's a flight tomorrow from Port Vila up to Pentecost Island, where she lives. How about we get it?'

'I need to be here for Jenny.'

'Yes, of course. Well, keep in touch, Harry. Let me know if I can do anything.'

He rings off, feeling weighed down by a feeling of impotence, and calls Bob Marshall, who tells him to come over.

They sit on the terrace, the shadows lengthening across the garden, Deb's cigarette stubs still there on a saucer on the table beneath the pergola. Bob nods at them. 'She came to see me this morning, knew we'd been talking on that phone. I had to tell her some of it. She said you'd told her Jenny's version of things.'

'Does she believe it?'

'No, Harry, not a word. She's dead set Jenny killed Palfreyman and you've been protecting her. She grilled me, Harry, like she was the superintendent and I was the constable, warned me off.'

'Well, sorry to have caused you trouble, Bob.'

Bob leans forward, grips Harry's arm and lowers his voice. 'I want to help, mate, but she'll be watching me closely now. No word of Jenny?'

Harry shakes his head. 'I have to find some way to protect her.'

'Deb will find her, and when she does I'll do my best to make sure she's given maximum protection.'

Harry nods, but he knows that's not good enough. With a bleak sense of the inevitable, he knows that there's only one way to protect Jenny now.

Bob is sliding an envelope across the table to him. 'This is all I could find out about Fogarty without arousing too much suspicion. Some of it's office gossip, but I reckon it's pretty reliable.'

'Thanks. Deb told me to leave town, get a new life.'

'Yeah, sure.'

'The night in the mental wing made me think,' Harry says carefully. 'I might take her advice, have a break, take a holiday.'

'That right? Anywhere in mind?'

'Vanuatu, I thought. Never been there.'

'Mm. Betty and I had a couple of weeks there the year before she died. The Grand. Try it, why don't you. Quite a decent pub.'

49

Harry reads through Bob's information. Ken Fogarty is a church-goer, apparently, partly because his second wife is a devout believer, but also because he lusts after a woman in the church choir, with whom he had a relationship between his two marriages. So the Fogartys and their two young children are regular attendees at evening service on a Sunday when the choir sings. They live in a quiet suburban house in Castle Hill. Fogarty has a close friend in the organised crime squad from his old drug squad days, a Detective Sergeant Eden Grimshaw, tall—two metres, six foot eight—and angular, very like the second man Jenny described. Grimshaw has form—several complaints of excessive force and an AVO from an ex-partner—for which Fogarty has always provided reassuring character references. Grimshaw has recently concluded a gruelling divorce, in which the Family Court judge stripped him of most of his visible assets, and is now living in a rented flat in Bondi. His rent is unnaturally low, given its location, and the apartment block is protected by CCTV.

Harry checks the times of church services on his phone and heads over to Castle Hill. The Fogarty house is in darkness in the gathering twilight. He goes around the back and uses his bump keys to enter through the kitchen door. There is a security alarm, but it hasn't been switched on. He pulls on gloves and goes inside. Something delicious is simmering in the oven. He quickly scans the ground floor rooms. The domestic scene unnerves him for a moment—the family photos, the Xbox on the floor in front of the TV, a Barbie doll—then he goes upstairs. In the parents' bedroom he investigates the wardrobe and takes a lightweight outdoor jacket of Fogarty's, a pair of old running shoes and a distinctive baseball cap with a large 'A1' logo. Downstairs again he goes through the laundry basket and retrieves male socks, handkerchief and sweatshirt.

He leaves and drives to Bondi, scouts around the block of flats, then returns to Nicole's house. She's had a few drinks and is feeling aggrieved.

'Harry, I never know when you're going to show up! Saturday night Abigail was so unsettled after you left. What's going on? Are you with us or aren't you?'

'Sorry, sorry,' he says. 'I got a call in the small hours and had to go. It was really important.'

She softens. 'Any word of Jen?'

He shakes his head. 'Listen, I need to go out for a couple of hours tonight, then I'll be back to look after Abigail. If anyone asks later, I'm here all evening, and with Abigail all night, okay?'

'Fine.'

'It's for Jen.'

'Sure, Harry. Whatever you say.'

After a couple of hours he leaves, drives to Bondi again. Grimshaw's flat is in darkness. Harry pulls on dark blue polypropylene forensic overalls and hood, gloves, overshoes, and Fogarty's jacket and baseball cap over the top, then approaches the block. He

189

uses his bump keys to open the lobby door, keeping his head down so the cap is clearly visible to the camera. On Grimshaw's floor he uses the keys again to open the door of his flat, and steps inside. A rapid but thorough search turns up a small plastic bag of what might be cocaine, a large commando knife in a sheath and a wad of banknotes. Harry stands by the window overlooking the street. What happens now depends on what he sees out there.

An hour passes, two, three. Then a taxi pulls up and Grimshaw staggers out. He is alone. Harry takes a deep breath and moves to the front door.

He hears the lift doors open, the rattle of keys dropped on the floor, picked up again, then turned in the front door lock.

'God forgive me,' Harry whispers, and as Grimshaw steps inside and closes the door behind him, Harry buries the commando knife in his chest and eases him to the floor. Blood is pumping everywhere. Harry scatters Grimshaw's banknotes and cocaine on the floor, then rolls him over on top of them. He takes Fogarty's running shoes and dips them in the blood and makes several prints on the floor, then wipes the handle of the knife carefully with Fogarty's sweatshirt, socks and handkerchief. He uses them again to touch things in the room—a bottle of scotch, two glasses that he half-fills—and the front doorknob. Then he leaves, making a couple more imprints from Fogarty's shoes on the way down. Outside in the street he discards the shoes in a nearby builders' skip, then drives back to Fogarty's house, where he tucks the cap and jacket in the bottom of their rubbish bin. He returns to Nicole's house and slips down to Abigail's room. She is uneasy, struggling against the bedclothes, and he picks her up and holds her close against his chest, rocking her until she settles and his own heartbeat returns to normal.

50

Deb Velasco grabs a breakfast cup of coffee and a roll from the stall in the lobby of police headquarters and heads up to the homicide suite on the eighth floor. She checks in with the administrative officer, who tells her that Dick Blake is in conference with the assistant commissioner and wants to talk to her about Slater Park when he returns.

'Okay. Nothing else?'

'There was a homicide in Bondi last night, called in a couple of hours ago.'

'Who's got it?'

'Stan Felder's gone out there. Thing is, victim was a cop, at home, off duty. Bloke from the organised crime squad.'

That stops Deb. Organised crime, like Fogarty. 'What's his name?'

The woman checks. 'Eden Grimshaw, detective sergeant.'

Deb doesn't recognise it, but still. She calls Felder, at the scene.

'Morning, boss. It's a flat on the sixth floor of an eight-storey apartment block. A neighbour on the same floor on his way to work at 5:30 am noticed that Grimshaw's door was open, knocked, looked inside and saw Grimshaw lying on the floor covered in blood. Local cops attended. They're door-knocking the other flats and surrounding properties. There's CCTV in the entrance lobby here and we're waiting for the property manager to give us access.'

'Have you spoken to organised crime?'

'Not yet, boss.'

'I'll do it.' She looks up the number for the head of organised crime. He's shocked to get the news. Deb says, 'Ken Fogarty works with you, doesn't he? Was he a friend of Grimshaw's?'

'Yes, indeed. He'll be upset big time. They worked together a lot. Friends from way back—in the drug squad together for years. I'd better let him know.'

Deb rings off and tells the admin officer that she's going out to Bondi to back up Stan Felder.

When she arrives she finds there have been developments. The lobby and the lift doors are draped with crime scene tape, officers escorting residents in and out. When she gets to the sixth floor there's more tape. Felder is waiting for her. He shows her footage taken from the lobby CCTV camera on his iPad.

'We're still checking the identity of all the other people coming and going last night, but I reckon this must be him, arrives at 21:48 last night and leaves at 1:27 this morning, just seven minutes after Grimshaw arrived home, at 1:20.'

'No image of the face?'

'No—head down, the visor of the cap hides him—but the neighbour who found Grimshaw says he's seen the logo on the cap before, a friend of Grimshaw's who's visited here. Doesn't have a name. We'll get him to work on a facial image.'

He leads her to the door of Grimshaw's flat. A crime scene team is working inside.

'The body has been rolled onto its back, the knife still in his chest. It's been removed for examination. You can see what was lying beneath him—banknotes and a packet of white powder. We've retrieved the victim's phone for analysis.'

'The knife, was it from the kitchen?' Deb asks, for a horrible thought is forming in her mind.

'No, more like a hunting knife. A leather sheath is lying over there next to the bedroom door.'

Felder's phone rings. He listens, nods, says he'll come down.

'They've found something nearby, a pair of shoes.' He points to the plastic number signs placed next to faint marks on the floor. 'Bloodstain footprints. Let's see if they match.'

Two uniforms are waiting outside the lobby door, one holding a plastic bag with a pair of white running shoes inside. White, that is, apart from dark smears of what might be blood.

'Found them in the builders' skip in the next street, boss,' one of the officers says.

Felder takes the bag and examines the soles of the shoes, holds up an image of the footprints from his phone for comparison and gives Deb a nod. 'Good,' he tells the men. 'Keep looking.'

Deb says, 'I'll let you get on, Stan. Keep me up to date, will you?'

'Sure. You have a particular interest, boss?'

'Yes. This may be connected to another case. But early days.'

She goes back to her car, checks Ken Fogarty's home address, then calls the local area command and asks for a detective to meet her at the Castle Hill address. They meet up outside, and together go to the front door. A woman answers their ring.

'Mrs Fogarty?'

'Yes.' Her smile fades a little as she looks them over.

Deb introduces herself and the other detective.

'Has something happened? Is Ken all right?'

'Yes. Do you mind if we come in for a moment?'

'Please.'

She takes them into a comfortably furnished living room,

removes a Barbie doll from the lounge and asks them to sit down. 'Ken's at work, if you're wanting him.'

'Yes. Someone else is contacting him. You see, a friend, a work colleague of his, has been murdered. Eden Grimshaw.'

'Eden! Oh, no, that's awful. Poor Eden.'

'You knew him?'

'Yes. We've known him for ages, through his ups and downs.'

She sees the query on Deb's face, and goes on, 'He went through a horrible divorce recently, and before that there was, well, a lot of bitterness. Ken did his best to help. He's been a regular visitor here.'

'Ah, yes. This weekend?'

'Yes, Saturday, he had dinner here with us.'

'Did Ken see him yesterday evening, do you know?'

'No. Ken didn't go out. We all went to church together and then came home for dinner. But why don't you speak to him?'

'Yes, yes, as I said, someone is doing that, but we just need to get as broad a perspective as possible, him being a police officer.'

Deb gets out her phone and shows Mrs Fogarty a close-up image of the A1 logo on the cap in the CCTV picture. 'Do you recognise this at all?'

'Oh…why, yes, it's Ken's cap.'

'Ah,' Deb sits back, 'I see. Is it here then?'

'I assume so. Ken keeps it in the wardrobe upstairs. Do you want me to check?'

'If you wouldn't mind.'

She leaves them, and the other detective looks at Deb, his face blank.

Fogarty's wife returns after a couple of minutes. 'No, I'm sorry, I can't seem to find it. Really you should ask Ken.'

'Yes, we will. I'm sorry to have bothered you, Mrs Fogarty. We're all chasing our tails this morning, going round in circles.'

'Of course. How awful. It's always a shock when a police officer is murdered. People don't appreciate what risks you run.'

She sees them to the door. As it closes behind them, Deb points to a pair of bins over against the fence. 'Do me a favour will you? Put on some gloves and take a quick look in there for me.'

'What am I looking for, boss?'

'Articles of clothing.'

She watches him lift the lids, crouch over the bins, then raise his arm to her. She goes over.

'Dark blue jacket stuffed down the bottom, and a baseball cap.'

'This one?' She shows him the CCTV image.

'Yeah, looks like.'

Hands behind her, she peers into the bin and sees it. 'Right.' Filled with a sense of disaster, she gets on the phone to homicide HQ, insists on speaking to Dick Blake. When he eventually comes on the line, she says, 'Chief, sorry, but we have a problem.'

51

'What made you come over here in the first place?' Superintendent Blake shakes his head, watching the search team going into Fogarty's house. Mrs Fogarty is standing at the front window, looking bewildered.

'The witness at the apartment block said he recognised the cap as belonging to a friend of Grimshaw's, and I thought I'd better check if it was Chief Inspector Fogarty's.'

'Which it was.'

'Yes, only his wife said he didn't go out last night.'

'And then you just happened to check his bins...'

Deb says nothing.

'Because?'

'Old habit of mine,' she says.

'Really? And the cap and jacket are covered in bloodstains.'

'They are.'

Blake shakes his head again. 'So Fogarty murdered his colleague?'

'Or else he's been set up. Fogarty's an experienced detective. Bit stupid to wear distinctive clothing to the crime scene, then dispose of it in his own bin.'

'Yes, that's what I was thinking. So we'll probably have to rely on forensics.' He ponders for a moment. 'Where is he now?'

'Still in his office at Parramatta HQ.'

'I know you're heavily committed with Slater Park, Deb, but I'd like you to handle this, at least for the first twenty-four hours. Why don't you and Stan have him identify Grimshaw at the morgue, then take him to the local station for a statement. Tell him you've found his jacket and cap, see if he has an explanation. Maybe they were stolen at the gym or something. I'd better inform the deputy commissioner.'

Deb does as he says, picking Fogarty up and driving him to Glebe. On the way he expresses his disbelief at what's happened, trying to pump Deb for information.

'Too early to be sure,' she says, 'but I'll get you to give us a formal statement of what you know of his recent movements. You were pretty close, I believe?'

'Yeah, yeah. We've been through a few situations over the years, some fairly tense. And then something like this happens, out of the blue. Unbelievable. I'll miss the big bastard.'

He sounds convincing, but then he's had plenty of experience.

Stan Felder meets them at the morgue and together they go to view the body. Fogarty gives a soft groan. 'You think you're invincible, and then bang, it's all over.' He turns to Deb. 'Stabbed, eh? Where?'

'His chest, the heart.'

'Quick then. Where did this happen?'

'In his flat, apparently.'

'Really? Well, there's CCTV down at the front door. Maybe that'll help.'

They go on to the local police station, an interview room. Deb checks the ERISP recording equipment.

'Formal, eh? Am I a suspect?'

'A potential witness. Take a seat. I have to caution you.'

'Go ahead.'

They get started. Fogarty says he last saw Grimshaw on Saturday. He came to watch Fogarty's son play a game of school football, then returned to Fogarty's home where they had drinks, a meal. Grimshaw left around eight. Fogarty says he doesn't know what plans he had for Sunday. They discuss possible enemies, Grimshaw's problems with money since his divorce, his drinking and gambling.

'Who might have had a key to his apartment?' Deb asks.

'A girlfriend, maybe? Don't know.'

'Yourself?'

'Yes.' Fogarty gets a bunch of keys from his pocket and shows them one for the lobby door of the apartment block and one for Grimshaw's flat. 'Just for emergencies,' he says. 'I never had occasion to use them. He always buzzes me up.'

When they've exhausted the routine questions, Deb closes her notebook and puts away her pen.

Fogarty sits back. 'You get the bastard, you hear?'

'We'll do our best.' Deb begins to rise from her chair, then turns to Felder. 'Oh, that cap image.'

Felder flicks through his phone and hands it to her.

'Yes. Do you recognise this, Ken?'

He frowns, surprised. 'I have a cap like that.'

Deb nods. 'Where is it now?'

'Where? In my wardrobe at home, I guess. Why?'

'When did you last wear it?'

'Hang on, why are you asking?'

'A resident on Eden's floor described one of Eden's visitors wearing a cap like that.'

'Oh, yes, that would be me. Last time I wore it would have been Saturday, at the boy's footy game.'

'Okay, well, thanks for your cooperation, Ken.'

At the door Fogarty pauses, checks his phone. 'Oh, the wife's been trying to get me. She must have heard the news.'

When he's gone, Deb goes out to her car and speeds off. On the road she calls the TIB at Potts Hill. 'Harry Belltree,' she says. 'We're tracking his phone, right? Where was he last night between nine pm and one am?'

After a few minutes they get back to her with an address. 'House belongs to a Mrs Nicole March. He's been staying there nights since last Wednesday.'

'Is he there now?'

'He is, or at least his phone is.'

Deb remembers the name—Harry's sister-in-law, widowed. She heads over there.

Nicole answers the door, a baby in her arms, and Deb introduces herself.

'I remember,' Nicole says coolly. 'You're Harry's colleague. We've met.'

'I need to speak to him, Mrs March.'

'I'm afraid you've missed him. He isn't here.'

'When will he be back?'

'I really couldn't say.'

'Can you tell me where he is?'

'Sorry.'

'Look, I really do need to speak to him urgently. What time did he leave?'

'After breakfast, around seven.'

Deb takes out her phone and calls Harry's number. From somewhere inside the house they hear a phone ringing. It stops when she finishes the call. 'His phone appears to be here.'

'He must have left it behind.'

Deb doesn't hide her impatience. 'Can you tell me where he was last night?'

'He was here, looking after Abigail.' Nicole strokes the baby's head.

'That's his daughter?'

'Yes, his and Jenny's.' Nicole looks defiantly at Deb. 'Abigail's quite demanding at night, wakes every couple of hours. Harry's very good with her. His bed is in the room with her cot.'

Deb stares at the small figure for a moment, the pink skin, the tuft of fair hair. 'Please get him to call me. It's urgent.'

52

Harry looks out of the window at the ocean far below, small clouds casting patches of shadow on the green ruffled surface. Three rows ahead on the other side of the aisle he can see the top of Kelly's head as she sips a glass of wine. Beside him two men are talking about the tragedy of a heavy-drinking friend who used to be a champion lawn bowler, 'Up there with Selby,' until he gave up the grog and completely lost the knack. The pilot announces their approach to Bauerfield Airport.

They collect their bags and take a minibus ride into Port Vila. It rattles and bumps over potholes, past strips of small workshops and homes, new signs for Chinese businesses. Their hotel overlooks the harbour. It has a casino and views out across the water to the resort island a short ferry ride across the bay. They take their bags up to their rooms, then meet in the lobby to walk to lunch at Brad's Hamburger Bar. As they stroll through the covered fruit market and out into the humid heat along the main street, Kelly sketches in Brad's background, a Tasmanian accountant who got a taste for the expat life during a stint in Papua New Guinea and fled a failing marriage to go troppo in Vanuatu. 'He knows everybody,' Kelly says, 'fiddles their tax returns for them when he's not serving them burgers and beer. I met him when I had a week's holiday out here once, and we hit it off. He had a greasy little shack on the harbour then, but he's gone up-market since.'

But not much up-market, Harry thinks, as they push through the plastic strips into a dark little bar on a back street. Two men in hard hats are sitting at one of the tables, drinking beer and eating burgers and chips. There's a strong smell of frying in the air, the sound of an argument through a doorway behind the bar. A man emerges, stocky, red-faced, wiping his hands on his apron.

'Kelly! You made it.' He gives her a kiss, shakes Harry's hand a little warily, waves them to stools at the bar. He opens a bottle of wine for Kelly, pours beers for Harry and himself and gets down to business. From a shelf beneath the bar he produces a stapled document, a copy of the local police report of an investigation into human remains discovered on Tuesday 16 September in the net of a fishing boat in ocean waters west of the island of Pentecost. They thumb through it, scanning passages that someone has underlined.

Forensic analysis determined that the remains comprised the right leg of an adult male in the age range 18–30, of Melanesian Ni-Vanuatu extraction. It was estimated that it had been in the water for 36–72 hours, and had been mauled, most likely by sharks. Cause of death could not be determined. There were no distinguishing marks to aid identification.

Subsequent enquiries by a VPF officer on Pentecost established that Selwyn Tamata, 28, whose family lived in the village of Panngi in south-west Pentecost, was missing. Selwyn had regular work as a tourist guide during the land-diving season from April to June, and out of season casual work with local fishermen as well as on the private

202

island of Maturiki, some 12 kilometres west of Pentecost.
No one had reported him missing until the police officer
came asking questions.

Brad points to the VPF officer's name. 'He's a regular in here. I told him that you were interested in the shark sorcerers for a story in your paper, Kelly, but he wasn't too happy about that. Apparently it's against policy to talk about sharks—bad for tourism—so he won't talk to you. But he suggested you could speak to Selwyn's sister Pascaline. He thought she was holding something back, and asked her if Selwyn had been in trouble with someone, but she wouldn't be drawn. Maybe you'll have more luck with her. She also has a casual job on Maturiki, so she may be able to fill you in on that.'

They discuss what they should do. There is a flight up to Pentecost that afternoon and they decide to go for it. Brad says he can't come with them today, but offers to contact someone who can help them. He flicks through a fat address book stuffed with business cards and handwritten notes and dials a number. Pastor Emanuel Dubouzet lives in a small village not far from Panngi, and knows the Tamata family. He also runs a guesthouse in which he would be happy to accommodate Brad's two friends.

53

Deb makes her way from the Strike Force Spider briefing to Superintendent Blake's office. He is poring over a new report from forensic services.

'DNA results,' he says, looking sombre. 'Not much room for doubt. The running shoes are definitely Fogarty's and it's their footprints all over the crime scene and on the landing and stairway. Fogarty's DNA on the knife and front doorknob.'

'Fingerprints?'

'Hmm...' He checks the report. 'No. That's about the only thing that seems to be missing. Oh, hang on—Fogarty's thumb print on the bag of white powder, cocaine.'

'What's the motive?'

'That's for Stan Felder to find out. You don't look convinced. You're not still thinking he's been framed, are you?'

Deb shrugs. 'Let's see how Stan gets on.'

'Maybe you should sit in with him, Deb. Reassure yourself.'

'Are we charging Fogarty?'

'Don't have a lot of choice. Not with this...' He taps the report.

For the time being the Grimshaw murder is being run from a room in the eastern suburbs local area command headquarters at Waverley. Deb takes a car out there and on the way calls the major incident room at Slater Park, asks for an alert to be issued for Harry Belltree if he should try to leave the country.

She gets a reply to the second request before she reaches Waverley. Harry Belltree left Sydney at 7:45 am that morning on an Air Vanuatu flight to Port Vila. She swears softly to herself, suddenly overwhelmed by a premonition of her career in ruins. She pulls in to the kerb and takes a deep breath. Think, focus, she tells herself, one thing at a time.

She calls Felder and tells him she'll be delayed and not to start talking to Fogarty till she gets there.

'His wife's been trying to call him,' Felder says.

'Has he been speaking to her?'

'No, he surrendered his phone to us for analysis.'

'He was happy with that?'

'He was cooperative. He's playing it pretty cool, not acting like a guilty man at all.'

'We'll see. I'm going to talk to his wife again, see how his alibi stands up.'

Deb turns the car around and heads for Castle Hill. The searchers are leaving, taking the clothes Fogarty wore yesterday. A woman constable remains inside with Brenda Fogarty, who is agitated, demanding to know what's happening. Deb tries to re-assure her that this is all routine in cases of homicide.

'I haven't been able to get through to Ken.'

'He's very tied up at the moment,' Deb says. 'A couple more questions and we'll be gone.'

'Good. I should be getting to work.' She has a job in a local real estate office, she explains, with a small, overworked staff.

'We need to be very clear about Eden's movements this weekend. Let's run through that again.'

Deb takes out her notebook. 'So Ken didn't see him at all yesterday, as far as you know?'

'That's right.' She repeats how they had spent their Sunday.

'And after dinner?'

'We watched TV for a while, the kids went to bed, and I went soon after, about nine. I was tired and hoping to get an early start at work this morning.'

'What time did Ken come to bed?'

'Um, well, I'm not sure. He usually stays up a bit later than me...' She hesitates, then says, 'I can show you what he does if you're interested.'

'Fine.'

She leads Deb to stairs down to a basement room, where she switches on the lights. Deb stares in amazement. 'Oh wow. He plays with a train set?' She studies the elaborate layout of train tracks spread on tables across the whole room—rolling stock, buildings, hillsides, a lake, all modelled in immaculate detail.

'Well, he wouldn't call it "playing". It's pretty serious, really, with all that electronics stuff controlling the points and signals and trains. He started it when the kids were small and they joined in. Then he was posted to Newcastle and we rented the house. When we came back the children weren't interested in the trains anymore, but Ken took it up again. He began to extend and develop it, as a form of therapy.'

'Therapy, yes, I can understand that.'

'He's found his new job really stressful. He doesn't complain to me, but I can tell. It's really got to him. The trains are a way of escaping, something totally absorbing and free of guilt.'

'Guilt?'

'Well, that's what police work is all about, isn't it? Guilt. I don't know how you can stand it.'

They return upstairs and Deb says, 'So, just to complete the record, Brenda, were you asleep when Ken came to bed last night?'

'I suppose I was. I don't remember. He's good at getting into bed without disturbing me—long years of practice—and I'd taken a sleeping pill.'

'And did you wake during the night at all?'

'Yes, I remember waking about four.'

'And he was there then?'

'Yes, certainly. What are you getting at?'

'It's what we do, establishing everyone's movements around the time of a murder, until we find the one that doesn't fit.'

'Well, Ken's in the clear, believe me. Now, can I get to work?'

54

The short flight up to Pentecost is in a seventeen-seater Chinese Harbin Y-12 twin-prop that lifts off sharply from Bauerfield into a deep blue sky. Kelly turns to look out of the window at the lush islands of the Vanuatu archipelago sliding past below in the shimmering ocean. At her side Harry appears to be studying the in-flight magazine, except that he isn't turning the pages. She senses that something happened before they left Sydney—his preoccupied air, his sudden decision to leave straight away for Vanuatu. The discovery of Amber's body at Slater Park must have been a shock, of course, but she wonders if there was something else. Maybe to do with Jenny. She prays that they haven't found her body too. That would be too much.

Pastor Emanuel Dubouzet is waiting as they get off the plane. A jolly, spherical man, he leads them to a small battered Nissan, slings their bags in the boot and squeezes in behind the wheel. He takes the short drive down the coast slowly, weaving to avoid the potholes, pointing out local attractions, which culminate in the strange muffin-shaped Captain Cook's Rock standing offshore.

Unlike most of the thatch and timber houses they've seen along the way, Emanuel's place is built of concrete blocks with a corrugated tin roof. Next to it he points out his open-sided chapel, and further away, almost on the edge of the beach, the small timber hut which is the guesthouse. It consists of just one indoor room together with a veranda and an outdoor toilet and shower attached. The room contains a double bed. Kelly glances at Harry, who says he'll take the ocean view room, and goes outside to drop his bag on the veranda.

'You will eat with us, of course,' Emanuel declares, and leads them back to his house to meet his wife Lydia, as plump and friendly as her husband. She offers them refreshments, but Kelly explains that they're anxious to speak to Pascaline Tamata as soon as possible. Lydia checks her watch and says that she's likely to be at the primary school at Panngi, where she helps out when she doesn't have a job elsewhere.

'She's a good girl,' she adds, 'loyal and respectful, and very sad since the terrible death of her brother. She's on her own now. Her mother died when she was young and her father is a wastrel. He's gone off, good riddance to him, off to Port Vila, two weeks after Selwyn died.'

Kelly says, 'What was Selwyn like?'

'A mischief when he was growing up, and went a bit wild when he was a teenager. He took those habits from his father, I suppose. Pascaline worked hard to get him to behave himself, and it was she got him the job on Maturiki.'

'Have either of you ever been out there, to Maturiki?'

'I have,' Lydia says. 'Once when their cook went sick I went out to help. They had a big party of visitors coming on a boat and we had to prepare a banquet. The island was so strange, so luxurious— a bit of a foreign country dropped into the ocean just out there. The kitchen was amazing, like a spaceship, all the latest gadgets. We had to work very hard, but they paid well. Maybe too well for Selwyn's good. He flashed his money around after he got his first pay packet there.'

'Do you think he got into trouble with other men around here?'

'You mean, was he killed and thrown into the sea for the sharks?' Lydia looks at her husband and sighs. 'Yes, it's possible. It certainly wasn't shark sorcerers who killed him, and he didn't go out to sea with any of the fishermen. The policeman who came here asked that question, but no one owned up.'

'Well, let's see what Pascaline has to say.'

'We'll walk,' Emanuel says. 'It's not far.'

But the afternoon is hot and very humid, and their clothes are soaked with perspiration by the time they come to houses lining the coast road and extending inland, dotted around lush green paddocks. The primary school has just finished afternoon classes, and a dozen small children are milling around outside, but Pascaline isn't there. Emanuel has a word with a teacher, and says, 'She thinks Pascaline has gone to tend to her brother's grave.'

They see her there as they approach the little cemetery beside the church, a slender figure kneeling beside a new white cross, arranging a large bunch of vivid yellow and orange flowers in a vase. She looks up and considers them with big intelligent eyes, then says to Emanuel, 'Selwyn liked parakeet flowers.'

He says, 'Pascaline, these are my friends, Kelly and Harry, who have come from Australia to see you. Will you talk to them?'

Pascaline gets to her feet slowly. 'If you wish me to, pastor. Are they police?'

Emanuel looks at Kelly, who says, 'Harry is an Australian police officer, Pascaline, but I'm not. We're here as friends of Amber. I believe you met her?'

'Yes, she was a kind lady. Is she well?'

'I'm afraid not. She died recently.'

'Oh, no, was she sick?'

'The police believe she was murdered.'

210

Pascaline's mouth drops open. She stares at Kelly. Then her legs fold abruptly and Harry and Emanuel jump forward to catch her as she falls to the ground. When she comes round they wait till she feels able, then help her to her feet and walk with her to a bench in the shade of a grove of palms. Kelly sits beside her, takes the bottle of water that Emanuel offers them and gets her to drink.

'Thank you,' Pascaline whispers. 'It was the shock.'

'Of course. Do you feel well enough to talk?'

The girl nods.

Kelly looks at Harry, who says, 'I was a friend of Amber's, Pascaline. We helped each other in the past, and I felt it very personally when she died. I'm determined to find whoever was responsible. I spoke to her in Sydney not long before she died. She told me she was hiding from her family because of things that happened on Maturiki Island. She told me some of the things, bad things. And then we heard that your brother had also been found dead, and we thought we should come and talk to you, to see if you could tell us anything that would help us.'

'I am afraid.'

Emanuel puts out a hand to reassure her, but she shakes it off, saying, 'They killed Selwyn and now Miss Amber.'

'Who did, Pascaline?'

She stares out to sea, towards the distant green blur of Maturiki Island. 'Those evil boys.'

'Boys? What boys?'

'Mr Nordlund's boys,' she whispers, 'Ryan and Hayden. Miss Amber ran away from Maturiki to escape them, after they killed Selwyn.'

'Why would they do that?'

'I don't know. I think because he spied on them, saw something he shouldn't. He wouldn't tell me what it was.'

'Did you see them kill Selwyn?'

'No.'

'Then how can you be sure?'

She looks back at her brother's grave. 'They sent their lawyer to Selwyn's funeral. Afterwards he came to see my father and me, and gave us money, five thousand American dollars each.'

Emanuel gives a soft whistle.

'He said it was in place of Selwyn's pension, a special gift from Mr Nordlund. My father was very happy. He got drunk, and the next day he left for Port Vila. I haven't heard from him since. He took my money as well as his own, but I don't care. I didn't want it—it was blood money.'

Harry says, 'Did the lawyer work in Port Vila?'

'No, he wasn't Ni-Vanuatu, he was Australian. He looked like a black kite, with a beak for tearing flesh. You know him?'

'Yes, he's a big-shot lawyer in Sydney. Mr Nordlund must have thought this was very important, to send him in person. What is Mr Nordlund like?'

'He is a cold man, very correct. Not like his wife, who is much younger and very beautiful and flirts with the men visitors like the Chinese man, Mr Deng.'

'Are there many visitors?'

'Yes, important men and women, especially during the land-diving season, when the tourists come to watch the men jumping from the high towers. That's when they need extra staff.'

'Is there anyone over there at the moment?'

'I don't know. Perhaps not. I haven't seen any boats lately.'

Harry gets her to describe the layout of the property. She isn't able to draw a plan, but she mentions various rooms that she's either seen or heard the cleaners talking about—a gym, a wine cellar, an office suite.

When she's finished they thank Pascaline and promise to keep their conversation secret.

They return to Emanuel's house where his wife is busy preparing a meal. Emanuel says something to her and then invites his guests

212

to sit outside on a veranda facing the ocean.

'Unfortunately,' he says, 'my religion forbids alcohol. However, the good book has nothing to say on the subject of kava. Have you ever had kava?'

Harry and Kelly shake their heads.

'Then you are in luck, for the very best, most noble kava comes from Pentecost, and it is best taken fresh. Ah...'

They turn to see Lydia emerging from the house with a pot and a dish containing some roots and a lump of coral. She sits with them, picks up one of the roots and begins to grind it in her hand with the coral, dropping the pulp into the pot. After grinding all of the roots she fetches a jug of water, pours some into the pot and stirs it. When she's happy with it she brings three glasses and pours the fluid into them.

Emanuel raises his glass and sips, nods contentedly. 'This is very good. Please try it.'

Kelly does, and gags. Emanuel laughs.

'You don't like it, Kelly? No, it's not really a ladies' drink. In fact in some places it's forbidden for women to drink it. Would you prefer a cup of tea?'

'If you don't mind, yes please.' Her tongue feels numb and she wants to wash her mouth out. She watches Harry take a sip too. 'You like it, Harry?' she asks.

'It's, um, growing on me, I think.'

The evening is hot, the air still and heavy with humidity. 'A storm is coming,' Emanuel says. 'Soon it will be the cyclone season.' As they drink he tells them stories of the islands. He was himself once a champion bungee jumper from the tall towers built up in the hills for the land-diving ceremonies. He sees the look pass across Kelly's face and he chuckles. 'That was when I was young and thin, before I tasted Lydia's cooking.'

They go indoors to sample it for themselves. During the meal Harry talks about their plans. 'There's a flight back to Port Vila tomorrow, but it doesn't leave till the afternoon. So I thought we might do a spot of fishing in the morning, if it's possible to hire a small boat?'

Emanuel says he thinks he can arrange it.

55

Ken Fogarty is sitting in an interview room with a cup of coffee. He looks quite relaxed, doodling on a pad of paper. Perhaps he's working on a problem with his train layout, Deb thinks, and apologises for keeping him waiting. She and Felder sit down opposite him.

'No dramas,' Fogarty says calmly. 'I expect you've got your hands full, what with Slater Park. How is that going by the way? Any leads?'

'Nothing solid.' Deb smiles resignedly, deciding to allow herself to be patronised. She takes out her phone, makes a show of checking it while Felder cautions him again.

Fogarty folds his arms and stares at Deb, waiting. When she puts the phone away he says, 'Brenda tells me you searched our home. What's that all about?'

'It was that cap business. She told us it was in your wardrobe but it wasn't.'

He looks at her as if she's stupid. 'I thought we cleared up the cap business. Didn't we?'

'Hmm.' She reaches into the bag at her side for a file, opens it and takes out a photograph of the bag of cocaine. 'Have you ever seen this before?'

He leans forward to inspect it. 'I've seen a thousand like it. I was in the drug squad, remember?'

'Yes, with Eden. But this was in his room, beneath his body. Ring any bells?'

He gazes at her, expressionless. 'Nope.'

'That's odd, because it's got your thumb print on it.'

A moment of silence, then Fogarty sits back and barks a laugh. 'Is that what this is all about? Jesus. Yes, it's possible I have seen it before. Saturday night I drove Eden back to his place after we'd had dinner. He offered me the bag of blow. I handed it back to him and told him not to be so bloody stupid.' He shrugs. 'But I could understand it. He's been doing it tough lately.'

'In what way?'

'Oh, money, divorce, work—you name it.'

'Brenda said you've been very stressed lately too.'

'Did she say that?'

'Anything special?'

'No. Where's this going? Are you seriously going to try to make trouble for me because my print is on Eden's packet of coke?' He looks at Felder for support. 'This is ludicrous. I want to see Dick Blake.'

Deb goes on, 'I'm thinking that you and Eden were both stressed, he offers you drugs, you have an argument that turns nasty, he pulls a knife, you struggle and the knife ends up in Eden's heart. Something like that?'

'What? You're crazy! For a start, I was nowhere near Eden's flat yesterday. I was with Brenda and the kids all day. She'll confirm that.'

'Yes, she does. The trouble is that she also says that she was asleep when you came to bed, so she can't vouch for your movements after about nine.'

Fogarty shakes his head, exasperated, mutters something.

'What was that?'

'I said go fuck yourself, Velasco. You are making one big bloody fool of yourself. You haven't got a shred of evidence to accuse me of anything.'

'Well, there's the cap.'

'The cap!'

'Yes, the cap, and the matching dark blue jacket, you know the one? They were worn by someone who appears on the CCTV at Eden's apartment block, arriving and leaving again late last night.'

'Ah…so that's what's bugging you? Someone with clothes like mine?'

'No, they are actually yours. We found them at your home, stuffed in the garbage bin, and stained with Eden's blood.'

Fogarty looks stunned. His face goes very pale as he takes this in. Finally he whispers, 'DNA?'

'Yours? Oh, yes, all over the place, the handle of the murder weapon…'

Fogarty seems to be having difficulty swallowing.

Deb reaches into her bag again and pulls out the pair of running shoes from the skip, now in a clear plastic evidence bag. She places them in front of him. 'Are these yours, Chief Inspector Fogarty?'

He stares at them, taking in the bloodstains, and says nothing.

Deb opens her file again, making a show of finding a document. 'Where were you on the afternoon of Monday October thirteen?'

He looks confused by the change of direction. 'What?'

'Just over two weeks ago—I have a witness places you and Grimshaw in the Blue Mountains that afternoon. Blackheath.'

Fogarty stares at her for a long moment, face frozen. Then, 'I want to speak to my lawyer.'

'Yes, I think that would be a good idea. You can tell him that you're being charged with the murder of Detective Sergeant Eden Grimshaw.'

56

They rise early, the air still sultry hot. Harry has slept more deeply than he has for months, due, Emanuel tells him, to the soporific effects of the kava. He warns Harry that they had a 'tudei' kava strain, so called because its effects can last for two days. Harry goes for a long swim in the ocean to wake himself up.

The boat that Emanuel borrows for them is a small aluminium dinghy with an outboard motor. Both boat and motor look as if they've been around for a very long time. He also provides a couple of fishing rods and some bait, and warns them of a storm front approaching from the north. 'You be back by noon, mind.'

Lydia supplies them with a bowl of laplap, the national speciality, a dish of pounded taro cooked in coconut cream, and some papaya. She also gives them bottles of water and two straw hats to keep off the sun and make them look more like locals. They coax the motor into life, and Kelly and Harry set off across a flat oily sea towards Maturiki.

Lydia has told them that the coral reef with its lagoon and beach lie on the far side of the island, with most of the buildings clustered around it, facing towards the west. The east side, which they are approaching, is fringed by mangroves, shifting sandbars and muddy beaches. After half an hour Harry throttles down and glides in through weed and roots to a place where the palm trees come closest to the shore. They wade up through the mud and tie the boat to a palm trunk, then set off up a shallow slope towards the centre of the island.

After struggling through thick scrub for a while they come upon a rough path. There is no sound, no indication of human life. They emerge into a large clearing paved with concrete, its centre marked with a large painted cross. 'The helicopter pad,' Harry murmurs.

From here a paved road winds through well-groomed groves of palm and hibiscus, but they stay clear of it, making their way through the cover of the lush landscaped garden, heady with the scent of frangipani, and approach the compound. They see white modernist buildings, two electric buggies standing at what might be the main entrance. Working around the complex, they get an idea of its layout—a kitchen wing and yard, a separate building for maintenance, what may be a guest wing, a staff block.

They reach the western side and see white coral sand running down to the lagoon, groves of pandanus trees with spreading aerial roots anchoring them to the sand, the line of foam at the reef, a brilliant blue swimming pool on a terrace. All is motionless, as if in suspense, waiting for the yachts and the helicopters to arrive.

And then a sudden burst of music—the Bee Gees, 'Stayin' Alive'.

They shrink into the shadows as a man comes around the corner of the building, lugging equipment, and kneels down by the edge of the pool.

'Jesus,' Kelly says. 'It's Craig Schaefer. Look at his left eye.'

Harry sees the black patch. 'So Karen Schaefer will be around somewhere too. The caretakers. I wonder who else.'

Kelly says, 'What's the plan, Harry?' She tried to raise this on the boat coming over, but Harry refused to be drawn, saying they had to assess the place first.

'If there are people here it'll mean that alarms are off, doors unlocked. I want to go inside, have a look at that office suite that Pascaline mentioned.'

They circle back to the kitchen side of the main building, where, sure enough, they see a door now standing open. It looks as if the Schaefers are just starting their daily chores.

'You stay here, Kelly.'

She tries to object but Harry is adamant. Two people double their chances of being spotted, he says. He leaves her there, hiding in the bushes, lopes silently across to the open door and then listens. There is a faint sound coming from within the house, one he can't identify.

He pulls on latex gloves and steps inside, moving through a utility room, looking quickly into the extensive kitchen that Lydia described, then going on, pausing to listen at each place that offers cover. That sound again, quite close. He guesses that it's someone cleaning a window. It stops and he slides in behind a door, hears someone walking past, the soles of their shoes squeaking slightly on the tiled floor. He waits, then steps out again, into a corridor. There's a bucket on the floor up ahead. He hurries past and finds himself in what must be the entrance hall of the house. The front doors are on his right and a huge lounge room to his left, over-looking the pool and beach. Four other doors lead off the hallway. Which one? He tries them in turn, discovers a home theatre and a games room. The third door opens into the office suite, with a room for staff and a more luxuriously appointed office with a large oval table with a dozen seats, and, at the far end, the boss's desk and high-backed chair. Harry hurries to that end, looks around the computer, the desk drawers. There is a small safe beneath the drawer on one side, an empty file cabinet on the other. He searches rapidly and entirely without result. There are no security codes, diaries, spare hard drives, letters or files. Then he tries to check the computer itself, which starts with an alarmingly loud musical chord and requires a password he cannot guess. After a fruitless search of a bookcase and a sideboard he admits defeat. He goes to the door, opens it, and freezes.

A woman is standing in the hallway. She has her back to him, and is arranging a large bunch of flowers in a vase. She is not Ni-Vanuatu, and Harry guesses that she is Karen Schaefer. He glances to his left, sees an open door and quickly steps across to it. He finds himself at the start of a corridor with doorways up ahead. Trying the first, he enters a bedroom with en suite bathroom. The next room is identical but reversed, equally anonymous and clearly unoccupied. The third is more interesting, with a panel covered in photographs and two framed and signed football shirts hanging on the wall. Harry goes in and examines the photographs, a catalogue of bragging moments in a young man's life—grinning alongside a football player holding aloft a cup, on a yacht with two beautiful models with familiar faces, in black tie and white tux at a roulette table. This room must belong to the other of Nordlund's sons, Harry guesses—Hayden.

There is a computer on a desk next to the window, through which he can see Craig Schaefer still working at the side of the pool. He doesn't try to start it for fear of being heard. Instead he goes through drawers. They are untidy, and there are a few items— printouts, some bills, business cards—that he stuffs in his pockets for later examination. It's disappointingly meagre stuff. He sits down at the desk, trying to imagine himself here, the owner, his hands resting on the keyboard. Without looking he lets his hands explore, running them across the desktop, then underneath, and in a corner his fingers touch something small and hard. He crouches down and sees a flash drive taped to the underside.

He pockets it, sets the chair back as it was and heads for the door. In the corridor he hears squeaky footsteps coming from around the corner and sprints in the opposite direction, towards an external door. He opens it, turns the corner of the building and runs straight into Craig Schaefer.

57

Deb hammers on the door, and after a moment Nicole cautiously opens it. 'Oh, what is it now?'

'Can I come in?'

'It's not convenient. I'm changing the baby's nappy.'

'That's all right. We can talk while you're doing it.'

'No thanks.' That defiant look. 'You'd frighten her.'

Deb sighs. 'Harry took a flight to Vanuatu yesterday morning.'

'Oh, really?'

'Come on, Nicole. You knew that, didn't you? I could arrest you for obstructing my investigation.'

'What investigation is that?'

'Murder, that's what I investigate, and you're being obstructive and uncooperative.'

'Should I be calling a lawyer?'

'Just tell me what his plans are.'

'I don't know. I remember him talking about someone advising him to get away and have a complete break. Maybe that was it, an impulsive thing.'

'Harry is never impulsive, Nicole. He always thinks things through, and he wouldn't have gone off and left you with his baby without discussing it with you.'

'Sorry, I can't help you.'

She starts to close the door, but Deb stops it with her foot. 'Get him to contact me. It's for his own good.'

Deb pulls in to the car park in North Ryde, shows her badge at reception and is directed through to the chief's office. Bob Marshall is standing by his desk, gathering up files.

'Ah, Deb. Just in time. I've got meetings. The TV campaign, the schools' program—'

'Have you heard about Detective Sergeant Eden Grimshaw?'

He looks at her with a sharp frown. She realises she sounds as if she's talking to a subordinate instead of a superintendent.

'He was murdered Sunday night,' she says, more measured.

'Grimshaw. Oh yes?'

'Stabbed through the heart. Forensic evidence all over the place, and all pointing to Ken Fogarty. In fact you could say it's almost a copycat of Terry Palfreyman's murder...'

Marshall stares at her, face impassive.

'Which Harry Belltree insisted was a frame,' she says.

'Where is Harry?'

'You haven't heard from him, sir?'

'No.'

'Skipped the country. Caught a flight to Vanuatu yesterday. We've asked the Vanuatu police to find out where he is. Could be anywhere by now. His sister-in-law is saying that he spent all Sunday night at her house, with the baby. Unfortunately the baby can't talk.'

'There's no need for sarcasm, Deb.'

'Actually the whole thing would be hilarious if it wasn't so bloody serious. We're being taken for a ride.'

'You don't know that for a fact.'

'No advice you can give me?'

'How about, don't jump to conclusions?'

'Well,' she says, 'I thought I should let you know.'

'I appreciate it. Scandal and rumour take longer to reach us out here.'

58

From her hiding place Kelly hears Schaefer's cry as he falls, hitting his head with a crack on the coral rocks edging the garden bed. Harry runs towards her and grabs her arm. As she spins around she sees Karen Schaefer standing open-mouthed at the front door, staring. They race off down the drive among the palms, reach the helicopter landing pad and find the small path beyond, plunging on until they realise they must have gone past the place where they cut through from the mangroves. Harry turns into the dense bush, crashing a way through tangled vines and roots. Kelly is behind him, but she feels her feet sinking into increasingly boggy ground.

'Harry,' she cries, gasping for breath, 'we're lost.'

'Keep going…'

She sees the sparkle of reflected light up ahead, and they force their way through to open ground, the spikes of mangrove shoots sticking through the mud like nails. Across a patch of heaving water they see the dinghy, tugging at its rope, and Harry splashes through the waves to it. She looks out across the water—choppy now—towards a darkening sky.

'Come on!' Harry reaches out a hand to Kelly as she struggles through the shallows, hauls her aboard and gets to work on the motor. Nothing. He pulls, adjusts the throttle, coaxes, waits, tries again, until, in an angry roar, it comes to life. He casts off and turns the boat out into the breakers. Behind them she hears a man's shout.

As they emerge into the open water they both turn to gape at the huge black storm front bearing down upon them from the north. Ahead in the distance the green hills of Pentecost are momentarily caught in a lurid bright light that fades as they stare at it. Harry teases the throttle and they bounce forward over gathering waves. Their concentration on the sea is suddenly broken by a crack and a zing. Kelly turns and catches a glimpse of Craig Schaefer on the mangrove beach aiming a weapon at them. A wave catches them and pitches them down as another bullet zips overhead. Kelly crouches in the hull, clutching the side, and prays the motor doesn't get hit. They are shipping water now and Harry bends down and reaches beneath his seat for the plastic bucket. He thrusts it at Kelly. 'Bail us.' She stares at him for a moment, uncomprehending, then nods and gets to work.

The heaving water saves them, tossing them in and out of sight until they are far off in the middle of the straits and struggling towards the Pentecost shore. As it comes closer Kelly makes out the figure of Emanuel, standing immune to the tugging wind and scattering rain, waiting for them. He lunges into the shallows as they approach and hauls them up the beach. His huge grin fades a little as he spies the puncture hole in the aluminium stern plate. Harry claps him on the shoulder and helps Kelly climb up onto the grass bank.

Later, during a hair-raising drive to the airstrip to catch their plane, Kelly says, 'Did Schaefer get a good look at you?'

'I don't think so,' Harry says. 'I hit him on his blind side.'

'I think Karen got a glimpse of us.'

They are just in time to catch the return flight to Port Vila, where they check in to their hotel on the harbour. In her room Kelly has a shower, changes her clothes and quickly checks her emails. Among the trash is a message from Brendon Pyle at the *Times*:

re: Fogarty
Kelly,

Sorry to have been so long getting back to you on Fogarty but things have been hectic as you know. I finally tracked down that story we discussed, spoke to old Houlahan who retired yonks ago. He told me that the Police Integrity Commission opened a file on Fogarty and his partner in the drug squad at the time, a detective called Grimshaw. Got that? The same Eden Grimshaw who was murdered Sunday night. The word is that Fogarty has been spending a lot of time since then helping the police with their enquiries. Also that the forensic evidence is compelling. What's this all about, Kelly? What do you know? Houlahan heard a rumour that the PIC investigation of Fogarty/Grimshaw was shelved after political pressure was applied. It would have to have been high-up political pressure. This was back in Warren Dalkeith's time as premier. So come clean, Kelly. Spill the beans!!!
Brendon

Kelly blinks, then goes to the *Times* website and reads the reports of the fatal stabbing of Eden Grimshaw in a rented flat in Bondi on Sunday night. She googles Grimshaw and comes up with pictures of a very tall man in police uniform. She reads other reports of the murder online, and thinks of Harry's sudden phone call at 4:00 am on Monday to say that he'd bought two tickets for the morning flight to Port Vila and would collect her in an hour.

She picks up the phone and dials the number of the room next door. 'Harry,' she says grimly, 'we need to talk.'

59

It's half an hour before Kelly hears a knock on her door and Harry comes in, carrying a bottle of scotch.

'Your call sounded serious,' he says. 'I thought we might need this.'

'After the day we've had we deserve it, but I want to be sober while you tell me about this.' She hands him her iPad with the email from Brendon Pyle.

He takes his time, reading it through twice, expressionless, then hands it back to her. 'Interesting.'

'Very, especially the timing. Grimshaw was stabbed just a couple of hours before you rang me out of the blue and told me we were catching the next flight out of Sydney.'

'What are you suggesting, Kelly?'

'Am I an accomplice, Harry? Are you a fugitive? Is that why we're here? Did you kill Grimshaw and frame Fogarty?'

Harry looks at her for a moment, an unnerving, steady look, then gets to his feet and searches her cupboards for two tumblers, which he half-fills with whisky before sitting down again.

'That's four questions. The answers are no, no, no and what if?'

'What do you mean?'

'What if Jenny's story of looking through Palfreyman's window and seeing him being tortured and murdered by Fogarty and a tall, thin accomplice was true? Do you believe it was?'

'How do you know Grimshaw was tall and thin?'

He smiles. 'Good try. Because I've met him in the past. Answer my question—did Jenny tell the truth?'

'How can I tell? She never told me her story. I've only heard it from you. Maybe you made it up to protect her.' Kelly hears a wobble in her voice and realises how rattled she is—the Maturiki business, the rush for the plane, and now this. Harry is holding out a glass of whisky to her. She's reluctant to take it because she knows that her hand will be shaking. She uses two hands and takes a gulp.

'They almost caught her on Friday night,' Harry says. 'After you called me about the new victim in Slater Park I went to check on Amber. She'd disappeared, and I found the man she'd been staying with dead. I called Jenny and told her to run. She managed to escape just as the police arrived where she was hiding in Marrickville.'

Kelly stares at him, decides he's telling the truth. She feels her heart pounding and whispers, 'You killed Grimshaw.'

'Yes, I did.' He reaches for his glass. 'It's a war, Kelly, and they aren't taking prisoners. If you hadn't called me so quickly there would have been two women killed that night.'

They fall silent. Harry is staring down at his drink, a look of resignation on his face. Kelly wonders what's happened to her moral compass. What would her housemate, Wendy, make of her, sitting here drinking with a confessed murderer and feeling sorry for him? No, not sorry, more than that. Devastated. Over the past two years they have been on a long journey together, and this is where it's brought them.

'What will you do, Harry?'

'I've done what I can for her. The best thing for everyone now is for me to disappear.'

'Out here? Or back up north?'

He shrugs. 'You should catch the first plane tomorrow for Sydney on your own. Tell no one that you were here with me.'

'We achieved nothing, did we?'

He reaches into his pocket and brings out some folded documents. 'I found these in one of the bedrooms of the house. It probably belonged to one of Nordlund's sons, Hayden.' He nods at her laptop. 'Can you find out what he looks like?'

Kelly brings up some images. Harry recognises some of them from the enlargements on the bedroom wall. 'That one.'

'Hayden, the younger brother, age twenty-five.'

'Right.' Harry spreads the stuff from the drawer on the table and they go through it. The computer printouts are web pages of online outlets for sunglasses and electronic gadgets; a couple show aerial views of unidentified buildings, images of luxury yachts. The bills and most of the business cards are for restaurants and clubs in Vanuatu, Sydney and Melbourne, but Kelly picks one out and shows it to Harry: *Doggylands Dog Breeders, Boarding Kennels.*

'I've been there,' she says.

'Me too. How come?'

Kelly explains about the leaflet she found in the Schaefers' mail, and then they tell each other about their visits to the kennels. 'Something's going on there, Harry,' she says. 'Something bad.'

They sip their drinks, staring at the bits and pieces on the table. Harry says, 'Not much for all that trouble going to Maturiki. There was also this…' He shows her the flash drive he found hidden beneath the desktop.

She takes it, a slender plastic stick. 'We'll need something with a USB port.' She tugs at the key ring at one end and the drive slides out of its case to reveal its body, studded with small keypad numbers. 'Oh, it's encrypted. We'd need the PIN number.'

Harry shakes his head in frustration. 'It's probably just porn, pictures of his girlfriends.'

Kelly sags back in her chair. She has the skeleton of a great story, which she can't use. 'Give me another drink, Harry.'

Later, back in his own room, Harry uses the hotel phone to ring Nicole. It's poor security, of course—Deb Velasco is probably monitoring her phone—but the whisky has given him a cold sense of fatalism.

'Harry, where are you? That detective, Velasco, has been to see me again, looking for you. She knows you left for Vanuatu yesterday. She says she needs to speak to you urgently.'

'Any news of Jenny?'

'No, nothing.'

'Abigail okay?'

'She's fine—you don't need to worry about us.'

'Good. I'm afraid you won't hear from me for a while. I just wanted to thank you for everything.'

'That's no problem, but—'

'I'm afraid I have to go.' He ends the call.

60

Deb checks the time, 11:13 pm, another fifteen-hour shift on Slater Park. The list of persons of interest has expanded to eighty-seven males and one female. Since dusk there have been intermittent reports of breaches of the electronic perimeter system. There's a colony of rabbits roaming about in the north-west corner of the park, and the odd fox, cat and dog. The police have their own dog patrol active at night, as well as the tours of the park roads by vehicles.

Her phone signals a text from Charity. *Home now. How u doing?*

Deb wonders where she's been, and immediately suffocates the little stab of jealousy that she swore she'd never allow herself to feel again for as long as she lived. But she cares.

Nearly done. How was your evening?

She stares at the screen, waiting, eyes watery from staring at screens all night.

Rubbish movie but fun with girls. When will u stop working and join us?

Deb smiles, then notices a new report arrived on her computer. It is the spreadsheet of vehicles entering Slater Park on the nights the last two victims were found. It lists the vehicle regos, names of their occupants and their source, times of entry and exit. Several of them repeat through the nights, vehicles from local stations incorporating a visit to the park on their regular night patrols. But as she checks through the schedule she notices some odd ones—vehicles from a local area command out in western Sydney, a long way from the park. There are two of them, one on each night, different patrol cars and different crews but from the same distant police station.

She rubs her weary eyes and silently tells Harry to stop fucking with her head. *Wherever you are.*

61

Early the following morning they part outside the hotel as Kelly's cab to the airport arrives. She gets in trying to dispel a hollow feeling that she won't see him again. He kisses her cheek and gives her the flash drive from Maturiki. 'I don't have the resources anymore,' he says, 'but maybe you know someone you trust who can open this thing.'

He makes his way to Brad's bar for breakfast, and has a talk. Brad considers the matter, makes some phone calls and comes up with a proposal. Harry settles down to wait.

After an hour a new customer walks in and shakes hands with Brad, who introduces him to Harry as Ginger, for obvious reasons. He has a thick New Zealand accent. After a brief conversation Harry hands over all his remaining cash and they leave. In the street a battered Citroën is waiting with the motor running, two passengers sitting in the back. Harry squeezes in beside them while Ginger gets in with the driver and they set off. He recognises some of the buildings along the way from their arrival two days before. When they reach the airport the driver takes them past the main car park at the terminal building and continues to a separate compound of small hangars and prefabricated buildings, where they get out. They wait in silence in the shade beside one of the buildings while Ginger goes inside. When he returns he leads them across the apron to the far side of a hangar where a small plane is waiting. They climb in, the four of them filling its tight seats, Ginger at the controls. When he's made his checks he turns to them. 'All right folks, all strapped in? First stop New Caledonia.'

It takes three hours for the Skyhawk to make this first leg to Nouméa, where they pause only long enough to refuel and make a comfort stop. When they reboard Ginger hands out bottles of water and packets of biscuits and sets off again across the great ocean towards the south-west. This stage is twice as long, and the sun is nearing the horizon as they drop down onto the little airstrip below Mount Lidgbird on Lord Howe Island. Again their stop is brief, and they are soon airborne again, heading directly towards the fading glow in the western sky. The other two passengers are soon asleep, but Harry remains awake, enveloped by the numbing drone of the engine and the dense blackness that surrounds them.

It's approaching midnight when the engine note changes and the plane eases forward into its descent. Harry makes out the glimmer of lights up ahead, becoming brighter and more distinct as they approach the New South Wales coast. Soon he can distinguish the pattern of streetlights below them, and the brighter gleam of the city centre over to their right. It recedes as they continue on, the lights becoming less dense. The other passengers struggle upright as Ginger warns them that they are about to land at Camden Airport in Sydney's south-west.

A big black Nissan Patrol is waiting beside the hangar, a woman behind the wheel. She kisses Ginger and they all pile in. One of the passengers asks to be dropped off in Liverpool, Harry and the other man opting for Central station. They separate when they reach the station, Harry crossing Elizabeth Street and striding up into Surry Hills. He walks past the end of his laneway, head down, surreptitiously checking the cars parked in the street. When he's satisfied he returns and moves quickly down the lane, keeping to the deep shadows. It's only when he's at the front door that he looks up and notices the sliver of light showing at the edge of the blind in the attic window high up beneath the roof.

He slides his key into the lock and eases the front door open. The interior is in darkness, silent. Harry closes the door and treads softly towards the stairs. At the first landing he pauses, hearing a sound, the thump of something heavy. He continues, hearing the tread of feet, the creak of floorboards as he gets closer to the attic. On the final flight he sees a line of light below the closed door. He bunches his fist, reaches for the doorhandle and barrels in. The figure at the desk gives a cry and turns. Harry stops short. 'Jenny!'

They hold each other tight, wordless. He looks around and sees the sleeping bag in the corner of the room, some clothes on hangers. Finally they sit down together and talk.

'This was the only place I could think to hide,' she says. 'I thought if they didn't actually break in here I'd be safe. I've become nocturnal—I creep downstairs in the middle of the night with the lights off and use the bathroom and get food, the way I used to do when I was blind. And…I just didn't want to run anymore. I wanted to come home, our home.'

'Yes. Nicole said you came here sometimes when you were staying with your mother.'

'That was different. You had left Sydney and no one knew where you were, and it occurred to me that if I was never to see you again I would have to explain to Abigail one day about the missing half of her family, who her father was, and her distinguished grandfather. And I realised that there were big gaps, things I knew little about, and I decided I should do at least a little research before everything in the house was disposed of.

'That's what I told myself anyway, although I think part of it was that I wanted to go back again to where we were happy together, before everything went so wrong.'

Harry says, 'Yes, I understand. I felt that too.'

'Is that why you came here tonight?'

He shrugs. 'I'm on the run too, Jen.'

She grips his hand more tightly. 'Why? What's happened?'

So he tells her about Grimshaw and Fogarty.

'Oh, Harry…You did this for me.'

'I had to stop those two. And I wanted the cops to realise just how wrong they were about you.'

'You told them my story?'

'I told Deb Velasco. She didn't believe it.'

'So you proved it could be done, and now she's after you.'

'That's about it.'

62

'You're exhausted.' Charity offers her a glass of whisky and sits by her side.

'I don't mind feeling tired. It's feeling things going out of control that I can't stand.'

'Do you want to talk about it?'

Deb shakes her head. 'I can't. That's part of the problem.'

Mid-afternoon, for the sake of thoroughness—for Deb is thorough—she phoned the duty inspector at the distant police station from which the two patrol cars originated. After a search of their logbooks he told her that no, the two cars had not been assigned on the nights in question. 'Do you know where they were?' she asked, and he replied, 'Here, locked up. Why?'

She told him that there was a discrepancy in their records and that someone on her team had obviously stuffed up. She mentioned the names and registered numbers of the cars' occupants as recorded by the officer on gate duty at Slater Park, and the inspector told her that one was HOD—hurt on duty, off sick with a broken pelvis—and the other was on overseas deployment in East Timor. Deb thanked him and apologised for wasting his time.

After several interruptions she got hold of the gate duty officers and questioned them about their shifts. Neither had a clear recollection of the uniformed occupants of the cars, although one thought the driver might have been unusually tall. There were no cameras operating at the gates on the first occasion, but one had been installed by the time of the second. She put in a request for the footage of that night, then thought for a long while before coming to a reluctant decision.

She went to see her boss, Superintendent Blake, and told him about the anomalies. He seemed more puzzled than surprised. 'So, how did you get onto this?'

She took a deep breath and told him it was Harry Belltree's suggestion.

'Belltree. I thought we were shot of him. How did he get involved?'

So she told him all about Harry, his claim that Fogarty framed Jenny, his being sectioned, charged, released. Blake's frown deepened with each new revelation. When she finished he was looking at her like someone wondering what to do with a disappointing piece of hardware.

He shook his head, irritated. 'Get him in here, Deb. I want to talk to him myself.'

Then she had to explain that unfortunately she couldn't do that, because Harry had left the country, current whereabouts unknown.

His expression darkened. 'You should have told me all this at the time. I want a full written report on what you've just told me. Every detail.'

'Yes, boss.'

'What's the situation with Fogarty?'

Deb explained that he was still in custody. He had refused to say anything further and his lawyer had applied for bail, which had been refused, decision to be reviewed after forty-eight hours to clarify points in the forensic evidence.

Charity squeezes her hand, whispers, 'Relax,' and Deb realises that her whole body has become rigid. She can't stop going over it again and again in her head.

'Sorry.'

'Is there nobody you can talk to?'

'No, no one.'

'What about your old boss, Bob the Job? He was a legend. I drove him a couple of times. He seemed very genuine, very sympathetic.'

Harry, Bob, damaged goods. She saw herself being tossed into the same sad bin of burnt-out cases. 'No, I don't think so. Doesn't matter, I'll sort it out.'

63

Sophie, her coat now glossy, torn ear healing, has learned some tricks while Kelly was away. She watches the pooch turning circles and rolling over to Wendy's commands, the two of them enormously pleased with themselves. In fact, Kelly realises, the bond between them has become much stronger than Sophie's bond with her. She doesn't mind, in fact is rather relieved. She claps and offers praise and rewards, which Wendy and Sophie accept with matching modesty.

'But you still haven't told me much about your trip,' Wendy says. 'I've always been fascinated by the land-diving on Pentecost, since I was at school back when the Queen visited. The locals put on a display for her, but it was the wrong time of year and the vines tied to the divers' ankles weren't flexible enough or something. One diver crashed and was killed. We discussed it in class—I think the teacher was making a point about the evils of colonialism, but we were just in awe at the Queen witnessing a horrible death.'

So Kelly tells her about Pastor Emanuel Dubouzet and his wife Lydia and the kava. Then, after another glass of wine, about poor

Pascaline Tamata and their hair-raising trip to Maturiki—scarier in the telling than it seemed at the time.

'Great background,' Wendy says. 'But what's the story?'

'Yeah,' Kelly says, suddenly glum. 'Good question.'

She tries to sketch the complexity of the situation with Harry, its improbable implications, without going into too much detail. After all they've been through together she trusts Wendy completely, but still, she has to be careful.

'You're not in love with him, are you?' Wendy demands.

'No, of course not!'

'Why are you blushing then?'

'Oh, shut up. The point is, the story is so outlandish, so scandalous, that it's only printable if I have overwhelming evidence that it's true, and there isn't any.'

'And you want to protect Harry. Do you want my opinion?'

'Okay.'

'You're a reporter, not a therapist. Harry can look after himself—go for the story.'

'I suppose you're right.'

'I am right. Impossible stories always have a loose thread somewhere. All you have to do is find the thread.'

'Wow. Who said that?'

'You did, long ago.'

Actually it was Bernie Westergard, her old boss at the *Bankstown Chronicle*. She remembers him wagging his finger at her when she was a rookie reporter. She smiles and resolves to pay him a visit one day.

'Well, I was absolutely right,' she says.

243

64

It had been eerie returning to the house. For three years after the crash left her blind, Jenny had lived there, rediscovering its geography by feel and memory and painful knocks. But when the inquest shook her from her torpor she returned there with her eyesight restored, and it was like being plunged back in time. Seeing it all again—the deep skirting boards, the burnt orange of the sofa, the gleam of light on a familiar vase—induced a deep nostalgic yearning for those days with Harry and his parents, before all the bad things happened. She realised how little she really knew about that family, beyond the public story. Her father-in-law had a little office in the attic, the judge's den, in which he worked in the evenings and at weekends. She had only been there a couple of times before the crash, and been impressed by the number of books, files, papers crammed into every corner. After the crash, when she and Harry moved in, she desperately wanted to explore it more thoroughly in the hope that something there might reveal why this had happened. But she couldn't see, and Harry, bitter with grief, avoided the place. Now at last she could look.

'And have you found anything?' Harry asks.

She shakes her head. Nothing pointing to a cause, or perhaps too much, for the judge had been involved in hundreds of cases during his career that might have provided motive. Certainly nothing in the way of a warning or threat—no abusive letters, no hints of anxiety or need for special care. It had come out of nowhere.

Harry says, 'So all we're left with is Palfreyman's stories, and his claim that he had proof that Konrad Nordlund killed his brother Martin, and that my father learned of it. But if Fogarty and Grimshaw didn't find it the day you disturbed them, they had plenty of time since to track it down. If that's what they were after.'

'The only confirmation of Palfreyman's story was that entry in your dad's diary on the ninth of August, 2002, the day Martin Nordlund's plane crashed. I'll show you.'

She goes to the pile of diaries on the side table and opens one of them to the date: *3:30 Norman Comfrey*. 'Just as Terry Palfreyman told me. It's the only part of his story I was able to check out.'

'He claimed that Martin Nordlund was at the same meeting,' Harry says, 'but we don't know that for a fact. Maybe we could check.'

'It's a long time ago, twelve years.'

65

Deb sleeps badly for a couple of hours, then wakes abruptly, lies rigid, head full of troubled thoughts about the Fogarty case. Beside her Charity breathes steadily in untroubled slumber.

Finally Deb slides out of bed and goes for a run through the darkened streets. She returns to the flat, showers, and discovers that Charity has washed and ironed her shirts.

When she gets to work at strike force HQ she finds the Slater Park entrance CCTV film downloaded on her computer, and scans through to the relevant time. She sees an over-exposed image of the patrol car caught in harsh lighting, deep shadows. The driver's face is visible—gaunt, bony. It looks very much like Eden Grimshaw.

Now what? She needs to think about how to approach this with Dick Blake, and leaves the office briefly to pick up a breakfast roll and coffee. She's eating, deep in thought, when she gets a message on her phone to get over to his office at Parramatta.

He's looking sombre, his big-boss-meeting tie on. 'Sit down, Deb. I had a long session yesterday with our assistant commissioner and Tom Bellamy, head of organised crime, to review your report.

They've both known Ken Fogarty over many years, and I must say they were utterly incredulous about what you had to say. Fogarty's record is impeccable, twenty-seven years in the force without a stain, two silver medals, regularly cleared in all the psychometric and other annual tests without a whisper of doubt. Grimshaw may be a different matter—his record is much more patchy—but they refused to believe that Fogarty was capable of what he's being accused of. And where's the motive, Deb? Why would an exemplary officer go so completely off the rails? He has a harmonious family life, high standing in his community, no significant debts or health issues that anyone's aware of.

'But both he and Grimshaw are in a challenging area of work in organised crime. Tom advised us that they're currently involved in an investigation into large-scale money laundering in Sydney for Colombian drug syndicates. Those people will stop at nothing, believe me, and it's entirely feasible that what we're seeing is a plot to neutralise two officers who were getting too close to the heat. And of course this whole business has been thrown into confusion by Belltree's maverick muddying of the waters.'

Deb tries to say something but Blake holds up his hand. 'If you're still not convinced, we now have solid proof that Fogarty is innocent.'

He passes a report across the table.

'Stan Felder gave this to me last night, Deb. Ken Fogarty's phone records for the night of Grimshaw's murder. You'll see the highlighted entries. Ken used his phone several times during the period when the intruder in the cap and jacket was inside Grimshaw's building, including a conversation with the duty officer at organised crime. Now, records show that all of those calls were made from a location at or around Ken's home in Castle Hill, forty kilometres away from Bondi.' Blake leans across and taps the report with his finger to make the point. 'Ken Fogarty was nowhere near the crime scene that night, Deb. He's in the clear.'

He sits back and considers her with a sympathetic gaze that makes her squirm. 'You are a first-class homicide detective, Deb. Extremely conscientious and self-sacrificing in pursuing your duties—perhaps too much so. I've been looking at the log details for the past couple of weeks, and the number of hours you've put in has been extraordinary. Quite excessive. And then there's the pressure with such a high-profile case as Slater Park. And not content with that, you drove yourself on to become involved in Stan Felder's Bondi case, and even, I understand, the Palfreyman case out at Blackheath.' He shakes his head. 'I blame myself for not paying attention to this sooner.

'Well, the assistant commissioner has suggested, and I concur, that you have a well-earned break. You're due three weeks' leave, and I want you to take it.'

'Boss, that just isn't feasible at this stage of Strike Force Spider…'

Again the hand. 'None of us are indispensable, Deb. It's only a job. No point in destroying your health over it. Brief Xavier Costas to take over Spider during the course of the day and then go.'

His phone begins ringing. He picks it up and nods for her to leave. She returns to her desk head down, thinking of the arguments she should have thrown at him when she had the chance. When she sits down she realises she's still holding the schedule of Fogarty's calls, and, mind elsewhere, runs her eyes over them again. She notices that, apart from the call to organised crime, he made one other call that night after his wife Brenda said she went to bed. It lasted from 23:10 till 23:56. Looking back over the list, which covers a week's phone activity, she sees that number recurring every day and often for extended periods. It belongs to someone living within a kilometre of Fogarty, a woman by the name of Michelle Crabbe. Deb checks her on the databases and the internet: forty-two, unmarried, no children, short auburn hair, unblemished driving record, a member of the same Uniting church that the Fogartys attend, address in a rented house shared with her mother Caroline.

Deb digs a little deeper: Caroline has been on an invalid pension for twenty-three years, following a car accident in which her husband, Michelle's father, was killed. After the accident Michelle abandoned a degree course at UTS and has had a succession of short-term jobs.

66

Kelly, back at work, catches up with what's been going on. There don't seem to be any new developments in the police investigation of the Palfreyman murder, but three members of the public have left messages for her saying that they know the mystery woman the police are looking for and how much would the paper pay for their story? She can find no references to Harry or Jenny Belltree, which she takes to be a good sign. There's an email from Husam Roshed suggesting a meeting. She calls him, leaving a message.

In her pocket her fingers close around the flash drive from Maturiki once again. She's unsure what to do. She spoke in general terms to one of the IT guys on the staff, who said he'd have to see the device to know if he could get into it, but she didn't know him that well and she hesitated. What if he found scandalous pictures of Konrad Nordlund, a part owner of the *Times*, and reported it to management? How could she explain where it had come from?

There have been several shootings and a kidnapping in western Sydney overnight, and she goes out to Parramatta to attend a police press briefing at which the wife of the missing man, a known drug dealer, makes a tearful appeal for his safe return. Fat chance, Kelly thinks. A text comes in from Roshed inviting her to come to Parliament House 'to see something interesting'. She confirms and drives back to the city.

Roshed is waiting for her in the lobby at Macquarie Street, and leads her quickly through to the exhibition hall in the heart of the building, with its display of important events in parliamentary history and stories of members who served in the Great War. He seems slightly furtive, checking over his shoulder as she examines the exhibits, wondering what this is all about. When he's satisfied that there's no one else around he hustles her down a corridor to a door marked *Meeting Room 3*, and takes her inside. The room is windowless, completely dark, and Kelly has a moment of panic as he closes and locks the door behind her. She gropes for her phone, but then he finds the switches and light floods the room. She sees seats and tables arranged around a central space in which stands a huge architectural model.

'Take a good look,' he murmurs, and they step closer. 'You see the river frontage over there? The main road on this side? The old buildings preserved in the centre?'

She slowly takes it in, the new buildings in pristine white, tall towers set in a green woodland, the small cluster of unpainted timber blocks representing the old buildings.

'It's huge,' she says. 'A whole city. It's not...?'

'Yes, it's Slater Park.'

'But it's so big.'

'The biggest vacant urban site left in Sydney. For a developer, worth killing for.'

'What's it doing here?'

'Last night the developers from Ozdevco—Maram Mansur and Konrad Nordlund supported by some technical guys—gave a presentation. It was supposed to be secret—selected government and opposition front bench members only.'

'Maram Mansur was there?'

'Yes, looking super-fit and brimming with confidence, I'm told. Nordlund looking tragic over the loss of his niece. A great double-act.'

'How did you hear all this?'

'It was supposed to be secret, but this is Parliament House. By this morning the whole place was buzzing like an excited beehive. I first got wind of it from the porters who helped carry this lot in. Then I cornered one of the crossbenchers and he told me what he'd heard. The premier is going to make a statement in parliament this afternoon. I'm told they've given the scoop to your rivals—photographs, images, Ozdevco interview.'

'Can I take a picture?'

'Go ahead. Just don't tell them how you got it.'

'Right.' She walks round, taking a dozen shots on her camera. 'What's the premier going to announce, do you know?'

'That they've agreed to sell the site to Ozdevco, I imagine. What else could it be?'

'What time?'

'Two-thirty.'

'I'll be there.'

67

Deb sits in her car, staring at the lavender front door, trying to bat down the jagged thoughts of *breakdown* and *wild goose chase* that keep popping up in her head.

A good five minutes pass before she opens the car door and walks across the street. The car in the driveway has a disabled parking sticker on its windscreen, and there's a steel ramp covering the step outside the front door. She rings the doorbell.

Michelle Crabbe opens the door. From inside Deb can hear the sound of voices on the TV. She says, keeping her voice low and serious, 'Michelle? I'm a colleague of Ken's.' She sees the swelling in the other woman's belly. Six months, she guesses, maybe seven.

Alarm flares on the woman's face. 'Oh! Is something wrong?'

A voice, frail but penetrating, calls from inside the house, 'Michelle? Who is it?'

'It's nothing, Mum.' She steps out into the porch and draws the door shut behind her. 'Is Ken all right? I haven't heard from him for days. I've been so worried.'

'He's had a few problems, Michelle, and I thought I should come to reassure you that it's going to be okay, but it might be a while before he can contact you himself.'

Deb, feeling oddly detached, watches the panic spread across the woman's face, her body gestures.

'What sort of problems? It's not about the money, is it?'

Deb gives her an awkward, sympathetic smile and shrugs.

Michelle hesitates. 'What, he confides in you?'

'He's been under a lot of pressure. Well, you know that. He hides it pretty well, but underneath...'

'Yes, yes.'

'One time he said something I picked up on. I felt I recognised the situation, something I'd experienced myself, and I told him so, and he opened up a little. No one else knows—well, except for Eden. He knew.'

'Eden...What happened to Eden? The police have been here, questioning me, searching. They wouldn't tell me why.'

'That would have been the homicide squad, investigating Eden's murder. They poke into everything. It's what they do.'

'They surely can't suspect Ken?'

'They suspect everyone.'

'But they must know that he's an honourable man.'

'Yes, I'm sure they do. But even honourable men do desperate things under pressure.'

Michelle puts a hand to her mouth, horrified, as if she's experienced a revelation. 'It's me. It's my fault. I've done this to him.'

'He's very fond of you, Michelle.'

'Yes, I know. But I've been selfish, wanting him so much.' Her hand drops to her belly, as if in explanation.

'You only get one life.'

'That's what he says!' A desperate smile. 'He said that it was only a little job, a private job, and then we'd be able to get everything sorted, and be free. But I was worried about Eden. I wished

254

he wasn't involved. Sometimes he's so…unreliable, out of control. I could tell that Ken felt that way too.'

'Yes, exactly.'

Michelle turns as they hear a cry from inside the house. 'I'll have to go.'

'Okay, Michelle. Don't worry, you'll be hearing from him soon.'

'Thank you, thank you so much for coming. Please, try to make them understand. Ken is a good man, an honourable man.'

68

The duty inspector is talking with one of the sergeants in the front lobby when she arrives. He tells her that he hasn't heard from homicide this morning, but that Fogarty is with his lawyer at present. Deb asks him to inform them that she wants to interview Fogarty again.

'Who's his lawyer?' she asks.

The inspector screws up his nose. 'Nathaniel Horn. Bad look for a cop, eh? Nathaniel Horn as your brief.' Deb asks if he can spare the time to sit in on the interview.

When they come into the room Deb notices the changes in Fogarty, his slack posture, pallid colouring, abstracted look.

As soon as Deb starts recording and makes the usual introductory statements, Horn says bluntly, 'I should say straight away that I've advised Chief Inspector Fogarty to answer no more questions.'

Deb ignores him, staring silently at Fogarty until he meets her eyes, and then says quietly, 'I've spoken to Michelle.'

Fogarty looks at her for a long moment, then he sags, and his head drops.

Horn, puzzled, says, 'What's that? What did you say?'

Deb is silent, waiting. Finally Fogarty sits up straight, as if with a huge effort of will, and says, 'I want to make a statement.'

Horn cuts in sharply, 'No, no, Ken. Do as I say.'

Fogarty doesn't look at him and says to Deb, 'This man does not represent me. I want him to leave.'

There are further protests from Horn, but Fogarty sits impassive until the inspector escorts the lawyer out of the room.

When he returns, Deb says, 'Go ahead.'

Fogarty takes a deep breath.

'Back in early September I was approached by Detective Sergeant Grimshaw about doing a private job together. It sounded simple, tracking down a document, something we've done in the course of our duties many times. The document had been stolen from a big company and contained information that could hurt them commercially. The thief was known, and I understood that it would involve entering his premises illegally for the purposes of a search, but there would be no repercussions because the document itself had been obtained illegally.

'The thief was a man called Terry Palfreyman and we used police resources to track him down to a cottage in Blackheath. When we reconnoitred the area we discovered that he appeared to be very friendly with a woman who was his next-door neighbour. On Monday the thirteenth of October we watched them going into a pub in Blackheath in the late afternoon, and when they ordered drinks we decided to take the opportunity to search Palfreyman's house.

'But it went wrong. Palfreyman came back much sooner than we'd expected and walked right in on us. Eden reacted quickly and violently, grabbing him and forcing him to the ground. He tried to get Palfreyman to tell us where the document was, applying some sort of wrist or finger lock that made him scream with pain. I was trying to tell him to take it easy—the bloke was making too much

257

noise. I was over the other side of the room, near the window, and something caught my eye. I turned and saw the woman outside, staring in at us. She saw me, turned and bolted.'

Fogarty's breathing has become ragged, sweat gleaming on his forehead, and the inspector gets to his feet and fetches him a bottle of water from the side table. Fogarty takes a few gulps and resumes.

'I yelled at Eden and ran out after the woman, who disappeared into the bush. I went after her—she was heading away from town, towards the cliffs overlooking the Kanimbla Valley—but I lost her, because the scrub was getting thicker and the light was fading.

'I turned back to the house and when I got there I couldn't believe what I saw. Palfreyman was on the floor with a knife sticking out of his chest, blood everywhere, Eden standing over him. I said, "Christ, what happened?" and he said, "You get her?" I said no, and told him how it would be hard to catch her, and he said, "Better be quick then."

'I said again, "What the hell happened?" and he replied, calm as anything, "She did this, mate. They had a fight…" He reached down and pulled Palfreyman's trousers down to his knees. "Tried to rape her and she turned on him. We need to fix up the evidence quick and disappear. Problem solved."

'He told me to go fetch the car while he went around laying an evidence trail between the two cottages. When he was satisfied we drove off. By then it was dark.

'I accept full responsibility for my part in this. That's all I have to say.'

Silence. Deb consults the notes she's been making. 'Just a couple of points I'd like to clarify. Who was the client who wanted you to trace the document?'

'I don't know. Eden didn't say.'

'Why did you accept the job, knowing it would involve illegal entry?'

'I…personal reasons.'

'How much were they paying you?'

Fogarty bites his lip. 'A hundred thousand.'

'Each?'

'Yes.'

'And did you find it, this document?'

'No.'

'Did you know the woman who saw you through the window?'

Fogarty hesitates, gives a reluctant nod. 'Yes, I'd seen her before. I believe she was the wife of Detective Sergeant Harry Belltree, who served in my command in Newcastle last year.'

'You were surprised?'

'Gobsmacked. I couldn't believe it.'

'And she recognised you?'

'I assumed so.'

'Did you tell Eden?'

'Yes.'

'And what did he say?'

'He said…we'd have to find her.'

'And?'

Fogarty shakes his head, looks away.

'And kill her?' Deb insists.

'Yes,' he says, voice barely audible.

'And did you find her?'

'No. When we heard that your prime suspect was a woman of her description we thought we were in the clear. I heard no more about her.'

'Last Friday night, late, towards midnight. Where were you?'

'Friday? At home, with Brenda.'

'We have you in a patrol car with Eden Grimshaw.'

'Friday?' Fogarty looks puzzled. 'No, no. What would I be doing in a patrol car? I was off duty. Check it. Last Friday Brenda and I went to see a show at the local club—some girls doing a take-off of the Supremes. Then home and bed.'

259

'Where was Grimshaw?'

'I've no idea. Look, I've made my statement. I was an accessory after the fact in the murder of Terry Palfreyman. That's all I have to say.'

'One more question, Ken. Did you kill Eden Grimshaw?'

'No, I did not.'

After he's taken away, the inspector turns to Deb. 'Well…did you see that coming?'

Deb shakes her head, trying to think it through. 'No.'

'Why did he confess?'

She hesitates, then says, 'Maybe because he's an honourable man.' Under the circumstances it seems an absurd thing to say, and yet she thinks it may be true.

69

Harry checks the brass plate on the wall of the sandstone building, goes inside and takes a lift up to the eighth floor. The receptionist shows him to a small meeting room and offers him a drink, which he refuses. After a moment a plump middle-aged man comes in.

'Mr Belltree, good morning. I'm George Schwarz. My father was the Schwarz in McKensey, Schwarz and Comfrey, the founding partners. I knew your father distantly—he addressed us on our graduation. A great man. How can I help you?'

'It's good of you to see me, Mr Schwarz. I was hoping to discuss something that involved my father and your Mr Comfrey. I believe they had a meeting on the day that Mr Comfrey was killed in that plane crash.'

'Did they indeed? I didn't know that. My office was two floors down at the time.'

'I believe it's possible that Martin Nordlund, the pilot of the plane, was at the same meeting.'

'Really? So what were you after?'

'I was hoping to speak to someone who was there.'

'Oh...Twelve years...My father might have been involved, but he died last year. Senior clerks?' He ponders, shakes his head. 'No. The other partner at the time was Hugh McKensey. He might remember something, I suppose. But he's retired now.'

'Would there be a record of the meeting?'

'Did it concern ongoing litigation?'

'I'm afraid I don't know.'

'We've been computerised and recomputerised since then, so...' He shrugs. 'We do maintain an archive of paper records, but space is limited and we cull ruthlessly. I think Hugh might be your best bet. I'll give you his number.'

Harry rings it and McKensey agrees to see him. He is currently working on a project, he explains, in the State Library just a couple of blocks away, and they arrange to meet in the café. Harry spots him at a table with a cup of coffee and a small pile of history books.

'Danny's boy, eh?' McKensey scrutinises him with a smile. 'How interesting. Take a seat. Let me get you a coffee.'

Harry thanks him and explains that he has been going through his father's papers and came across a reference to a meeting with Norman Comfrey on the day he died in the plane crash.

'Aha, thinking of a biography of Danny, eh? Excellent idea. Tricky, though. Wouldn't write it yourself, would you? Bit of a challenge to write objectively about your old man, eh? I see George W. Bush has had a go. Wonder what that'll be like.'

'I'm not sure what to do, but I've been going through his stuff, trying to decide what to keep, and I was intrigued by that reference.'

'Yes, a tragic day. I remember it quite well, of course, the last time we saw poor Norman. Devastated us all, his family, the firm.'

'Were you at the meeting?'

'No, that was just Norman, the judge and Martin Nordlund, who piloted the plane.'

'Norman was Martin's solicitor?'

'Yes, the Nordlund family solicitor. I understand Nathaniel

Horn has taken over that role since.' McKensey barely hides his grimace.

'Do you know what the meeting was about?'

'No idea. Some Nordlund family matter, I suppose.'

'Why would my father be involved?'

'Norman knew him quite well. I assume he was seeking his advice on some legal question. I remember seeing your father that afternoon when he arrived for the meeting. We had a bit of a chat. Norman and Martin were delayed, you see, over lunch, and I had to hold the fort. Let me see, what else can I remember...?' He ponders for a moment. 'I think we just talked about personal matters—yes, both our wives were having back problems or something like that. When Norman and Martin finally arrived I had the impression that the wine had been flowing at lunch. Oh...' He stops with a frown. 'I'm sure not enough to affect Martin's capacity to fly that plane. I didn't mention it at the inquest, and neither did Bernard.'

'Bernard Nordlund?'

'Yes, he'd been at the lunch. I remember one of them mentioned it when they arrived. Then I had to go off to an appointment of my own, and I never saw poor Norman again. I think about it quite often, his remains still lying somewhere out there in the bush.' He sighs.

'The next day, when we heard, your father called me. He was very distressed, of course. He came into the office to commiserate, and we met up several times in the following weeks, at the memorial service and elsewhere.'

'And he didn't say what they had discussed?'

'No, though I remember he did ask if Norman had left any record of the meeting, any notes to be typed up. We searched, but there was nothing.'

Later, with Jenny, Harry says, 'We keep meeting a blank wall. And yet Terry Palfreyman claimed to have discovered something incriminating. What did he call it? A dossier. How had he got hold of that?'

'I know, I keep wondering that. Did he really have something to show me, or was it all talk?'

'Well, Fogarty and Grimshaw must have believed he did.'

'Yes, and presumably they didn't find it after I disturbed them. So they've probably been back again to have a further look, wouldn't you think, after the police finished?'

'You'd think so, but it would be risky for them. They wouldn't know whether you'd got word to the cops.'

'Maybe we should go back and take a look.'

'Yes,' Harry says, 'that's what I'm thinking.'

70

The message comes in as Deb is sitting with Superintendent Blake in his office, working out how best to handle this. He lifts up the phone, listens, then turns, eyes wide, to stare at Deb, and even before he murmurs, 'How?' she knows what's coming.

He says, 'Thank you,' rings off and says to her, 'Fogarty, found in his cell. Ripped up his T-shirt to make a noose. The bugger's dead.'

A long silence.

Deb says, 'Who's going to tell the women, Brenda and Michelle?'

'Don't know.'

'I'll do it.'

71

Kelly takes a seat in the press gallery in the chamber of the lower house. Below her the members' benches are packed. A government minister is reading from a document in a monotonous drone, but no one is listening. Heads are down, whispering, nodding, waiting.

Her eyes roam over the half-empty visitors' galleries and come to a stop at the figure of a man in a grey suit, sitting motionless, eyes fixed on the scene below, his hair and complexion pale, almost anaemic. Konrad Nordlund. Kelly takes a picture.

The droning voice comes to an end and the whispering stops abruptly as the familiar figures of the premier and deputy premier stride into the chamber. The premier pauses to say something to the speaker, then takes his place on the government front bench. The speaker announces that the premier will make a statement. He rises to his feet and speaks in a firm, steady voice. After intensive and thorough negotiations, he says, the government has reached an agreement with a major development consortium to put an end to the scandalous and tragic neglect of a major public asset. Subject to strict planning guidelines, which will ensure that the public interest is safeguarded, Slater Park will be transformed from its present pitiful state into a vibrant new community. It will be designed and constructed to the highest standards, following international best practice.

As he pauses to let this sink in, applause breaks out from the government benches. He raises his hand and continues. At the end of business today the consortium will present its proposal, prepared by prestigious international architects, at a briefing for all members of the house, to be followed by a press conference. He is also pleased to advise the house that the Nordlund family, who have suffered directly as a result of the recent tragic events at Slater Park, will be represented in the development consortium. He informs the house that Mr Konrad Nordlund is present in the visitors' gallery.

Heads turn towards the gallery and clapping breaks out again, this time on both sides of chamber, rising to a crescendo, with cries of 'Bravo!' and 'Hear, hear', members getting to their feet. Konrad Nordlund also stands and bows his head in acknowledgment of the acclaim.

Kelly takes more pictures with the zoom lens she picked up at the *Times*. Should the headline be *Extraordinary Scenes in State Parliament*? Or maybe something less boring: *The Slaughter of Slater Park*? On the strength of Kelly's scoop—the photo of the development model—Catherine Meiklejohn has given her the lead story, which will go online as soon as she's written it. Brendon Pyle will also have a piece on the bloody history of the park, while the property and environment desks will assess the proposals.

Kelly hurries out of Parliament House and finds a seat at a café nearby where she rapidly composes her piece and sends it through to the office with a note to her editor. Catherine responds quickly, approving the article and asking her to cover the premier's press conference. A call comes in from Husam Roshed, asking if she wants to meet beforehand, somewhere they won't be seen together. He suggests the Art Gallery of New South Wales, across the park, the nineteenth-century Australian room. She walks over there and takes a seat facing Streeton's *Fire's On*, the heroic scene of blasting a tunnel for the railway to the Blue Mountains in the blazing summer heat.

'That's the real Australia, isn't it?' a voice says behind her. 'Anglo pioneers grappling with nature, before they let us wogs come in and spoil it all.'

Kelly turns as Roshed sits down beside her. 'Are you going to spoil it all, Husam?'

'Given half a chance. You heard of the Haddad boys?'

Kelly thinks. Haddad, the name's familiar. 'Hakim Haddad was one of the Crows, wasn't he?'

'Their sergeant-at-arms, shot dead in the car park of the Swagman Hotel last year. His sister had two boys, Amal and Khalil, idolised their uncle.'

'Okay. So?'

'You asked me about Kylie McVea, sister of Frank Capp, vice-president of the Crows. Well, according to a well-placed source, namely my mum, Amal and Khalil Haddad now work for Kylie, somewhere out west, on a property or something.'

'Doggylands Dog Breeders, Boarding Kennels, yes, I've been there.'

'Really? Dog breeders? I'd have thought those boys would have been more at home pushing dope in a Kings Cross nightclub.'

'Right. Well, thanks for the tip.' She's not sure what she can do with it. Then she remembers the flash drive in her pocket and a thought strikes her. 'Do you know any tech whizz-kids who could open a pin-protected flash drive?' She takes it out and shows him.

He turns it over in his hand, examining it. 'I might. What's the deal?'

'I'm not sure of the provenance, but it may contain something—emails, photos, I don't know—relating to the Nordlunds.

268

Thing is, not knowing what's on it, I don't want to give it to anyone who's going to blab or make copies, see?'

'Right,' he says. 'Absolute discretion. I think I can do that. Leave it with me.'

72

The train leaves the plains of western Sydney and climbs up into the Blue Mountains. A perfect spring day, blue-domed, sparkling. At each of the small towns—Wentworth Falls, Leura, Katoomba, Medlow Bath—the passengers on the platforms are cheerful, untroubled, and Jenny begins to relax. But when they get off at Blackheath and make their way through the familiar streets the sense of dread returns. What if they're there, waiting?

They walk quickly through to the western area of the town and follow the road into the bush, a few houses visible to left and right. Wary now, they come to the turning onto the dirt road, and Jenny stops, gasps. Ahead there is nothing but trees, the two cottages gone.

'What happened?'

Harry is pacing on ahead and she hurries to catch up. As they get closer to the site she begins to make out the blackened, burnt-out ruins.

'Someone's torched them both.' Harry walks over towards the fallen metal roof sheets, the charred stumps, peering into the remains. There is a strong, acrid smell of burning hanging in the still air, no sound of birdsong.

Jenny circles around her cottage, making out the remains of the mattress on which she slept, the kitchen sink, then moves to Harry standing beside the ruins of Terry Palfreyman's place.

'Well,' he says, 'they did a pretty good job. If there ever was a document hidden here it's gone now.'

Near the place where the back door would have been, Jenny recognises a pile of cracked and blackened wine bottles, the cardboard box in which they were stacked now disintegrated around them. 'In vino veritas,' she says quietly. Harry goes carefully into the ruin, his feet crackling on shattered glass, dust and fumes rising around him. 'Hopeless,' he calls back over his shoulder. 'It must have been quite a blaze.'

Jenny is still staring at the bottles, recollecting Terry's voice, his impish tone of conspiracy. The image of him kneeling on the floor begging for mercy. Her heart is pumping and she lifts her head, staring up into the cobalt blue sky, trying to breathe.

Harry is by her side. 'You all right?' he asks. 'We shouldn't have come.' He takes hold of her and begins to turn her away.

She says, 'The bottles, Harry. Check the bottles.'

'What?'

'Please.'

She watches him kick at the pile of blackened bottles, some shattered, then pick his way through to the more intact ones below. He straightens, holding one up to the light. Through the mottled green glass she can make out something inside. He tells her to turn away, and she hears the sharp crack as he hits it against a brick. She turns back and sees him picking among the pieces of glass.

'A message in a bottle,' Harry says, carefully drawing out a blackened roll of paper. As he lifts it up it disintegrates into charred flakes, crumbling between his fingers. 'Damn,' he murmurs, 'the whole thing's burnt through.' He's left with just one barely legible brown fragment, a piece of what seems to be the cover page, which had been coiled tight in the centre of the roll. He reads: *Record of interview with Joseph Doyle, signed and witnessed by Terry Palfreyman, 10 September 2014.*

'Terry's dossier,' he says. 'It did exist. But not anymore.'

Jenny stares at it for a moment, then says, 'Let's get out of here, Harry.' She hears the shake in her voice. This place is too silent, too sinister.

He takes hold of her arm again and together they walk quickly back towards town.

'You okay?' he asks. 'Do you want to stop and have a drink?'

She shakes her head. 'People will recognise me here. Let's just get on the train.'

The station is deserted. They wait far down the platform and when their train arrives find a quiet corner of the carriage. As it continues on its journey, winding through native bush and small townships, Jenny says, 'In vino veritas—Terry was telling the truth after all. He did that interview while Amber was at Maturiki, and he never had the chance to tell her.'

'And Joseph Doyle is the key,' Harry says. 'But we have no idea where to find him. I wish we could have seen his letter to my father that Amber discovered. There might have been something in it to tell us more.'

'It could be at Kramfors, don't you think? Amber probably hid it there, somewhere private, personal to her, where other people wouldn't come across it.' Jenny pictures the family homestead in Cackleberry Valley. 'It's a big place. It'd be hard to find anything hidden there, even if we could get in. I'd like to see it again, the valley and Cackleberry Mountain. When we were there last year I had to imagine it all, hearing and smelling it, but unable to see.'

73

Something Brenda Fogarty says sticks in Deb's mind. She goes to see her accompanied by a mature woman constable who looks as if she's done this sort of thing many times. After the shock, the confusion, the disbelief, Brenda, choking through the tears, frames the question. Why? Why did he do it?

'We're not entirely sure at the moment,' Deb says. 'We believe he'd got himself mixed up in something that he shouldn't, something he was ashamed of.'

'Eden Grimshaw,' Brenda says bitterly. 'I always knew he was trouble. I warned Ken often enough.'

They wait until her sister arrives to be with her. As the two officers are leaving, Brenda says, 'Eden made a remark last time we saw him, something about his evil little mate, and I could see it made Ken unhappy. I said to Eden, maybe you should watch yourself, and he said, don't worry, I have insurance tucked away, nice and safe. I don't know what he meant by that.'

Neither does Deb, but when she gets back to the station she contacts the leader of the crime scene team and asks for an update.

A thorough search of Eden's flat has yielded nothing beyond some doubtful pills and a bit more cash, both at the lab for tests. Deb asks him to go back there with her for one final search.

'What are we looking for?' he asks when they enter the flat.

'I don't know. Grimshaw said he had insurance tucked away somewhere safe. It sounded like something physical. A photograph? A letter? A memory stick? I really don't know.'

They work their way through the small flat checking everything that might have been missed, anywhere a cop might hide something small. They unscrew the light switches and power sockets, tap the skirtings, strip the backs off the TV, refrigerator and microwave, dismantle light fittings, and find nothing.

'What about his car?' Deb says.

'It was downstairs in the parking bay in the basement car park. Been taken to the workshops for examination. I'll make sure they do a good job.'

'Let's go down and have a look.'

They take the lift to the basement and he shows her the empty parking bay. Bare concrete floor, wall, column and ceiling. Sprinkler pipes and heads running under the ceiling, a bulkhead light and conduit on the wall. Deb goes over to the light, pokes the back of it with her screwdriver and snags a bit of plastic. She teases it out, a small plastic packet. Inside is a folded envelope, and inside that a fifty-dollar note. They stare at it, then the man says, 'What's that smudge?' He takes out a magnifier and peers closely. 'Looks like a blood smear, with a fingerprint in it.'

Deb wonders how that would work. And then it comes to her— victim's blood, killer's print. That would do the trick. That would be insurance. 'This is priority,' she says. 'For God's sake don't lose it.'

74

It takes a while to track down Bernard Nordlund. The faculty office thought he might be away at a conference, but eventually it transpires that he's working at home. They give Harry a phone number, and when he rings, Bernard invites him to come round. Harry remembers Amber describing her uncle's home as an art deco flat in a block in Potts Point, but the description seems too modest for what he finds there. Spacious, immaculate and filled with furniture, artworks and fabrics of the 1930s, it looks as fresh as it must have done when first bought by Bernard's grandfather Axel. He welcomes Harry and takes him through to the lounge room with its view over Sydney Harbour, only partially spoiled by more recent developments, and offers him a cocktail from a shaker that once belonged to F. Scott Fitzgerald.

'No really,' Bernard insists, 'I bought it at an auction in New York.'

Harry refuses all the same. Bernard chuckles. 'Ignore me, I'm just a dilettante. And I take comfort in retreating to the past when faced with today's barbarisms. Poor Amber. Do the police have any ideas at all?'

'I'm afraid I don't know. I'm persona non grata at the moment.'

'A shame. Amber thought very highly of you. So how can I help you?'

'It's probably nothing, but I've been going through my father's old papers and I discovered a reference to him meeting with your brother Martin at your then family solicitor's offices in Sydney. The date was rather significant, the ninth of August 2002.'

Bernard's face, usually animated, suddenly becomes still. 'Indeed significant,' he says finally. 'The day my brother died.'

'Yes, and I've been wondering what their meeting could have been about.'

Bernard shrugs. 'A legal matter, I suppose. Your father was an expert.'

'One of the surviving partners told me that you had lunch that day with Martin and the solicitor Norman Comfrey, who also died, and I wondered if they talked about the meeting with my father.'

'Did I? To tell the truth, the terrible news from Kramfors drove everything else out of mind. I really can't remember.'

'So, did my father know your family?'

Another shrug. 'In those circles, Sydney is a very small town. I'm sure he must have come across members of our family from time to time, along with most other families of significance.'

'Yes, I suppose you're right. Well, I'm sorry to have interrupted you.'

'Not at all.' As they go out to the front hall, Bernard says, 'It sounds as if you too have been looking into the past, Harry. As someone who's made a career of it, I should warn you that it's beguiling but dangerous. Better to look to the future. Remember that freedom is the recognition of necessity.'

'Sounds profound. Who said that, Abraham Lincoln?'

Bernard laughs. 'Friedrich Engels. I understand your wife has recovered her sight, a wonderful boon. You should concentrate on enjoying it.'

Harry nods, then says, 'Oh, by the way, do you remember someone called Joseph Doyle from that time, twelve years ago? He may have been connected with your family.'

'Joseph Doyle?' Bernard looks vague. 'I don't think so. Why?'

'Oh, I just came across a letter he sent to my father. Wondered who he was. Doesn't matter.'

Harry returns to Surry Hills and approaches the lane carefully, cap and dark glasses on, head down. When he's satisfied it's safe, he goes quickly to the front door and lets himself in.

'Hi.' He kisses Jenny, still feeling that little moment of surprise that she can now see him. 'I got some groceries on the way.' He tells her about his meetings, and the slightly odd, evasive tone of the conversation with Bernard. 'I asked him if he knew of Joseph Doyle and he said not, but I don't think he was telling the truth.'

'Tomorrow,' Jenny says. 'Tomorrow we should go back to Kramfors.'

75

'I know it's late, Bob.' Deb hesitates, thinking she may be making a mistake. 'Just wondered if I could call by and have a yarn.'

'Now?'

She imagines him in bed, groping for his glasses to see what the time is.

'We could leave it till tomorrow.'

'No, no. Now's fine.'

'Fifteen minutes?'

'Sure.'

Long enough for him to wash his face and get dressed. She's sure now that this is a bad idea.

She picks up a bottle of wine on the way, and when he opens the front door and sees it he says, 'Going to be a long night, is it, Deb?'

'A peace offering for disturbing you.'

As he leads her through to the living room she catches odours from the direction of the kitchen. 'That smells good. What did you have for dinner?'

'Beef cacciatore. New recipe. I suppose you made do with a burger?'

'Cold pizza.'

He chuckles. 'Want to try it? I can heat some up for you.'

So they go to the kitchen and she sits at the table feeling like a little girl being indulged by a doting uncle. She pulls herself together and pours the wine. He puts a plate down in front of her.

She picks up a fork and takes a bite. 'Oh, that's really good.'

He beams at her as she wolfs it down. 'So, how have you been, Deb? How's things at the pointy end?'

'Bit chaotic.'

'Apropos?'

'Apropos Harry Belltree.' She wipes her mouth with a napkin and takes a gulp of wine. 'Ken Fogarty has confessed in interview to murdering Terry Palfreyman.'

'Jeez. I'd have liked to have been at that one.'

'Be my guest.' Deb calls the video file up on her iPad and hands it over to him.

When the recording's finished Bob shakes his head. 'Why did he confess?'

'I think he'd just had enough. They took him back to his cell and he hanged himself.'

'Dear God.'

'Thing is, we're inclined to believe what he said. And if that's the case, Jenny Belltree's innocent. It'll have to be cleared through the big bosses, but I think we should tell her she's off the hook. Trouble is, I can't. We don't know where she is, or Harry. For all we know they're on the run together. Could be anywhere.'

'Maybe that's the best thing for them.'

'Maybe, but I'd like them at least to know it's safe to come home if they want to. Their kid's still here, Bob, with Jenny's sister. They're bound to try and get her out.'

'Have you told the sister?'

'No, neither her nor the other person Harry might be in touch with—Kelly Pool at the *Times*. We're not making this public yet—maybe never, given the reaction from above. I can't see the commissioner fronting the cameras on this one, can you? She's not happy.'

'Well, I don't think I can help you, Deb. Harry hasn't been in touch with me and I have no means of contacting him. But I could have an informal word with Kelly and the sister, in case he contacts them.'

'Thanks. They wouldn't believe it from me, anyway. They'd think it was a trick.'

Bob frowns, points to the iPad. 'What was that about Fogarty being in a patrol car with Grimshaw?'

'As well as claiming Fogarty was responsible for Palfreyman's murder, Harry also suggested to me that he was mixed up in the Slater Park killings. He claimed that the only way the killers of the last two victims could have got the bodies into the park, under our noses, was in an authorised vehicle.'

'Smart,' Bob says.

'Ridiculous, I thought. But I checked anyway, and came up with two unauthorised police patrol cars entering the park—one on the night of the third murder and the other on the night of the fourth. On the most recent occasion we had CCTV working at the gate. The driver was Eden Grimshaw, although that wasn't the name on the ID he showed. The camera didn't pick up the face of the man sitting beside him.'

Deb reaches for her iPad and brings up the image. 'But...' She zooms in on the passenger's hand. 'He has a ring on his third finger, see? And a Rolex watch. Ken Fogarty had neither.'

Bob peers at the screen. 'Interesting. Ken Fogarty had no idea what he was getting himself into. Jeez, Deb, I wish I was back there with you.'

'So do I, Bob. Let me top you up.'

Later, when they've exhausted all the angles they can think of, she says she'll call a lift. When it arrives he sees her out, watches as the car interior light comes on when she opens the front passenger door. A woman driver. For a moment it almost looks as if Deb gives her a kiss, then the car moves on. Bob frowns, shakes his head. 'No, can't be.'

76

They decide to drive up to Kramfors, borrowing Jenny's parents' Holden. Since her father died, her mother has hardly driven it, complaining that there is too much traffic on the roads these days. 'Mum won't notice that it's gone,' Jenny says. 'Though it may not start.' Friday is her mother's big bridge day, and by the time the bus delivers them to the end of the street she has already left home. Jenny leads the way down the side of the house, finds the key hidden beneath a pot of coriander. Inside the garage they find the car keys on the hook, start the car and open the garage door.

Soon they are on the motorway heading north, then bypassing Newcastle and on to the Bucketts Way towards the country town of Gloucester. Harry, driving, notices how absorbed Jenny becomes in the passing scenery, greedy for the sight of it. They discuss what they'll do when they reach the homestead, how they might talk their way in and find an opportunity to search Amber's room. It all sounds very implausible.

From Gloucester it's not far along Thunderbolt's Way to the turning for Cackleberry Valley and Kramfors. The road has been improved in places, Harry notices, dramatically so when they come to the section through the Cackleberry Forest. What used to be a narrow dirt road, heavily pot-holed, is now a broad, straight highway cutting through the dense bush.

They see the timber thinning on the far side of the forest, and a sign that Harry remembers: *PRIVATE PROPERTY.* But now there is a high chain-link fence and closed gates blocking entry to the road across the paddocks beyond. A small demountable building stands next to the gates like a sentry post, and a man comes out as they approach.

Harry lowers his window. 'G'day. Can we get through?'

The man, wearing a hi-vis orange shirt, bends to look into the car. 'What's your business, mate?'

'We want to visit the homestead.'

'What for?'

'We're just tourists.'

'Sorry. There's no access.'

'Why not?'

They're interrupted by a large truck arriving from inside the fence. The man opens the gate, waves to the driver. As it roars through they see the huge tree trunks it's hauling.

'They're cutting the timber,' Jenny says.

The gate man returns to Harry's window and tells him he'll have to turn and go back. Harry does so, slowing when he gets to the mouth of a small side trail into the forest. He turns into it and parks the car in the bush, hidden from the road. 'Let's take a walk.'

They follow the trail into the forest, the ground gradually rising. Sunlight filters down through the tree canopy to pick out rock outcrops, the glistening of dark leaves, the twist of vines and new growth struggling up towards the light. Occasionally they get glimpses out towards the valley, see a column of ochre smoke from a fire smudging the blue of the sky.

They grow hot, struggling through increasingly rough country, the trail barely visible. Then another path joins them from the valley side and it broadens, climbing more steeply, until they come to the base of a wall of rock rising vertically through the forest.

'I think I remember this,' Harry says, and in his head he hears Amber's voice: *There are snakes.*

He leads the way along the base of the cliff until they reach a break, a narrow gully. Tumbled rocks form giant steps and they clamber upward, using hands and feet, panting with effort. They arrive at a rock shelf and Harry points to a faded black circle painted on the boulder facing them. 'That's the all-seeing eye that guards the approach to an Aboriginal sacred site. Amber brought me up here, to the eagle cave. Nearly there.'

They climb the final section to a level rock platform partly sheltered by an overhang that forms the entrance to the shallow cave. From here there is a clear view out over the whole of the valley towards the dark egg-shaped hump of Cackleberry Mountain on the far side. Jenny turns towards it, then stops, pointing. 'Harry, look. What's happened?'

Harry sees the familiar dark line of the landing strip for small planes, but the landscape around it has been torn apart. The stands of trees are gone, smoke rising from the razed ground. So too are the horse paddocks and fields of grazing cattle. And most shocking of all, Kramfors Homestead itself has disappeared, a heap of rubble all that remains. Large trucks and earthmovers are roaming over the site like mechanised dinosaurs, ripping the ground, stripping the topsoil, and exposing the first strata of black coal that lie beneath.

Jenny says, 'How could Konrad do this, destroy the family home, his grandfather's heritage?'

'This must have started months ago,' Harry says. 'They must have been waiting for Amber to be incapacitated so they could get on with it. She had no idea...'

'I wonder. Do you remember how she was that last time we saw her? Almost as if she knew she was doomed. She told you to come up here, didn't she?'

Jenny turns towards the overhang. Beneath its shelter they see the Aboriginal rock art, the large red ochre figure of the eagle, the guardian of the valley, surrounded by the shapes of other animals and handprints. She moves further into the shallow cave, studying the images, most of them old and faded: snake, turtles, goanna, kangaroo. 'Here's another of your guardian eyes,' she says.

Harry looks at where she's pointing, low down on one side. He doesn't remember it from the last time he was here, and it seems oddly placed, almost out of sight. 'It looks new.' He crouches and picks up a charcoal stick lying below the symbol among a small pile of stones. He pushes them away to reveal a small black tin box, which he carefully picks up and prises open. Inside is an envelope, grubby and folded. He lifts it carefully out and unfolds it, sees the handwritten address: his father's chambers. Inside is a letter and a curling piece of paper. A photograph, Polaroid, black and white.

He takes it out into the light, smoothing it flat, and shows it to Jenny. A white shape lies in a tangle of undergrowth and tree trunks. He peers more closely and makes out the letters painted on its side: *VH–MDX*.

Harry unfolds the accompanying letter, written in a careful script.

Dear Judge Belltree,
As arranged I will meet you at 2 pm on the 26th of next
month at the place we first met up. I enclose the photograph
I spoke of and will make a sworn statement.
Yours faithfully,
Joseph Doyle

285

Harry examines the postmark on the envelope: *Moree NSW 24 May 2010.*

'It's like Amber told us. Joseph was planning to meet my father on the twenty-sixth of June, the day he died.'

'To tell him about what happened to flight VH–MDX,' Jenny says. 'Terry was right. But how did Konrad get hold of this in the first place?'

'Greg,' Harry says.

Jenny frowns, reluctant to believe that her sister's husband would have done such a thing—despite everything they've learned since his death.

'We knew that Greg betrayed Dad,' Harry went on. 'We just didn't know exactly how. He stole this from Dad and sent it to Konrad, who then made sure that Dad never made it to the meeting. This is the reason why they died, Jenny—why you were blinded for three years.'

77

'Where the hell did you get this, Kelly?' Roshed drops the flash drive into her palm.

'You got into it?'

'Sure did.'

'So? What's on it?'

Roshed looks over his shoulder around the café, then takes out his phone, flicks at the screen until he finds what he's looking for, and hands it to her.

'Oh my God!' Kelly stares at the picture, a dog of some kind with its throat torn open, another dog, bloody teeth bared, standing over it.

'There are quite a few of those.'

'I don't want to look. Any people we can identify?'

Roshed flicks through the images. A heavily muscled man is holding back a snarling Rottweiler on a chain. Foam is drooling from the dog's jaws and the man is grinning at the camera, holding up a wad of banknotes in his other hand. 'This guy.'

'I don't know him.'

'I do. Amal Haddad, remember? You asked me about Kylie McVea and I told you about Amal and his brother Khalil working for her.'

'Her kennels, yes. So this is what they do out there.' There's another figure in the background, a man holding a can of beer. When she looks more closely Kelly recognises him, the black patch over his left eye. 'I know that bloke. His name's Craig Schaefer, mechanic, works for the Nordlunds. Is it all about the dogs?'

'There's pictures of girls, showing their all…Lot of flesh, but not too many faces.' He finds a picture of a woman ogling the lens.

'No, don't know her. That all?'

'I've saved the best till last.' He shows her three people lounging in front of a pool, a crisp white modern building in the background, a pandanus tree.

'I know where that is—Maturiki Island in Vanuatu. Owned by Konrad Nordlund. That's him there, isn't it?'

'Yes. Who's the Asian guy, any idea?'

'I think his name is Deng Huojin, a Chinese businessman, part of the development consortium for Slater Park. Who's the woman between them, in the bikini?'

Roshed doesn't answer and keeps flicking through the images, looking for another. 'Aha…here she is again.'

The woman in a room, lying on a bed, looking off camera. The bikini top has gone. Kelly would put her age at around fifty.

'And number three.'

A man is lying on top of the woman, both naked. Roshed zooms in. The woman is staring fixedly into the man's eyes, gripping his black hair. 'Don't recognise her?'

'She sort of looks familiar…' The man looks twenty years younger.

'But you don't recognise her without her clothes on. Her name's Susan Aguilar.'

'What!'

'The New South Wales minister for infrastructure and planning. I believe the boyfriend is Konrad Nordlund's elder son Ryan.'

Roshed grins at the look on Kelly's face. 'You're trying to write the headline, aren't you? Something like *How to Screw the NSW Government?*'

'Dear God.'

'So, Kelly, where did the flash drive come from?'

'I don't reveal my sources. But I believe the images may have been taken by Nordlund's other son, Hayden.'

'He's got a hidden camera in the guest bedroom?'

'Could be.'

'Well, we should talk about strategy.'

78

They get off the motorway into the northern Sydney suburbs, heading towards Frenchs Forest. Harry slows down as they turn into the end of Jenny's mother's street.

'Stop,' Jenny says suddenly. 'Oh, fuck.'

He pulls into the kerb. Up ahead they see Bronwyn, Nicole at her side, pointing to the open garage door, the empty space inside. Bronwyn is gesticulating, agitated, and talking into her mobile.

'Okay,' Jenny says, 'turn round.'

She gets him to drive to Chatswood rail station. 'It's best if you're not involved, Harry,' she says, 'Mum being how she is. I'll go back and explain that I just needed to use the car. They'll understand. I can depend on them. Actually it'll be a huge relief to be able to tell them I'm okay. You catch a train back into the city and I'll ring you.'

She leans across and kisses him, thinking that every time she does this she wonders if it will be the last time. 'See you this evening.'

He waves as he disappears into the station and she turns the car and retraces the route back to Frenchs Forest. Her mother and sister are still outside in the drive, someone else with them. They turn as she pulls in at the kerb, and her mother cries out as she recognises Jenny getting out of the car. It's only then that Jenny realises the third person is a uniformed policeman. As she meets his gaze she hears the whoop of a police siren, and a patrol car sweeps in behind her.

79

The house phone is blinking when Harry gets back to Surry Hills. He listens to the message. The voice is hesitant, as if telephones are a modern mystery the speaker hasn't quite come to terms with.

'Harry, my dear chap, Bernard here...Um, look, I'm sorry, I think I was rather abrupt last time we met. I was a bit pre-occupied...A paper I'm writing...Um, anyway, look, something you mentioned...a letter—Joseph? It occurred to me afterwards, it did ring a bell. I think I need to talk to you about it. It may be significant. Can you call me? Thanks...um, bye.'

Harry dials the number and Bernard answers immediately. He sounds relieved.

'Thanks for ringing back, Harry. I think we need to meet. Would it be too much trouble for you to come to my flat again tonight? About eight? I'm so glad. I think this is important for both of us. And could you bring the letter? Excellent, excellent, goodbye.'

Harry waits but Jenny doesn't call. He imagines the three of them, mother and two daughters, reunited with one another and with Abigail, and feels regret. He is surplus.

Eventually he goes out into the darkening city, the streetlights coming on, laughter and music from the busy pubs and restaurants, as he walks briskly to Kings Cross. There he pauses to buy a burrito and Coke, standing in the shadow of a doorway while he eats, watching the passing crowd for any sign that he's being followed. When he's done he wipes his fingers and mouth with the paper napkin and sets off again for Potts Point. The front door of the apartment block clicks open as he presses Bernard's buzzer.

Music comes from the open door of Bernard's flat as Harry steps out of the lift—Duke Ellington, 'It Don't Mean a Thing (If It Ain't Got That Swing)'. Bernard seizes his hand, guides him into the flat, eager with relief. He seems very anxious or excited—it's hard to tell which—his cheeks glowing pink, eyes unnaturally wide, talking fast without pause. 'Come in, Harry, come in. I'm so glad you could come. Sit, sit. I've made us gin rickeys—Fitzgerald and Zelda's favourite cocktail. Have you tried it? You must. You must. Here, here. Cheers.'

Harry takes the fizzing cocktail glass, tastes the tart lime, the strength of the gin. 'Cheers. You seem in high spirits tonight, Bernard.'

'Oh, I suppose I'm in hope of revelation, Harry! From you!' He lowers the volume of the music, 'Sophisticated Lady' now, and turns back to Harry. 'The letter—did you bring it?'

Harry takes it from his pocket and hands it over, watches Bernard eagerly snatch it out of the envelope and then listens to him read it aloud.

'...*will make a sworn statement. Yours faithfully, Joseph Doyle.* What do you make of it, Harry? And where's the photograph? Do you have it?'

'Not with me.' The gin certainly has a kick.

'But you've seen it?'

'Yes, I've seen it.'

'And what does it show?'

'A small plane, a Cessna, number VH-MDX.'

'My brother Martin's plane! The one he died in, yes?'

'Yes.'

'And where was the picture taken? Was Martin with the plane?'

'I guess he was in the cockpit, but you couldn't see him. The plane had crashed, you see, the wings sheared off. It was half-buried beneath debris on the forest floor.'

'But…' Bernard's mouth drops open. 'You mean *the* crash? The one that took my brother's life? How is that possible? The wreckage has never been found.'

'Apparently it has. I guess that's what Jacob…' Harry pauses, frowning.

'Joseph?'

'Yes, Joseph. I guess that's what Joseph wanted to make his sworn statement about.'

'To the judge—your father?'

'My father, yes.'

'Do you know where Joseph is?'

'That's a secret.'

'What do you think this means, Harry?'

'I think it means that something about your brother's crash stinks, don't you?' Harry stares into his glass. 'Hell, Bernie, you and Zelda certainly know how to mix a cocktail.'

'Here, let me top you up. So where is the photograph? I'd like to see it.'

'Wrong question, Bernie. God, I feel tired.' Harry rubs his eyes with his free hand, clumsy, trying to focus. The music, the cocktail…Hell, he tells himself, he's even beginning to sound like Philip Marlowe. 'The right question is, who killed Martin? Wasn't you, was it, Bernie?'

There is a glow about Bernard's pink face, a halo of golden light, and Harry stares at it, fascinated. He tries to order his thoughts and has to close his eyes to concentrate. When he opens them again something very strange has happened to Bernard. He now has hair—black, slicked back—and his features have grown lean and menacing. Very like Nathaniel Horn's in fact. Harry remembers that he has to ask Horn a question, but he can't for the life of him remember what it was.

Someone is searching his pockets. He tries to frame an objection, push them away, but his limbs feel incredibly heavy and he finds he can barely move them.

'It's not here,' someone says, far, far away. 'Call the boys. Get him out of here.'

80

Kelly watches Husam Roshed get to his feet to cries of 'Sit down!' and 'Get him out!'

'My question is directed to the minister for infrastructure and planning. I would like the minister to tell the house what her relationship is with the Nordlund family.'

There are groans and cries of 'Shame!' as Susan Aguilar stands up with a smile. 'Mr Speaker, I can assure the house and the member for Campsie that my relationship with the Nordlund family is purely professional and does not conflict in any way with the fulfilment of my ministerial responsibilities.'

Roshed hesitates, seems as if he might sit down, then says, 'Has the minister ever been a guest on board Mr Konrad Nordlund's luxury super yacht *Princess Estelle*?'

'Yes, I have attended a function on board Mr Nordlund's boat, in Sydney Harbour, accompanied by other members of the government and opposition.'

'And has the minister ever been a guest on Mr Nordlund's private Pacific island, Maturiki?'

Aguilar seems startled, then says firmly, 'No, Mr Speaker, I have not.'

Roshed attempts another question, but is drowned out by an eruption of angry cries. 'Enough!' 'Get him out!'

The speaker bangs his gavel, shouts, 'Order, order!' The noise subsides and he goes on, 'Will the member for Campsie now resume his seat.'

Roshed says, 'Mr Speaker, in view of the rumours that have begun to circulate around Sydney, I feel obliged to give the minister the opportunity to respond to one final question.' The word *rumours* seems to quieten the chamber, which goes still as Roshed asks, 'Has the minister had a sexual relationship with Mr Nordlund's son Ryan Nordlund?'

A moment of stunned silence, then another eruption, louder and angrier than the last. But some on the opposition benches have noted the strange expression on Susan Aguilar's face, something like panic. Through the roars of 'Withdraw!' and 'Shame!', a lone opposition voice calls out, 'Answer, answer!' Then others, cautiously at first, begin to take up the cry.

When the speaker finally restores order he says, 'I'll give the minister the chance to respond to that last question and then we shall move on to the next matter.'

Aguilar, very pale, says nothing. She reaches for a glass of water, raises it part way, then returns it to the table, perhaps because her hand is shaking. Finally she lifts her head and speaks into the silence. 'That is absolutely untrue.'

Kelly rushes back to the *Times*, dictating her story in the taxi on the way. When she's satisfied with it she takes it up to Catherine Meiklejohn's office and waits while she reads it.

'Looks like a fun evening in parliament, Kelly, but is any of it true, these so-called rumours? I must say I hadn't heard anything. Can we trust Roshed?'

'I believe we can, and I think they are true. Look.'

She hands Catherine a hard copy of the picture of the three people by the pool. 'We have a couple of old images on file of Nordlund's villa at Maturiki that show a similar background. That's Konrad Nordlund, his Chinese business partner Deng Huojin, and Susan Aguilar.'

'Hmm. So she may have told a fib. Anything else?'

Kelly shows her a second photo, Aguilar in bed with Ryan Nordlund.

Catherine whistles. 'You going to tell me where you got these?'

'I can't.'

'Why would Aguilar be stupid enough to let someone else see her in bed with him?'

'The suggestion is that Nordlund's other son, Hayden, spied on the guest bedroom.'

'Well, if it's genuine it'll break Susan, possibly the government too. But digital images are so easily manipulated...We'll need to get them checked out, see if anyone's tampered with them. Do we have an exclusive on these?'

Kelly thinks of the copies on Roshed's phone. 'For the moment, yes. But if we don't publish them, they'll go elsewhere.'

'How long have we got?'

'Twenty-four hours.'

'So we've got the Saturday editions...if we decide to use them. And you know the other problem, of course.'

'Konrad Nordlund owns thirteen per cent of the *Times*.'

'Exactly. Leave it with me, Kelly. I'll have to talk to people. But well done. This is good work.'

81

Jenny is in a holding cell, 1.5 metres square, a clear plastic door in a heavy steel frame so that her every gesture can be observed. She feels calm, resigned. She gave it her best shot, but in the end something like this was bound to happen. Ironic that it happened because she stole her own mum's car. Her poor mother, almost hysterical at recovering her lost daughter one minute and having her snatched away again the next. Her cry as Nicole tried to console her, 'Why has all this happened to us?' She'll blame Harry, of course, another travesty to add to all the rest.

A police officer comes in, looking tired and bored. She's leading an old man who shuffles along, head down. She tells him to take his shoes and socks off, then bends to pick up the socks in one gloved hand, holding her nose with the other, and dumps them in a sink. Sighing, she fills it with water, then turns off the tap and leads him into the holding cell next to Jenny.

She unlocks Jenny's door. 'Mrs Belltree, this way.'

Jenny follows her out to the prisoner reception area. There are several uniformed men out there, big bulky blokes with big guns and big boots, sharing a laugh. With a jolt she realises that one of them is Bob Marshall. She's not sure whether she should show she knows him, and he ignores her. It's only when her guard leads her to the man behind the counter and Bob hands him some paperwork that she realises he's here for her. She doesn't take in everything that the counter man reels off, something about conditional police bail and home detention, but she signs the document he gives her. She takes the bag with her possessions and Bob says, 'Follow me.' He waves goodbye to the others and they walk out together. After the relentless electric glare inside the station she's disoriented to find that it's night outside, the air fresh and cool.

She gets into the car beside Bob, who throws his police cap into the back and grins at her. 'Well, Jenny. You're not looking too bad, considering.'

'What's happening, Bob?'

'You're in the clear, pretty much. They can't say it openly as yet, but they will. In the meantime, say as little as possible and stay out of trouble.'

'But…what about Palfreyman?'

'Fogarty confessed to murdering Palfreyman with Grimshaw.'

'My God.'

'Then he committed suicide, in a police cell. Much embarrassment all round.'

'That…that's wonderful. I mean, about being in the clear. I must tell Harry.'

'Do you know where he is?'

Jenny nods. 'He'll be at Surry Hills, our house.'

'Okay, let's go and tell him.'

He starts the car and they set off at a steady pace, mindful of the five rules of road safety, until Bob mutters, 'Oh bugger it,' switches on the siren and lights and puts his foot down.

The house is in darkness at the end of the lane, no lights in any of the windows. Jenny fumbles with the key in the door and finally pushes it open, switches on the light, and gasps. The hall cupboard doors hang open, its contents thrown across the floor. The raincoat that hangs on the peg is on the floor too, with the phone. She steps through the mess to the living room and stops, seeing the greater chaos inside.

Bob is at her side. 'You've been done over properly.'

'Harry,' Jenny says. 'Where's Harry?' She starts calling his name, running from room to room—the kitchen, the bedrooms, the bathroom, all trashed and no sign of Harry. Bob catches up with her in the attic study, where all the judge's notebooks and files are scattered.

'They've done a very thorough job,' he says. 'I'll call it in.'

They return downstairs. In the kitchen the fridge and freezer doors stand open, the contents all over the floor. The same with the pantry, the crockery and cutlery drawers, everything. Then a terrible thought strikes Jenny. She goes to the phone on the hall floor, finds it's still working and calls her sister.

'Jenny! I'm so glad you've called. I was going to try to visit you. Where are you?'

She explains, then asks, 'Nicole, is your house all right? You haven't had any intruders?'

'No, no, everything's fine.'

'Abigail's all right?'

'Yes, we're sitting here—Mum, Abigail and me—thinking of you.'

'Has Harry been in touch with you?'

'No, we've heard nothing. Are you all right?'

'Yes, I'm coming home to you, but someone's broken into our house in Surry Hills, so I'll have to deal with the police first.'

Bob, who has been on his own phone to report the break-in, is looking at the damage. 'They went to a heap of trouble to find something. Did you have anything valuable here, Jenny?'

She joins him, pulls a chair upright and sinks into it, suddenly exhausted. 'I think I know what they were after. It's in that bag they gave me at the police station.'

She nods at the plastic bag she dropped in the hall. Bob picks it up and brings it to her, and she unzips it and rummages around her possessions for the tin box. She hands it to him, watches him open it carefully and take out the photograph.

'What is it?'

'It's Terry Palfreyman's secret, the thing that Fogarty and Grimshaw killed him for.'

Bob frowns at the image. 'But what is it?'

'It's the remains of the plane that Martin Nordlund and his lawyer died in, back in 2002, up in the mountains north of Gloucester. It's supposed to have never been found, but someone did, and took this photo.'

'I see. But is this worth killing for?'

'There was a letter with it, addressed to Harry's father, arranging to meet him on the afternoon he died in the crash. It's possible this is to do with how Martin Nordlund died, or maybe why Harry's parents were killed, or maybe both...I don't know, Bob. I don't really understand it, but I think that's what they were looking for.'

'So where's the letter?'

'Harry had it in his pocket.'

'And where is Harry? Has he got a phone?'

'No. Inspector Velasco is after him and he didn't want her to trace him.'

'That's a shame.'

Police arrive, Bob briefs them, then turns to Jenny. 'We can't do anything here. Let's get you to your sister's place.'

'Yes, Harry will know to find me there. Was he here, do you think, when this happened?'

'No, I don't think so. There's no breakages, no bloodstains, no signs of a fight. Just a very thorough and systematic search. I'll come back here later and see if the crime scene people find anything.'

They drive through the city centre, the towers glowing in the night sky, across the Harbour Bridge and through North Sydney towards Nicole's suburb on the lower North Shore. Jenny feels exhausted and disoriented—her arrest, the jail, the ruined house. Bob won't be able to find Harry unless Harry wants to be found, but she tells herself that he can look after himself and will contact her when he can.

After dropping Jenny off at Nicole's house and witnessing the tearful reunion with her baby, Bob returns to Surry Hills. He speaks to the leader of the crime scene team who confirms his reading of the situation—no fight, no violence, just a very thorough search by intruders who were careful enough to wear gloves and probably overshoes too.

'There's one message on the house phone,' she says. 'It might mean something to you.'

He listens to the call, notes the name, Bernard, and the number, then tries to ring it. It goes straight to voicemail. Bob thinks for a moment, then calls Deb.

'Velasco.'

'Deb, Bob Marshall here. I picked Jenny Belltree up as we agreed and brought her to her house in Surry Hills, where she was expecting to meet Harry. He's not here and we found the place broken into and turned over. Nothing to do with you, is it?'

'No, Bob, not me.'

'You looking for Harry?'

'I'd like to talk to him about the Grimshaw murder, but so far he's not on our wanted list. I didn't know he was back in the country. I think he's trying to avoid me.'

'Yeah, I guess so. There's one message on the phone here, someone called Bernard asking Harry to meet him at his apartment. Could you track it down for me? I'd get onto the TIB myself, but I'd have to go through channels. You can do it quicker.'

303

'Sure, Bob. I'll get right back to you.'

He feels humiliated having to ask Deb to do this, wonders if he shouldn't have bothered.

She rings back fifteen minutes later. 'Unregistered mobile, Bob. At the moment it's on a property out near Dural, a place called Doggylands Boarding Kennels. Jenny has a seeing-eye dog, right? They're probably giving it a holiday.'

'Oh, right.'

'Sorry, not much help. You know Harry, Bob. He'll show up when it suits him.'

He rings Jenny's sister's number. Nicole answers and he asks to speak to Jenny.

'We're just going to bed, Bob,' Jenny says. 'Thanks so much for looking after me. It feels so wonderful to have Abigail in my arms again. Is there any news of Harry?'

'No, I'm afraid not. Listen, you have a dog, don't you?'

'Yes, I do.'

'Were you planning to put it in the kennels?'

'No. Why?'

'Oh, just that someone left a message on your phone at Surry Hills from a place called Doggylands Boarding Kennels.'

'I've never heard of it, Bob. Harry must have been in touch with them. Our Labrador has been staying with my mother. Maybe he wanted to give her a break.'

'Yes, that must be it. The man said his name was Bernard. Ring any bells?'

'The only Bernard I can think of is Bernard Nordlund. Harry met him a couple of times, I think. But it couldn't be him, could it?'

'No, guess not.'

82

He wakes with pain in his arm and shoulder, lying awkwardly on the hard ground. Tries to lift his head and chokes back a wave of nausea. It's pitch dark, but he's not alone. He can make out sounds: heavy breathing, grunts, a muffled snore.

As he tries to sit up there's a metallic clunk and a rattling noise as his foot strikes something hard, then faint sounds of movement around him. He reaches a hand to the obstacle and realises it's a metal bucket. When he slides his hand over the lip he touches water, fresh and cool. He struggles upright, cups water in his hands and splashes his face, takes a cautious sip, then a grateful gulp. Something makes him look up suddenly and his eyes meet another pair, unblinking, very close.

He says, 'Hello?' and is answered by a deep growl. Beneath the eyes he can make out two rows of large white fangs, bared.

He backs away, feeling the hard concrete beneath his palms. His watch, his shoes and socks are gone, and everything from his pockets. He lies back and tries to focus. His brain isn't functioning properly. This is a dream, right?

83

Kelly blinks at the illuminated numbers on the clock, 3:22 am. She gets up from the couch where she's fallen asleep, fires up the computer and logs into the *Times* online and begins searching. Nothing in the headlines or main stories. Eventually she finds it, under local politics, a short article beneath a picture of Husam Roshed, 'Consternation in State Parliament'. The tone is humorous, mocking Roshed's reputation for wild claims, in this case that a government minister has been having a sexual relationship with a member of a developer's family. In a press statement the premier has laughingly dismissed the claim as 'lurid nonsense'. There is no mention of Susan Aguilar, Konrad Nordlund or Kelly Pool. The author is the paper's political editor, Maurie Stevens.

Kelly calls Catherine Meiklejohn's mobile. A sleepy male voice answers. 'Hello?'

'Can I speak to Catherine, please?'

'Look, she's just got to sleep. Can it wait?'

There's a sound of a voice in the background, a muffled conversation and then Catherine comes on. 'Kelly. You've seen the paper?'

'Yes, I—'

'I would have spoken to you but you'd gone by the time we made the decision, and I thought it could wait till morning. I'm sorry, but it was a political story, not a crime, and Maurie was adamant there was nothing in it.'

'But the photographs.'

'Who took them? How credible are they? How do we know some teenage geek didn't cook them up on his computer? There's just nothing to substantiate them, Kelly. I'm sorry, but you were a bit out of your depth on this one. Stick to crime.'

Kelly rings off, chilled by the change in Catherine. There's been pressure, she thinks, from above. She dials Roshed's number. 'Husam? I'm sorry, I've just seen the *Times* online. I'm furious.'

'It's okay, Kelly, I've seen it—it's kind of what I expected.'

'What shall we do now?'

'It's already done. Keep an eye on the *Post*.'

'You've given it to them?'

'Yep.'

'You should have talked to me first, Husam. I can't have my name on an article in another paper.'

'It won't be in your name, Kelly, don't worry. They'll write the piece, use the pictures. They won't mention you.'

'But...it's my material! It's my story! You shouldn't have made a copy of what was on that memory stick.'

'Your paper got first shot at it and wouldn't play ball. Not surprising when Konrad Nordlund sits on your board. This is the only way to play it. If you want to take credit for the pictures, be my guest.'

'I can't do that.'

She rings off, tight with anger and frustration. Stick to crime, Catherine told her. It's what she wants to do, what she was doing. So what now?

84

A pale light slowly grows. Harry gets clumsily to his feet, legs cramped, and tries to make out his surroundings. His eyes begin to identify features in the dimness—steel posts and frames, dark bodies huddled on the paler concrete. His fingers clutch chain-link and he realises that he is in a cage, one of a row disappearing into the gloom. His cage has a steel-framed gate. It resembles a temporary holding prison they built at the base in Kandahar. There is a strong smell of urine. He begins to do exercises to get his body moving once again.

The light grows and he sees that he is inside an industrial shed. Sounds can be heard from outside the building, a vehicle starting up, a radio. Now he sees that all the huddled bodies in the cages around him are large dogs. The nearest ones stare at him malevolently.

Eventually a door opens with a clang at one end of the shed, letting in a shaft of morning sunlight. The figure of a man appears, pushing a wheelbarrow. The animals stir and begin squealing and barking with excitement. The man stops at the first cage in the row and scoops something from the barrow, then continues, stopping at each cage in turn. When he reaches Harry he sneers. Harry recognises Kylie McVea's son Gavin, who fills the scoop and tips it through a hole at the bottom of the cage.

'Here's ya breakfast, dog,' he says, and laughs, moving on to the next cage. Harry sees a pile of dried dog food lying on the concrete.

When Gavin has reached the end of the row he turns back, and as he passes Harry's cage he says, 'If ya want a shit, go out there.' He points to a hatch in the wall at the back of Harry's cell. When the shed door bangs shut again Harry goes to the hatch and slides the cover up. Crouching, he sees a patch of dirt outside, surrounded by a high chain-link fence. He crawls out and sees three dogs in the yard. They stare at him, snarl, then one charges, followed by the others. Harry ducks back into the cage and slams the cover down as the animal throws itself against it.

85

Deb wakes slowly, reluctantly. Stretching out a hand, she feels the bed beside her empty, cold. She sighs and closes her eyes again.

Lying there, still only half awake, she finds her thoughts drifting to Bob Marshall. Poor Bob. Sad. She wishes she could help him, but there's no way—office politics saw to that. If Dick Blake thought she was in touch with his predecessor he'd think she was undermining his authority, leaking information.

She hears the bang of the front door closing, then Charity is there, flushed with health and exercise, in her running shoes, shorts, T-shirt, her phone strapped to her arm. 'Morning,' she says. 'I'll make some tea.'

When she returns with the mugs she has a newspaper tucked under her arm. She tosses it to Deb. 'Look at this. You'll love it.'

It's the *Post*, a rag Deb never buys. 'I was lucky to get a copy,' Charity says. 'Everyone was buying them.'

She points to the picture on the front page under the single-word headline *Screwed*. 'What a shocker,' she says cheerfully. 'Poor Susan.'

But it isn't Susan Aguilar Deb is staring at, it's her boyfriend's wrist and hand, caressing her cheek—the Rolex watch and the thick gold band on the middle finger. Ryan Nordlund.

'Do you have to go in to work today, love?' Charity says. 'It's a beautiful day. We could take a ferry, have a picnic?'

'I wish. It won't always be like this. It's just there's a mountain of stuff waiting, and I have to be there to deal with it all.' She reaches out her hand for Charity's. 'Soon, I promise. I'll take leave. Where would you like to go? Bali? Fiji? There's this great resort in Thailand someone told me about.'

But when? Since Fogarty's confession they've let her back in to the Slaughter Park investigation, which is a never-ending data-grind now, with no prospect of an arrest in sight. She looks again at the Rolex watch in the picture. If only life were that simple, she thinks.

86

Bob rises late, feeling at odds with himself. He makes breakfast, low carbs, fruit, because he's been putting on weight, sitting on his arse behind a desk all day. He wonders what he can do with himself this Saturday morning. Bit of shopping, get a haircut, lunch in that little place that's just opened. Or he could go into the office and do some work on the budget report. He groans. Not like the old glory days in homicide, when Betty was alive. Then the days were always busy, full of something new, feeling fulfilled.

'Jeez, Bob,' he mutters. 'Stop feeling sorry for yourself. And stop talking to yourself, will you? People'll think you're senile.'

Doggylands. Stupid name. Keeps scratching at his brain. Has he heard it before? He gets his computer going and looks it up. *Proprietor Kylie McVea.* That Kylie McVea? Monster half-sister of Frank bloody Capp? Now he's got it.

'Might just go out there and take a look this afternoon. What do you reckon?'

87

Kelly is thinking about Harry. She hasn't seen or heard from him since parting at Port Vila. Is he still out there? Or has he returned and is he right now opening the *Post* and wondering where those pictures on Maturiki came from? She owes him an explanation big time. The least she can do is try to explain. Maybe Jenny's sister has heard something.

Nicole answers her call. 'Hi, Kelly, how are you?'

'I'm fine. I just wondered if you'd had any news of Harry or Jenny.'

'Yes! Jenny's right here.'

'Jenny?'

'Yes, wonderful news. She's in the clear. I'll let her tell you herself.'

Jenny comes on the line. 'Yes, Kelly, it's true. The police arrested me yesterday and then released me. Apparently they now believe what I told them about Terry Palfreyman's murder.'

'But how come?'

'That man Fogarty I recognised at Terry's house? It seems

he confessed to murdering Terry with another detective called Grimshaw.'

Kelly is startled. 'What? I've heard nothing of this.'

'No,' Jenny says, 'I think they're keeping it quiet at the moment.'

Not for long, Kelly thinks. Catherine told her to concentrate on crime, and this is it. The Palfreyman murder, her baby.

'Tell me the whole story,' she says, and Jenny does. When she's finished, Kelly says, 'But what about Harry?'

'Yes, I'm worried sick. When Bob Marshall took me home to Surry Hills, Harry wasn't there, and the house had been broken into and ransacked. I haven't heard from him since.'

'That's terrible. You have no idea where he might be?'

'No. The only thing Bob could find was an odd message on our phone from a dog kennels somewhere.'

'Dog kennels?'

'Yes, called Doggylands. Silly name. Someone said they wanted to meet Harry. I don't know what that was about.'

But Kelly does. She says, 'Do you have Bob Marshall's mobile number, Jenny? I might chase him up, see if I can learn more.'

'Okay, I have it here.'

Bob answers her call with the cop brush-off voice he reserves for the press. 'Yes, I remember you, Kelly. You gave Deb Velasco some grief if I remember, and got into a bit of trouble yourself. Sorry, bad time. Can't talk now. On my way out.'

'To Doggylands?' Kelly says.

Silence on the line. Then he says, not very convincingly, 'What are you talking about, Kelly?'

'Kylie McVea. I'm coming too.'

'Not a chance.'

'I've been there, Bob, to the kennels. I can help you. She has a son, not too bright, loves guns, and two muscle men, Amal and Khalil Haddad, nephews of the sergeant-at-arms of the Crows who was killed at the Swagman Hotel last year. Remember?'

Of course you remember, Kelly thinks, because you were in charge of the Crucifixion Creek mess.

Another silence. 'Where are you, Kelly?'

She gives him the address and he says, 'I'll pick you up in an hour.'

88

The sun is high overhead now, sending patterns of light through the dirty windows of the shed. The dogs have gone, let loose into the pens, leaving behind a pungent animal smell and the sound of barking.

Some cocktail, Zelda. He wonders what was in it, can still feel the effects—an ache in his head and an uncoordinated clumsiness in his movements.

With a screech the door at the end of the shed opens and a waft of country air gusts in. Two men, identical, huge bulky upper bodies and arms, shaved heads, Middle Eastern complexion. They roll up to his gate and slide the bolt. 'Out.'

Harry stays where he is, sitting on the concrete floor, back to the shutter.

One of them comes in, turning sideways to fit his shoulders through the opening. 'I said out. Git on ya fuckin' feet.'

Harry gazes blankly up at him, still doesn't move. The man steps closer to deliver a kick, and as it comes Harry grabs the foot and yanks it hard, tipping the man back against the wire side of the cage with a crash. As the other man rushes in, Harry jumps up and punches him hard in the face, ducks to one side, hits him again in the ribs and trips him down onto his companion.

He runs towards the external door, where he is confronted by a third man holding a shotgun pointed at Harry's chest. The man has staring eyes, a wild grin, as his finger tightens on the trigger. Harry stops, raises his hands, and a blow from behind throws him to the ground, out cold.

He wakes spluttering, water running down his face. A man, one of the Lebs, is standing in front of him holding a bucket, a nasty expression on his face. Harry's arms are stretched above him. He looks up and sees rope around his wrists tied to the roof truss of another shed, a workshop by the look of it, bits of equipment scattered around. The man drops the bucket with a clang and punches Harry hard in the belly. Harry gasps, trying to get breath. The man steps forward, hisses, 'Fuckin' dog. Have ta train ya.' He moves back and his look-alike steps forward and kicks Harry in the crotch.

The beating goes on for a while, the two men taking turns, until they've had enough and walk away, leaving Harry hanging there, licking the blood running down from his nose, willing the pain to ease.

Eventually someone else comes into the workshop, his figure silhouetted against the glare of light at the far end so that Harry can't make out his face at first.

'My God, Harry. What have they done to you?' A familiar voice.

'That was some cocktail, Bernie,' Harry mutters, spitting blood as he speaks. One eye has swollen closed, but he can still see Bernard's pink plump face, full of concern.

'You mustn't provoke them, Harry,' Bernard says, whispering close to Harry's ear. 'This is all so unnecessary. Just tell me where the photograph is, and where we can find Joseph, and that'll be the end of the matter. They'll let you go and won't bother you again, I promise.'

'So you're in charge, are you, Bernard? You were behind it all.'

'No, no, not exactly. In some ways I'm as much a victim in all this as you are. I just wanted a quiet, spoilt life, like everyone does, but I'm…implicated, and I have to play the part allotted to me, as do we all.'

'Money is the master, is it, Bernie? Money writes the play?'

'Something like that.'

'What if I tell you that I have no idea where the photograph and Joseph are?'

'I won't believe you, and neither will anyone else. You'll have to do better than that, Harry. Please don't play games with them. They're not nice people. I'll leave you to think about it for a little while.'

He turns and walks away.

89

Deb returns to strike force base and is immediately hit by a storm of questions, demands for meetings, signatures, decisions. It's some while before she can make time to send the rather odd request to the technical branch to track down the photograph in the *Post* and assess it against the CCTV image from Slater Park. They come back a couple of hours later.

The tech's name is Paul—'Which is pretty significant actually,' he says, sounding quite pleased with himself.

'How come?'

'Well, the reason I'm called Paul was because my mum was mad keen on Paul Newman.'

Deb shakes her head. 'I don't…'

'I'd better explain. The *Post* gave us the original digital image they used for that picture in the paper, and it was pretty sharp. The watch was, as you said, a Rolex. A Cosmograph Daytona, in fact, with the three small chronograph dials inside the big dial— very distinctive. They come in three series, the first four-digit series produced from 1961 to 1987 being the earliest and rarest, and the rarest of all have what's called the Paul Newman dial, because he was an enthusiast and had one.'

'Ah. And the one in the picture is…?'

'Yep, it's one of them, a Paul Newman Daytona, rare and expensive. Your guy's got money.'

'Yes. What about the other picture?'

'Not nearly so clear, but the three chronograph dials are there, and although we can't make out all the markings, it's very similar to the series one watches.'

'Very similar?'

'I'd stand up in court and say ninety per cent. And then there's the gold ring. We estimate that the thickness and width of the rings in the two pictures are identical.'

Deb thanks him, asks for a report and hangs up. She checks records and finds that Ryan Nordlund was arrested in 2011 for assault and breaching the peace while celebrating after driving in a V8 Supercar event at Eastern Creek Raceway. Which means that they have his fingerprints on record. She asks for a match with the thumb print on the bloody banknote found in Grimshaw's block of flats, and waits, biting her lip. When someone tells her she's due at a briefing for the new shift she shakes her head and tells them to get Col to do it.

It's a match. Grimshaw's insurance. Deb takes a deep breath, traces Ryan's registered mobile phone number and asks for a location. The answer, when it comes back from Potts Hill, hits her like a slap in the face: Ryan Nordlund is currently at Doggylands Boarding Kennels.

Later, when she has made the connection to Kylie McVea and her dead brother Frank Capp, and is planning the next move, she wonders about contacting Bob Marshall. But no—office politics. Instead she speaks to Dick Blake, who is shocked.

'Are you absolutely sure, Deb? You're saying that Konrad Nordlund's son was involved in the Slater Park murders?'

'Well, if he wasn't, I'd like him to explain how we have his thumb print in Christie Florian's blood.'

'Don't rush into this, Deb. Check and double-check. His movements, phone records, social media.'

'Boss, we know where he is now. But if he gets wind of this…'

'How can he?'

'We don't know that Fogarty and Grimshaw were the only cops on their payroll.'

Blake makes a face like he's got acid heartburn. 'Just take it steady, Deb. Nice and steady.'

Back at her desk she does what she's told, organising the checks, itching with impatience. This isn't how Bob would have done it, she thinks. Bob would have been out there with his TOU mates armed to the teeth for the big arrest.

90

'The others have gone on ahead, have they, Bob?'

Kelly is riding in the passenger seat of Bob's Ford, heading north and west on the Pacific Highway through the suburbs. He doesn't seem dressed for the part, somehow—jeans, a light jacket, no uniform, no radio, no bulletproof vest. More like an old bloke going out to the pub.

'What others?'

'The SWAT team, the TOU, the nasties, the black ninjas.'

He shakes his head. 'Nothing like that, Kelly. We're just going to take a little gander, that's all. A recce. Sniff around. You and me.'

'I've already sniffed around. I told you. It's not a nice place. Can't imagine anyone would kennel their pet pooch there. I think they have some kind of...I don't know, gatherings out there.' She realises it's Saturday today, and remembers the leaflet in the Schaefers' mail, about a Saturday event at 8:00 pm last December at Doggylands.

'What you got in that backpack of yours?' Bob asks.

'Oh, just survival stuff—sandwiches, water.'

'Good thinking.'

Actually she also has a still camera and a movie camera, both borrowed from the staff photographers at the office, as well as a sound recording machine with a long-range microphone. But she doesn't think Bob needs to know that she's hoping for a scoop.

'You did at least bring a gun, didn't you, Bob? Those guys are tough, and they have guns.'

'Yes, I've brought a gun, Kelly, but you don't need to worry. There's not going to be any shooting.'

91

Still hanging from the roof truss, aching all over, Harry sees the dark shape of another man appear in the doorway and come towards him. He recognises Nathaniel Horn, who stares at his battered face with detached interest.

'Mr Belltree.'

'Mr Horn.' Harry finds it hard to form the words through his damaged mouth. Something seems to be wrong with his teeth.

Horn gets a small metal case from his pocket. 'Do you smoke?'

'No.'

Horn takes out a cigarette and lights it.

Harry says, 'Was that an offer for the condemned man?'

Horn blows smoke off to the side. 'Not quite yet. But you haven't got long. You were no help tracing Amber. I suggest you make up for it now. So listen very carefully. Four years ago I received a package from your brother-in-law, containing an envelope he had taken from your father's study. In the envelope was a letter from a man called Joseph, together with a photograph. I passed these on to Konrad Nordlund, who put them in his safe. Sometime earlier this year they disappeared. Now we discover that envelope and the letter in your pocket. Where is the photograph?'

'I don't know. I haven't got it.'

'But you described exactly what it showed. Does your wife have it?'

'No. Amber gave them to me. She said she was keeping the photograph hidden somewhere, as insurance.'

'Where?'

'She didn't say.'

'What about Joseph? You told Bernard you'd met him. Where is he?'

'No, I didn't. I said it was a secret. I have no idea where he is.'

Horn shakes his head. 'I've met far better liars than you, Belltree. You'll have to do much better than that, and quickly.'

There is a sudden interruption from the doorway, someone calling out, 'Nat? Nathaniel? You in here?'

Horn frowns, annoyed. 'Yes, Ryan, I'm here. What is it?'

Harry recognises Konrad Nordlund's son pacing towards them, waving a newspaper.

'Look at this, for God's sake!'

He thrusts the *Post* at Horn, who scans the front page, frown darkening, turns to the follow-up story inside. 'Maturiki…how the hell did they get hold of this?'

'I don't know. I've no fucking idea.' Ryan looks round at Harry as if noticing him for the first time. 'How are you going with him? Could he have something to do with this?'

Horn considers this. 'The intruders on Maturiki that the Schaefers reported…Get Karen in here.'

Harry's head is throbbing, trying to read the situation, to find the right answers he'll have to give. He's struck by Horn's manner, by the way Ryan Nordlund defers to him, as if the roles of client and consultant are reversed, Horn giving the instructions.

Ryan returns with Karen Schaefer, who looks startled when she catches sight of Harry's face. Then she peers at him and says, 'Yes. It's him. He's the one we saw running away from the villa.'

Ryan pushes close to Harry, menacing. 'How did you get those pictures?'

'She's wrong,' Harry says. 'I could never have taken pictures like that.'

Doubt shows on Ryan's face. 'Yeah, he's right. How could he?'

Karen says, 'Unless...'

'What?'

'Well, your brother...you know, that spy camera he's got.'

'I'll kill him!' Ryan pulls out his phone and walks away, begins shouting into it. 'Well, you get over here!'

Now Bernard arrives, carrying a copy of the paper. 'My God, Nathaniel, this'll finish us.'

'Nonsense,' Horn snaps. 'We'll say the pictures are fakes, intended to discredit the Nordlund family. We'll sue the paper. The government will back us—they'll have to.'

'Yes...' Bernard says doubtfully. 'I suppose you're right. Has Konrad seen it?'

'I'll get onto him right away.'

Again that deference to Horn, Harry thinks. They're all in thrall to him.

Horn, Ryan Nordlund and Karen Schaefer all hurry away, leaving Bernard chewing his lip, staring at the newspaper.

'It's all falling apart, Bernard,' Harry says.

'Be quiet,' Bernard mumbles, still hypnotised by the front-page image. 'You're in enough trouble.'

'I'm the only hope you've got.'

'Don't talk nonsense.'

'I'm not just talking about corruption, Bernard. I'm talking about murder, multiple murders—your brother Martin, my mother and father, Terry Palfreyman, Amber...'

'No, no. Not Amber, that was the Slater Park murderer.'

'Your family is mixed up in the Slater Park murders, along with the policemen Fogarty and Grimshaw. They kidnapped Amber, chopped her up and smuggled her body into Slater Park in a police car. My colleagues in homicide know that now, I've spoken to them. That's their major line of inquiry.'

'I knew nothing of this.'

'They won't believe you. You'll go down with the others. Your only hope is to get me out of here and in return I'll convince them you're innocent.'

'It all happened so quickly, Harry, I couldn't control it. When Martin came up with his bizarre proposal, Nathaniel stepped in. It was he and Konrad arranged for the plane crash, not me. And your parents—I was shocked when I heard what they'd done to them, you must believe me. I would never have agreed to it.'

'What was Martin's proposal? Why did my parents have to die?'

'Bernard!' Horn's voice echoes in the metal shed. 'Come!'

'He talks to you like a dog, Bernard,' Harry whispers. 'Help me and I'll help you.'

'I must go.' He hurries away.

Harry hears them talking, then silence, broken only by the endless barking of the dogs.

92

There's a major accident on the M2 and they sit in the motionless car, Bob drumming his fingers on the steering wheel. They've been stuck here for almost two hours now and all around them motorists have got out of their vehicles. Kelly watches them on their phones, calling family and friends, drinking from water bottles as the hot afternoon drags on.

'Tailgating probably,' Bob grumbles. 'Or speeding. Too many cowboys on the road.'

'Shouldn't we get a few of the local cops to meet us there?' Kelly asks. 'Help us search for Harry?'

'We've absolutely no evidence that he's there, Kelly. All we know is that he's been talking to someone called Bernard, who happened to be at Doggylands when we checked his phone.'

'Maybe we should check it again. He could have moved.'

Bob sighs. 'Just relax, Kelly. Okay, looks like we're on our way.'

People are getting back into their cars, starting up their engines. They begin to move, slowly at first, then more steadily, past the scene of a large truck that's lost its load on a bend. They reach the junction with the M7 and head north, the bush becoming denser, the buildings more widely spaced. The sat nav tells them to turn off before they reach Dural and they take a winding country road between fields and market gardens. They reach a filling station and make a turn onto a narrow dirt road through thick scrub.

'Yes, I remember this,' Kelly says. 'It's just up ahead.'

They come to the bullet-holed sign for the kennels. A man is standing at the entrance to the property, a machete in his hand. Bob pulls up alongside him. He's heavily built, shaved head, a walkie-talkie radio clipped to his belt. He peers into the car.

'Help ya?'

'G'day. Just passing,' Bob says. 'Thought I recognised this place. Does Bernard work here?'

'Bernard? Na.'

'Oh. Doing a bit of pruning, are you?' Bob nods at the machete.

'Yeah, pruning.'

Bob drives on. 'One of the Haddad boys presumably. Not much of a PR.'

'He was put at the front gate for a reason, Bob. There was no one there when I came. Something's going on.'

When they're well clear of the place Bob pulls off the road onto a fire trail leading to a small clearing, where he stops. 'All right, let's look around.'

They get out of the car, Kelly hoisting her backpack, and begin to make their way through thick bush towards the distant sound of barking dogs. They pick their way over fallen branches, feet crunching on bark and leaf litter, and eventually come to a two-metre-high chain-link fence. They follow it for a while until they find a place where it crosses a shallow gully, dry now, and there they squeeze beneath it with some grunts and puffs. 'Just like the old days,' Bob mutters.

They're getting closer now to the sound of the dogs, whose barking is interrupted by a sudden burst of gunfire, followed by a raucous cheer. Bob mutters, 'Jeez.'

'What is it?'

'Sounds like an M4 carbine.'

'I told you, Bob. We need backup.'

'No panic. Could be a practice range. Let's check it out.'

They move more warily, treading carefully over and around obstacles. The sun is low now in the western sky, sending long shadows across their path.

Finally they reach the edge of the dense bush, open space visible through the trees. They creep forward and Kelly recognises the back of Kylie McVea's house, with a rotary clothes line, a barbecue, and the rear veranda facing across a rough paddock in which lies the empty swimming pool she noticed on her earlier visit. And again that discordant element, the floodlights on tall poles, as if for a spectacular swimming gala that will never be held. Beyond the paddock she sees the further clearing, where more than a dozen vehicles are now parked, utes and four-wheel-drives, many with racks of hunting spotlights and antennae. The large pile of fallen timber has had extra fuel added to it, and groups of men—all men—are clustered around it, talking, drinking from bottles and cans. Kelly takes the camera out of her backpack and snaps off a few pictures.

'Hey!' A voice close at hand.

'Whassa matter, Charlie?'

'Thought I saw someone in the bushes over there.'

Bob drops flat to the ground. 'Bugger.'

Kelly whispers, 'Come on, Bob, let's go.' She sets off at a crouch through the tangled undergrowth, clutching camera and backpack, adrenaline sending her heart racing. She hears more shouts and struggles faster, ripping her shirt, then throws herself behind the trunk of a huge twisted angophora, gasping for breath. The shouts have died down, the bush suddenly very quiet and rapidly darkening.

'Bob?' she says in a loud whisper. 'Bob, where are you?'

But no one answers.

93

Nathaniel Horn is accompanied by Ryan Nordlund, the two Haddad boys following.

Harry sees that Horn is smoking again, must be worried. Horn says, 'Time for answers, Belltree. Three things now. We want the photograph, we want Joseph, and we want the flash drive you stole from Maturiki.'

Harry tries to speak but the words don't come.

Ryan pushes into Harry's face, bellows, 'Tell the man, arsehole!'

Harry manages to get his throat to work. 'Piss off.'

Ryan's eyes glitter. 'Do you know who I am?'

Harry mumbles, 'Yeah. A prick.'

Ryan steps back, looks at Horn, then takes the cigarette from his hand and turns back to Harry, grinds the burning tip into Harry's throat, watches his body jump.

He smiles, says, 'Say again? Who am I, arsehole?'

Harry stares at him through watering eyes and whispers, 'A total prick.'

'Enough!' Horn steps in. 'This isn't the way. Bring him outside.'

They release his arms and catch him as he sags to the ground, grip him under the armpits and drag him out into the open. The evening light is fading fast, but dazzling floodlights illuminate the paddock. In front of him he sees the pit of a disused swimming pool, tiles grimy and stained. Beyond he makes out groups of silent figures, staring at him.

They stop at the edge of the pool. Horn says, 'This is where you're going to die. Tonight there will be a party here—a special party. Invited guests have come to see a spectacle, down there. Dogs fighting, to the death. It's a regular event, and the guests are people with a highly developed taste for that sort of thing. They pay well to come, and even more to bet on the results. Tonight they will witness something special. A man being torn apart by the dogs. The betting is already quite frantic. How long will you last?'

Horn looks at his watch. 'You have less than an hour to give me answers to my questions.'

Harry says, 'Why should I tell you anything, if I'm going to die?'

'Because it's the only way you can save your wife Jenny. If you don't give me true answers, she will be the star of the next show here.'

Harry stares for a moment at the fouled tiles below his feet, then whispers, 'Go to hell.'

Horn lights up another cigarette, draws deeply on it. 'Think about it. Take him back inside.'

94

'Oh, Harry,' Kelly murmurs. 'Harry, what have they done to you?'

She had been looking for a good vantage point, and managed to haul herself up through the limbs of a tree to a fork where she could safely perch, high enough to give her a view over the clearing. She had just pulled her video camera and a long-range microphone from her backpack when the first two men emerged from the shed on the far side of the paddock, hauling a third between them.

As two others followed, Kelly had switched on the camera and scrambled for the earphones that went with the microphone, to try to pick up what the men were saying, but in her haste she fumbled and they fell to the ground below. She aimed the microphone anyway and pressed record, hoping it would pick something up, though she couldn't hear it.

And it's only now, as the men are carrying their victim away again, that she can make out the battered features of Harry Belltree.

'Oh, Harry,' she groans again. She has no idea what's happened to Bob or if he's been able to see this. She pulls out her phone and dials triple-O. 'Please,' she whispers, 'tell them to come quickly.'

Half an hour passes, three-quarters of an hour. No sound of howling sirens. No police megaphones. It's quite dark now. She tries triple-O again. 'Are you sure they've got the right place?'

'I'll tell them again,' the operator says. 'Don't worry.'

There has been a steady stream of vehicles arriving and the crowd around the bonfire pile is much larger now, men laughing, shouting, drinking. Then a great cheer goes up as two men appear down the path from the kennel area, each with a huge Rottweiler. The dogs react to the noise, howling, straining against their chains. The men get them to the edge of the pool and push them over the edge. Another man appears with a bucket, throws bits of scarlet flesh down to them.

95

As the minutes pass, Harry feels despair grow like a slow, cold death inside him. He is sitting on the concrete floor of the shed, wrists bound behind him with tape. The two body-builders are sitting over at a side table counting money and betting slips that Kylie's son brings in to them. The sounds of the crowd outside grow louder all the time, joining the barking of the dogs in a hellish chorus. He has tried everything to wriggle and tug his wrists out of the tape, but has made no progress at all.

From a side door an unlikely looking figure in this setting, portly and somewhat ungainly, comes in and has a word with the two men, handing over money and receiving a slip. It's Bernard, placing his bet. He ambles over to Harry and squats down beside him.

'The consensus seems to be eighteen seconds, Harry. The more optimistic ones hope you'll last longer, but you're not exactly starting in good shape, are you?'

He makes a funny little lip-smacking sound, like a fat baby at the teat. Sighs.

'Oh, Harry, be a sensible fellow, dear chap, please. Tell me what you know.'

'Bernard, there's nothing I can tell you that will satisfy them. Not a thing. If you won't help me, at least get word to the police to save my wife and baby.'

Bernard shakes his head. 'They don't trust me, Harry. Horn has ordered them to take my phone away. There's nothing I can do. I'm sorry.'

Harry feels Bernard's warm breath against his cheek, as if he's stooping to kiss or bless him. Then he gets up and walks away.

Harry tries to struggle upright, feels a sharp stab of pain in his palm, the stickiness of blood. He investigates carefully with his fingers and discovers a razor blade.

After five minutes the McVea boy comes in and whispers something to the money-counters, turns to look at Harry with a glint of excitement, trots away again. The men finish what they're doing and get to their feet. One picks up the machete and they walk over to Harry, lift him to his feet. Harry says, 'What's the machete for, mate?' and the man smiles. 'Gotta give the dogs a little taste of ya first, *mate*.' He grins, and Harry slashes him across the throat with the razor blade. As he reels away with a scream, blood spurting from his severed artery, Harry turns and chops the second man with the edge of his hand at the base of his throat, on the bulb of the carotid sinus, sending a massive shock to his brain which abruptly stops his heart. His knees fold and he falls to the ground. Harry picks up the machete and heads for the door.

He thinks of Afghanistan—rising before dawn, pulling on the gear and going out to face who knew what. Why did we do it? Let the bastards have their way. It's natural selection, evolution.

An image comes into his head: Amber, her poor body used as a business ploy, a bargaining chip. He reaches the door, ahead of him a dazzle of lights, a dense crowd in a horseshoe staring his way, expecting him. But not like this. Several men stand in front, looking at him in surprise. This isn't how it was supposed to be. They turn to each other, and in that moment Harry sees Ryan Nordlund among them, Amber's nemesis. *Who do you think I am?* He raises the machete and charges at him with a roar, sees a muzzle flash, hears the bang as Ryan fires. A jolt in his left hip, his momentum carries him on and he brings the blade down.

96

From her eyrie in the tree, Kelly sees the melee on the far side of the pool. Chaos, screams, bodies falling into the pit, scrabbling for a grip, dogs howling. Then two loud bangs and a voice: 'Police! Step back! Hands in the air!'

From the shadows of the bonfire tower a lone man walks through the crowd, which parts in front of him. She recognises the figure of Bob, holding a pistol, marching towards Harry, whose assailants get slowly to their feet and back away. *But where are the troops!* she screams silently to herself. *Where are the black ninjas!*

Bob has reached Harry's side. Kelly watches him in close-up through the lens, saying something to Harry, a silent movie in slow motion, trying to get him to his feet. But something is wrong. Harry's trying, but he can't get up. As Bob reaches down to help him Kelly sees a movement behind him. Hayden Nordlund has picked up the machete. He steps forward to stand over Bob, raises the blade with both hands above his head. A rumble of anticipation passes through the crowd as Bob, unaware, struggles to lift Harry. And then something strange happens—a point of brilliant red light glows briefly in the centre of Hayden's chest, there is a gunshot, and he is hurled backwards.

And now armed figures in black are running in from all directions, shouting, herding the crowd.

Kelly gives a whoop. *At bloody last!* She recognises Deb Velasco among the police, giving orders. This is her operation, Kelly realises, not Bob's. She films for a little longer, zooms in on Deb, then switches off, stuffs the equipment into her backpack and begins the tricky descent from the tree. She's about halfway down when she hears a crashing through the bush somewhere nearby. She peers down into the gloaming and sees a bobbing light, makes out a figure, a woman, desperately fighting through the tangle of undergrowth. As she gets closer Kelly recognises her—Karen Schaefer, making her escape.

No way. Kelly grits her teeth and jumps, landing with a crash on Karen. Gasping, she rolls off and struggles to her feet. 'Got you,' she says, then notices the strange angle of Karen's head across a fallen branch. 'Come on,' she urges. 'Get up.'

But Karen isn't moving. Kelly drops to her knees beside her and reaches gingerly for her throat, feeling for a pulse. Absolutely nothing.

Kelly sits back on her haunches, mouth open. She looks at Karen, then at the backpack, containing the scoop of the year, of the decade. She reaches forward and turns Karen's flashlight beam towards the paddock, gets to her feet and sets off through the bush. After twenty minutes she emerges onto a road, looks around and sees the filling station they passed on the way in. A couple of men are standing in the forecourt, watching ambulances and police cars racing past.

Kelly goes up to them. 'What's going on?' she asks.

They turn to her in surprise. 'Something at the kennels. Sounded like guns firing. Always knew that was a bad place. What are you doing out here?'

'Car broke down. I've got a family emergency in the city. Have to get there fast. Can I get a cab around here?' She rummages in her bag and pulls out her purse, shows a bunch of banknotes.

'No worries,' one says. 'Raj can take you, can't you, Raj?'

'Sure, no worries. I drive like the wind.'

'You're very kind.'

97

In the following days Jenny Belltree does what she can to contain the damage, physical and psychological. Around her the whole state seems to be going through the same process. Each day new revelations in the *Times* under Kelly's byline stoke the flames. The remnants of the Nordlund family have gone into hiding; the minister for infrastructure and planning has resigned, as has the premier and half the government front bench; ICAC has announced urgent new corruption investigations; the police commissioner has revealed a string of arrests arising from the work of Strike Force Spider, including that of Sydney legal identity Nathaniel Horn, following the shocking film and audio clips released by the *Times* online; Detective Inspector Deb Velasco, head of Spider, has become a celebrity, pictured raiding Horn's offices in the CBD and a meat-processing plant in western Sydney owned by a subsidiary of one of the Nordlund group of companies. She is equalled in public esteem only by Detective Superintendent Bob Marshall, hero of the hour.

On Tuesday there is a report of a light plane owned by Nordlund Resources and piloted by Konrad Nordlund taking off from a small airfield in the Hunter Valley and tracked by RAAF radar crossing the coast and heading out across the Pacific. The following day it is confirmed that it has not landed on Lord Howe Island, the only seaward destination within the plane's range, and an ocean search is begun; it appears that more than one passenger was on board, though their identities are in doubt.

Among the extensive research material recovered from Bernard Nordlund's office and transferred to the university archives is a thick file dating back over a year on the history of the Slater Park Hospital for the Insane and its notorious inmate, Cador Penberthy.

Several well-known authors confirm that they are racing to bring books on the Nordlund family tragedy into print in time for Christmas.

But Jenny's concerns are more personal. There is the house in Surry Hills to put right, but more importantly, Harry is in hospital with the bullet wound to his left hip, among other complications. It isn't only the physical damage that worries Jenny; it's as if the accumulation of blows and setbacks over the past two years, coming on top of earlier traumas in the army and police, have finally knocked Harry flat. He's become withdrawn, hardly moving, locked inside a troubled shell she cannot penetrate. Only Abigail, all budding life and innocence, seems to make an impression on him, and Jenny hurries to prepare the house for his discharge so that the three of them can retreat there together, and she can coax him back from his dark places.

Towards the end of November, when the first serious heatwave has the east coast in its sweltering grip, Harry is released from hospital. He walks with crutches, and is a pale shadow of the robust bushman who came out of the Queensland rainforest ten weeks before. Bob Marshall is with him, and together they go out to Bob's car and head for Surry Hills. When Jenny opens the front door to them she is struck by how Bob too has been transformed, now fit and full of

342

energy, revitalised by his rapid promotion to assistant commissioner in charge of state crime command. While she and Bob talk in the kitchen, making coffee, Harry sits on the living room floor in silent communion with Felecia the dog, while Abigail crawls around them with her toys. Later, when Bob has gone and Abigail is down for a sleep, Jenny and Harry sit outside in the small yard, beneath the shady Japanese elm, together in silence.

It's another month, the run-up to Christmas, before Harry refers to what's happened. He's been to the gym, abandoned his crutches for a walking stick and seems finally to have some energy. He joins Jenny in the kitchen, helping her chop garlic for the evening meal, when he suddenly says, 'So, after all that, we never solved it, did we? We still don't know why Mum and Dad died, and we don't know who Joseph was.'

She looks at him, trying to gauge if he's really up to this, then says, 'I've got something to show you.'

She wipes her hands and they go upstairs to the attic, his father's study. 'After the break-in I had to go through everything, every broken book and scattered bit of paper, and try to put it all back again as it was. And I found something. Look.'

She shows him a photograph, a formal group portrait of a couple of dozen people standing together on the steps of a building. 'I'd seen it before, but it meant nothing to me. It was in a frame, behind glass, and the glass had been broken by the intruders. So I took it out of its frame, and when I looked at the back, I saw this…' She turns it over and shows him.

Family and staff at Kramfors Homestead on the occasion of Carl Nordlund's 80th birthday, 5 May 1990.

Jenny points to one of the names set out beneath, in rows corresponding to the individuals in the photograph: *Joseph Doyle.* She turns back to the photograph and points him out, a young Aboriginal man.

Harry studies the image carefully. 'It must be him, don't you think? But what was this doing in Dad's study?'

'I found something else. Joseph's letter was postmarked Moree, and that made me think of the 1965 Freedom Ride for Aboriginal rights that your parents took part in. Moree was one of the towns they went to. I tried to find any references to it in your father's papers here, but there was nothing except a note about a speech that he gave to the Law Society in 2005, on the fortieth anniversary of the ride. So I talked to their librarian, and she found a copy of it in their annual record of proceedings for that year. I've got the whole text, but the relevant bit is this…'

She shows him the document, turned to page three:

After the success of Charlie Perkins and the others in gaining access for the Aboriginal kids from Soapy Row into the previously segregated town swimming baths, we broke up to prepare for our planned public meeting in the Memorial Hall that evening. Although it was a very warm February day I decided to take a walk to become more familiar with the town of Moree. Not far from the thermal baths lay the railway station, a modest little brick building beside the tracks on a wide, barren, flat area, baking hot, and there, standing outside, was a strange sight, a solitary little Aboriginal boy dressed in his best clothes, white shirt and socks, clutching a small suitcase.

I went up to him and introduced myself and asked him if he was lost, for that was how it looked. He said that his name was Joseph and he was aged seven years. As he told me his story I realised that he was one of the stolen children, as I had once been, taken that morning with other children from their families living on a mission out west of Moree with much confusion and tears, and sent off in a bus to this station for transportation to the white families who

had agreed to take them in and turn them into white fellas.
Except that Joseph was bound not for a family in Sydney
or Newcastle like the other children, but for the Kinnerlee
Boys' Home near Port Macquarie.

Now I had heard of this institution and its reputation
as a dark, brutal place, and I remembered how fortunate
I had been to avoid such a fate and instead be taken in by a
warm, loving couple such as the Belltrees. It appeared that
the people who were escorting the other kids had somehow
overlooked little Joseph, who was now abandoned here. So
I straight away went to the public phone there in the station
and telephoned my adoptive father, Len Belltree, and told
him of the situation. He told me, in his usual calm way,
to feed the boy and put him on the next available train
to Sydney with some sandwiches and water, and he and
Ruby, his wife and my adoptive mother, would collect him
at Central. So that's exactly what I did.

When I returned to Sydney, my parents told me they
had indeed met Joseph and taken him home with them.
After staying a few days he was taken to the family they had
arranged would adopt him, who lived up-country in New
South Wales. I don't know if any of this was legal, nor have
I ever heard from Joseph again. But I like to think that our
intervention gave him a better life than was in store for him
and that it was a positive footnote to the greater events that
were taking place in Moree on that historic day.

When he's finished reading, Jenny says, 'Len and Ruby Belltree,
your grandparents, took care of Joseph and found him a family
somewhere up-country.'

'Yes.'

'Now look again at the names on that group photograph, the
family members, there...'

Harry reads them: Carl Nordlund, in 1990 the patriarch of the family, with his second wife, Trixie, and his three sons, Martin, Bernard and Konrad. Martin and Konrad are with their wives, and nearby a nurse is standing with their young children, Amber, Ryan and Hayden. The other staff member present is named as Joseph Doyle, holding the bridle of Carl's champion horse Bucephalus. There is also an elderly couple, Len and Ruby Belltree.

Harry looks at the photograph again. 'I really wouldn't have recognised them. They were already middle-aged when they adopted Dad, and elderly when I was born. I have some memories of them, white-haired and kindly, on a beach somewhere, and in the big dark old house in the eastern suburbs where Dad grew up. He was always very respectful towards them, very grateful that they'd given him a privileged life when so many other Aboriginal children had much less happy outcomes. He was very young—less than a year old—when they took him in, and he had no memories of his Koori birth family, from somewhere out west beyond Cobar, Ruby told him.'

Jenny says, 'But somehow they knew the Nordlunds well enough to be invited to Carl's eightieth birthday bash up at Kramfors. And I'm wondering if this was what your father's meeting with Martin that day he died was all about. Was Martin maybe thinking of setting up a trust or a scholarship or something in their name, and he wanted your dad's approval?'

'Yes, I suppose that's possible.'

'And then when Joseph, many years later, wanted to come clean about what happened to flight VH-MDX, he thought of Danny Belltree, the young man who rescued him at Moree and who was now a famous judge. He intended to meet him on the day of the crash. Moree is a five-hour drive from Gloucester, so I assume Danny planned to drive us there first, meet Joseph, then go back to Armidale for the night.'

'Makes sense,' Harry says. 'Which would mean that we now know what Joseph looks like, or at least looked like twenty-four years ago, and we also know the place where he wanted to meet—the place they first met, Moree railway station.'

'According to your father's speech he'd be fifty-six years old now. We should be able to find him.'

Jenny sees the life go from Harry's face.

'No,' he says. 'We've done enough digging. Let Kelly and the cops sweep up the pieces. I'm finished.'

She takes his hand. 'Of course, if that's what you want.'

They sit in silence for a long while before Harry speaks. 'Go on then, say it.'

'What?'

'That we still don't know why Mum and Dad were killed.'

98

But it seems that Joseph Doyle doesn't exist. Jenny uses all her legal researcher resources—birth, marriage and death records, Medicare, car registrations, police records, social security—to try to find him, but discovers no one who seems to fit.

'Unless he's out of state.'

'Or changed his name,' Harry says. 'The Nordlunds were after him. Maybe he went into hiding.'

'Back to his original family?' Jenny suggests. 'On a mission out west of Moree, that's what your father said.'

They mull it over, decide to make the trip. Jenny asks Nicole to look after Felecia. They'll take Abigail with them.

The temperature has moved into the high thirties as they leave the New England Highway and head west, out across the broad inland plains of rich black soil. On each side fields of cotton, sorghum and wheat stretch away to the horizon. They have been driving for almost eight hours by the time they reach Moree, up towards the Queensland border. As the sun sets they drive along the main street, Balo Street, neatly landscaped and decorated with Christmas lights, to the Imperial Hotel at the central crossroads. They book in and take a walk through the town, finding their way to the railway station, much as it was when Harry's father met Joseph, fifty years before, then they return to the hotel for a drink and a meal.

The next morning they find the office of the local paper, the *Moree Champion*, further along Balo Street, and place an advertisement in the personals.

———

JOSEPH DOYLE
Harry Belltree would like to meet you
at the place you first met his father. He will be there
at midday each day, until Christmas Day.

———

Then they walk back along the street, stopping at shops and cafés, the community library, the shire council offices and the local Aboriginal land council to make enquiries, handing out printed copies of the ads for shop windows. A couple of Santas are also working the strip, sweating in their scarlet costumes.

At noon Harry is standing in the sun at the station, conspicuous on the empty platform, while Jenny and Abigail sit in their car in the car park watching passers-by. They stay for two hours, then set off with more leaflets for small settlements in the surrounding country—Pallamallawa, Biniguy and Garah.

In the following days they cover all the pubs and social clubs, the schools and churches. No one can help them, and no one comes to the railway station.

Finally it is Christmas Day. Over breakfast in the hotel they exchange presents. They have bought the same thing for each other, new wristwatches. Jenny smiles. 'A new time,' she says. 'A new start.'

No canvassing today, their last day. 'We're in the lap of the gods, Harry,' Jenny says. Towards noon they return to the station, the sun blazing down from high overhead.

Jenny has Abigail on her knee, giving her a drink, when she notices a dark-skinned man walk across the tracks towards Harry. They talk for a while, shake hands, then Harry points to the car and the two of them walk over. Jenny gets out.

'Jenny, this is Joseph. His name is now Monti Anaywan. He's agreed to talk to us.'

Jenny shakes Monti's big hand, scarred by heavy manual work. He looks the right age and his face does resemble Joseph's in the photograph. His expression gives nothing away.

'Monti wants us to go to his place, where we can talk.'

Jenny feels a tremor of alarm. 'Is it far?'

'About a hundred kilometres, he says, over the border.'

'I have the baby. You go, Harry. I'll wait in the hotel.'

But Monti shakes his head. 'You should come too, Jenny,' he says, voice low. 'There's someone specially wants to meet you.'

'Who?'

He just smiles enigmatically, points at a dusty white ute farther down the car park. 'You follow me, okay?' He walks away.

Jenny looks at Harry, who shrugs. 'We've come this far, Jen.'

They head out of Moree on the Carnarvon Highway, north and then west across the plains towards the Queensland border.

After an hour and a half the sat nav tells them they are approaching the border town of Mungindi. They drive through a small grid of streets, low bungalows on large plots, until they come to the Barwon River marking the state boundary, then cross over the river into another street grid, larger grass paddocks, some of the cottages on stilts. On the outskirts the ute leads them off onto a dirt road, long and straight, through grass, scrub and scattered trees. Another turn, kicking up clouds of dust in the hot, still air, towards a solitary cluster of metal shacks beside a dam. The ute comes to a halt, Harry pulls in alongside. A smell of roasting meat hangs in the air. Monti grins. 'Barbecue. Come inside.'

He leads them through a screen door into a dark interior hallway, and a room in which an old woman sits in a wicker chair beside the window.

'I want ya to meet me aunty.' He steps closer to the chair where the woman is still staring out the window. 'Aunty Pearl?' He touches her shoulder and she gives a start.

'What? Oh, Monti. How are you, darlin'?'

'Brought some folks to see ya, Aunty. Harry Belltree and his wife and baby.'

'Oh?'

She peers, and Monti waves Harry forward, whispers, 'Eyes goin'.'

'Are you really Harry Belltree?'

'Yes, Aunty, I am.'

Monti says, 'I got some business with Harry, then we'll come back and see ya. Okay?'

The old lady nods and turns back to the view out over the dam.

They go through to the kitchen and sit around the table. Monti pours them glasses of cold water from the fridge. 'So you found the letter I sent your dad?'

'Yes, eventually.' Harry gives him a short account of what's happened.

Monti shakes his head. 'So one murder led to another, and another, and on and on.'

Harry says, 'Martin Nordlund was murdered then?'

'Yes. I didn't understand at first, but later I worked it out.'

'Tell us what happened.'

'It was a Friday, ninth of August, a cold winter afternoon, when things started happenin'. The day staff had gone home for the weekend, and we—the ones who lived in the cottages at Kramfors—were packin' up when Mr Konrad came out and got

351

hold of the chief mechanic, Billy Stokes. Billy was a black fella, like me, but smarter. He and Mr Konrad went to the airstrip, and went off in the helicopter, over towards Cackleberry Mountain. When they came back I asked Billy what they'd been doin', but he wouldn't say.

'Early the next morning, before dawn, Billy came to my room and shook me awake. They'd heard that Mr Martin's plane had come down somewhere in the bush during the night, and we were to go out and try to find it. He had kit packed in the Land Cruiser and we got in and drove across the property to a fire trail up into the forest below Cackleberry Mountain, as far as we could go. Then we got out, pulled on two big backpacks, and set off on foot, into this real thick bush. I asked Billy how we were supposed to find the plane, and he showed me an instrument he was carrying, said it was a tracker would help us.

'We struggled through that bush for a couple of hours, right across to the far side of the mountain, until Billy reckoned the signal was getting close. Not long after, we came on a steel box lying there on the forest floor, like it had just dropped out of the sky. It had big black letters on it: *NDB*. Billy opened it up and pulled a switch, then said the plane should be nearby. We searched for another twenty minutes till we found it, half buried in a gully. It was a hell of a mess, the propeller crushed, the wings ripped off. We took off our packs and Billy told me to wait. He got a Polaroid camera out of his pack and went down into the gully and took pictures. Then he came back for some tools to open the cockpit that was jammed closed. While he was gone I looked at the pictures he took—about a dozen of them—and I put one in me pocket as a souvenir.'

There is a sudden sound from outside the house of young children squealing. 'Me kids,' Monti says. 'I started late. Had a lot of catchin' up to do.

'So anyway, Billy came back up from the plane carrying a smart leather briefcase. I asked if they were dead, and he said, "Oh, yeah. Nuthin' we can do, mate," but he was lookin' kinda sick. He got on the radio and spoke to someone he called boss—I guess Mr Konrad. When he was done we went back to the steel box and Billy got to work with his tools, takin' out parts and putting them in his backpack along with the camera and briefcase. Then he strapped the steel box with the rest of its equipment to the frame of my back-pack and said we were goin' back to the property. I tell you, my load was pretty damn heavy, and I was buggered by the time we reached the Cruiser.

'Billy drove us straight to the vehicle workshop, where Mr Konrad was waiting. We unloaded our gear and Billy gave him the briefcase and the camera and photos. He looked pretty serious—well, he'd just lost his brother. But he said he was pleased with us, and would give us a big reward for our efforts. He was lookin' at Billy when he said this, and I had the feelin' they'd already talked about it. Then he said he would organise a proper rescue party and Billy would lead them to the plane. He wanted me to go back to work with the horses and not talk to anyone about what we'd done.

'Later, when I was in the horse paddock, I saw the cars comin' in from town with people wanting to join the search. While they were gathering I saw Billy drive the Cruiser out to the airstrip and work on a bit of equipment out there by the helicopter pad. And that's when I remembered seeing that box with the letters *NDB* before—out there by the airstrip. But I didn't know what they meant.

'That evening I watched the search party return, tired as, and disappointed. I asked Billy what happened, and he said he hadn't been able to find the plane. They'd try again the next day. That's when I told Aunty Pearl all about it.'

A sound of splashing water, more children's laughter, and Monti stops to look out of the window, calls out, 'Sam, you go easy on your sister, hear me?' He goes to the kitchen sink. 'Reckon I'll make a pot of tea. You folks?'

He talks while he busies himself. 'I should tell you about me and Aunty Pearl. Back in '65, when your dad found me at Moree station, he put me on the train to Sydney, where his folks were waiting for me. Imagine me, a kid from the bush, arriving at Central station, eh? I'd never seen such a huge building. Then Sydney, and later they took me to the beach. I'd never seen water bigger than a farm dam. I was a country boy, and I loved horses, so they said they knew people on a farm with horses would look after me. They bought me new clothes and we set off to Kramfors, and when we got there Mr Carl Nordlund, the big boss, welcomed me and handed me over to Aunty Pearl, who gave me a room in her place and became a mother to me, though I never forgot my real mother and aunties out west.

'So, back to that Saturday, the day after Mr Martin's plane crashed. The one person I could tell about what Billy and I had done was Aunty Pearl. I was pleased with myself because of Mr Konrad's promise of a reward, and I said I'd share it with her, but she wasn't happy at all. She knew Mr Konrad, see, and she didn't trust him one bit. When I told her about the steel box on the airstrip she said Mr Martin once told her what it was when he bought it— a radio beacon, so the plane could find its way home at night or in bad weather.

'Aunty Pearl told me she had a bad feeling about all this, and told me I had to leave Kramfors, right away, that night, and she would come too. We left when everyone had gone to bed, walked to Gloucester and caught a train in the early hours, ended up in Moree where Aunty Pearl had a friend, and we began a new life. It was Aunty who saw something in the paper a few years ago about the judge, Mr Belltree, a black fella like us, and she suggested that I contact him to tell him what had happened to Mr Martin Nordlund. The judge replied to my letter and we arranged to meet, as you know, but he never showed up and I heard that he'd died in an accident, just like Mr Martin.'

Jenny says, 'Did you ever meet a man called Palfreyman, Monti? Terry Palfreyman?'

'Yes, I knew him from Kramfors, an engineer working with Mr Martin on some kind of machinery. He got in touch with me again a couple of months ago. Miss Amber had shown him the photograph I got of the plane wreck, and he wanted to know what really happened. He tracked down an old friend of Aunty Pearl who was still in touch with her, and asked her to ask me if I would talk to him, and I agreed. We met in Moree one day and I told him the whole story. He got it all typed up proper and I signed it. I hoped it would bring Mr Martin some justice.'

Monti looks up suddenly and gets to his feet. 'Aunty, you okay?'

The old woman is in the doorway, shuffling forward with the help of a stick. Monti helps her to a seat at the table.

'My legs,' she sighs. 'My eyes, my ears, all crook.' She looks at Abigail, asleep in Jenny's arms. 'What's your baby's name?'

'She's Abigail.'

'Nice name.' To Harry, 'Did your dad tell you where he came from?'

Harry shakes his head. 'He told me he was one of the stolen children, but he didn't know where he came from or who his birth parents were.'

Pearl frowns, says, 'I knew your father.'

'Did you?'

'Only for a little while, Harry. Too little a while—four short months. He was my son.'

Harry stares at her in astonishment, then at Monti, wondering if she's rambling, but Monti nods. 'It's the truth, mate.'

Harry looks again at Pearl, her weather-beaten face, and catches a look in her eyes—sharp, intelligent—he hasn't noticed before. 'Tell me,' he says.

'My folks were Worimi people from around Gloucester, maybe Yoongooar, the original owners. My dad worked as a stockman for

355

the first Nordlund settler, Mr Axel, and saw them building Kramfors Homestead and attended the church service when Queen Victoria died. When I was old enough I served as a housemaid to the Nordlunds, so I was there when Mr Carl, Mr Axel's son, returned from the war against the Japanese. He was a big hero, tall and strong. I was sixteen, a pretty girl so I was told, and Mr Carl took a fancy to me. I fell pregnant, a familiar story in them days. Mr Axel and the rest of the family knew, I think, especially when the baby, your dad, arrived and was so pale skinned.

'While I was pregnant, Mr Carl became engaged to his first wife, Hannah, a young beauty from Sydney society, and I suppose his dad, Mr Axel, wanted to avoid any complications. His wife, Mrs Greta, had a nephew and his wife living in Sydney—the Belltrees—who couldn't have children but wanted one, and he decided that they should adopt my baby Danny. I never saw him again, and he never knew I existed.

'When Mr Carl died in 2001 he had three other sons—Martin and Bernard by his first wife, and Konrad by his second. Before he died he told Martin that he had an elder brother, and told him the story. He said he felt guilty about how Danny and I were treated, and asked Martin to make amends, if he could. Martin took over the family businesses, and in the following year he decided to carry out his father's wish. That August he told me what he had decided to do. He was going to see his lawyer in Sydney and they would draw up a plan where Danny and I would be recognised as full members of the Nordlund family, and he and Danny, as the senior brothers, would jointly have control of the family businesses. When they had the details arranged, he would speak to his brothers and explain what he had decided.

'And that was why they killed him, Konrad and Bernard. After his plane disappeared there was no record of what he had planned. When Monti came and told me what he and Billy had discovered in the forest I knew that we were in great danger, and I told him

356

we had to leave. Later I heard that Billy died soon afterwards in another "accident".'

The old lady turns to the child sleeping in Jenny's lap. 'So you are my grandson, Harry, and Abigail is my great-granddaughter. From what I hear, you brought down God's vengeance on the heads of the Nordlund family. You made good for your father.'

She reaches out and takes Harry's hand. Jenny sees him take a deep breath and then relax, as if for the first time in years.

'And now I am very tired,' the old lady says. 'We hope you will stay with us tonight, and we can talk more.'

She gets stiffly to her feet, and Monti helps her to the door. When he returns he sticks his hand out to Harry. 'Well, congratulations, mate. I guess that makes you the head of the Nordlunds now.'

99

In the aftermath of Slaughter Park and the Doggylands affair, the Nordlund business empire collapses. Shunned by their Chinese backers and property developer partners, by investors, politicians and shareholders, its companies fall into bankruptcy one by one, many of them subject to ongoing police and ICAC investigations. Slater Park is saved as public parkland, while mining in the Cackleberry Valley is stopped and its landscape restored.

After a formal search, Harry Belltree is confirmed as the senior surviving member with a claim on the Nordlund family trust, and after apportionments to other surviving members he ends up with the only significant remaining asset, the thirteen per cent shareholding in the *Times* newspaper. Thus Harry becomes, in effect, Kelly Pool's boss, a quirk of fate that appeals to them both. Kelly has no need of his patronage, however, as the recipient of a Walkley Award for excellence in journalism and a legend in Sydney crime reporting. The income from Harry's *Times* shareholding goes to a foundation run by Jenny Belltree, to develop and distribute new technologies to help the blind.

Harry, Jenny and Abigail often travel up to Mungindi to the farm that Monti has bought with Pearl's share of the Nordlund inheritance, and have become a close part of their family. On one of these trips they detour through Newcastle, Gloucester and on to Thunderbolt's Way. It is the twenty-sixth of June 2015, the fifth anniversary of that day when, early on a misty morning, the car in which Jenny sat, gazing idly out of the window at the trees rushing past, was hit by an overtaking truck and sent over the edge in a howl of screaming metal. They pass the spot, an awkward bend above a steep hillside, and Harry pulls into the next layby. He straps Abigail onto his back and together they walk to the fatal place and climb down to the great blue gum against which his father's BMW finally came to rest. Jenny remembers it all clearly now, the deafening, nightmarish plunge, the glimpses of Danny and Mary in the front seats tossed like puppets. There are deep gashes in the blue gum's massive trunk, and she reaches out her hand to touch them. She thinks of the invisible scars that day left, and all the other people, innocent and guilty, whose lives were changed by that shattering moment, and she weeps.

ACKNOWLEDGMENTS

Writing the Belltree trilogy was a new experience for me. I had never written a story spanning three books before, nor one set in the world of the New South Wales police. I am indebted to many people for their generous help with this project, and have acknowledged many of them in the first two books. In addition I would give my special thanks to people whose insights and advice have helped shape *Slaughter Park*, including Alex Mitchell, Dr Tim Lyons, my agent Lyn Tranter, my editor at Text Elizabeth Cowell, and especially my wife Margaret.

31901063574810

CPSIA information can be obtained
at www.ICGtesting.com
Printed in the USA
LVHW03s0826200818
587000LV00002B/2/P